In The
COMPANY of
CROCODILES

Maggie Brown

BELLA
BOOKS
2017

Bella Books, Inc.
P.O. Box 10543
Tallahassee, FL 32302

Printed in the United States of America on acid-free paper.

First Bella Books Edition 2017

Editor: Cath Walker
Cover Designer: Linda Callaghan

ISBN: 978-1-59493-533-6

Other Bella Books by Maggie Brown

I Can't Dance Alone
Mackenzie's Beat
Piping Her Tune
The Flesh Trade

Acknowledgments

I'd like to thank Bella Books once again for the production of this book. Many thanks also to Cath Walker for her editing skills in guiding me through the intricacies of the plot. I tend to run away with the story and she skilfully brings me back to earth.

Lastly, I'd like to pay tribute to the fascinating unique wildlife we have in Australia. Approximately 90% of our native animals are found nowhere else in the world.

Twenty-one of the twenty-five most venomous snakes live in Australia.

The swamps, rivers and estuaries across the north are croc habitats. Protected since 1970, the crocodile population has increased with a vengeance. It is estimated that there are probably more than one hundred and fifty thousand Australia-wide. Experts say that we can now assume any body of water in the far north will contain a saltwater crocodile, and this includes fresh water.

About the Author

Maggie Brown is a writer who thinks wit and humor go a long way.

Is she intelligent, model-like, mega-super-important? Hell no!

She is an Australian alien life form, who drinks too much coffee, sits too long at the computer, and sometimes is a hot mess when struck down by writer's block.

She hopes you enjoy her book as much as she enjoyed writing it.

Dedication

To my family.

CHAPTER ONE

The day was a scorcher. Vivian Andrews pinched the shirt material off her skin and flapped it to create a breeze. It had little effect. Heat still lapped around her like a blanket. She eventually ignored the trickling beads of perspiration to concentrate on sliding the boat down the ramp. Nearer the water, the salty tang in the air thickened. As she sucked in the smell, the thoughts of nearly forgotten summer holidays crept in. Nostalgia was a luxury, but today she let the memories linger. Why she didn't know, for she didn't want to relive the past. There was too much pain there and she had moved on.

Seaward, small sandbars rose like mounds of flesh through the blue-green water and she stopped a moment to admire the sight. She wasn't religious, but for her, this was as close to heaven as you could get. This afternoon there was no activity on the water except for a trawler that listed in a shallow stretch like a beached whale. She wondered who had been stupid enough to be caught in that part of the bay by the outgoing tide. Whoever it was would have to wait. The vessel was there to stay until the tide came in again.

"Come on, Ned, concentrate," she called out. When there was no answer, she poked the teenager.

He pulled the headphones off and fiddled with the iPod in his breast pocket. "What's wrong?"

"Make sure the esky and the rest of the gear are secure and let's get the show on the road. We want to be fishing while there's plenty of light left."

"Right ya are, Viv."

The motor purred into life at the first pull. She steered the compact three-seater aluminium boat past the pier, wove through the sandbars and cruised around the headland to the mouth of the river beyond. Her favourite fishing spots were the waterways in the delta. Twenty minutes later as they moved inland, she wriggled uncomfortably. The air was even hotter and more humid in this transitional world between land and sea, the estuary channels being well protected from the southeasterly winds by thick marsh vegetation. Her nose wrinkled as she caught a whiff of hydrogen sulphate fumes that hung sullenly like eggs rotting in the sun. The smell was more noticeable where the tall stilted mangroves met the water in a tangle of snaking roots.

Half an hour later Vivian switched off the motor. She stood up, planted her heavy boots on the tin bottom and took off her battered Akubra to fan her face. "Throw the anchor out here. It looks as likely a place as any."

"Got it." Ned leaned forward casually to drop the weight over the side, its ripples spreading towards the bank.

Vivian studied the olive-green trees that crowded the edge. She'd never been quite so far up this particular channel. She pulled the tackle box onto the seat, took out the rods and with practiced twists threaded prawns onto the hooks. They hung lifelessly on the barbs. She passed one of the rods over. "Give this a go. And watch what you're doing. Someone saw a big croc around this part of the creek last week."

Ned grinned as he balanced his legs for the throw. "Ain't enough meat on my bones to tempt him."

"Don't get too cheeky. Just keep your hands out of the water."

The line snaked out in an arc and landed in the middle of the channel with barely a splash. After Vivian had completed her cast, they settled down to wait.

Moments later, Ned fidgeted on the seat, sniffing the muggy air like a retriever. "There's a bad stink comin' from the bank somewhere. You smell it?"

"Ummm…Yes, I do."

"Whatcha reckon it is?"

"I have no idea. It doesn't smell like fish."

"Could be a dead dugong, maybe?"

"Perhaps. Reel your line in. We'll pull up the anchor and have a look."

The engine coughed into life and the boat eased forward to carve a passage through the brine. Ned leaned over the side, his eyes narrowed. "Phew! It's getting worse." He pointed a stubby finger. "Look. Something's under that clump of branches over there."

Vivian swung the bow towards the bank and killed the motor. "I think we'd better have a look. Chuck out the anchor and hand me the grapple."

The stench was stronger here, overpowering the mangroves oozing sulphur and muddy odours. Uneasily she wriggled the hook between the roots to prise them apart, on high alert now. The foul smell had nothing to do with sea-life. She knew the fetid odours of fish and prawn heads rotting in the heat. This was different. She ignored her heaving stomach as she worked the debris away with the grappling iron until a pile of filthy garbage was exposed.

"There's something there. Pass me the flashlight." The glow picked out a glimpse of pale blue material, jumbled up with something dirty yellow. The colours were barely definable amongst the mud and grey-green leaves. Vivian's skin prickled. She prayed it was just a load of rubbish, but she doubted it was. Blowflies swarmed over the rags. "I've got a shitty feeling about this, Ned," she muttered. With a flick of her wrists, she caught the top of the cloth protruding above the water line. She gave the rod a sharp jerk. With a slurp, a bulky mass slid free from its tomb and bobbed to the surface.

When Ned yelled, Vivian fought to stay calm. Half submerged, a man's body floated out, his bloated face turned directly towards the boat. She swallowed the bitter taste that shot into her mouth as she peered at it. The corpse looked like it had been there for at least a week. Part of the left cheek was eaten away by fiddler crabs, which still clung to the tattered skin. Sightless eyes bulged grotesquely from the puffy flesh. Vivian forced herself to study the face. Distinguishing features were too hard to pick at this stage of decomposition, but a moustache hung like a dirty strip of seaweed beneath a beaked nose. She turned quickly to Ned. "Turn away. This poor bugger will give you nightmares."

Loose strands of hair stuck to the perspiration on his face, which was now two shades paler. His freckles stood out in sharp contrast. "Do you recognize him, Viv?"

"It's a little hard to tell, but I don't think it's anyone from around here. He's not a local anyhow. No one has a moustache like that."

"What'll we do?"

Vivian looked at the youth with sympathy. A fifteen-year-old shouldn't have to see something like this. Wild-eyed, he was half-perched on the seat like a gazelle ready for flight. "There's nothing we can do. He's too far gone to get him in the boat. Besides, we wouldn't be able to put up with the smell. After I take a couple of photos, we'll push him back into the roots and go home. I'll tie something on the branch to mark the spot and notify the police when we get to town."

She took the small phone out of its waterproof bag and snapped off some shots from every angle she could manage. Then Vivian manoeuvred the body back between two roots in the thick mud with the grapple and an oar. Once it was wedged in tightly, she lassoed a rope over a hanging branch, pulled it tight and tied one of the orange life jackets to its tail. She stood back satisfied. Coupled with the coordinates on the GPS, the body shouldn't be hard to find again.

She looked around. The personality of the river had become far less welcoming. Shadows striped gloomily across the channel in the late afternoon light, and despite the heat, she shivered. Then an imperceptible flicker of movement in the water caught her eye. She stopped to listen, but heard only the benign sound of water lapping under the boat.

"Come on, let's go!" Ned's strident tone brought her back to action.

Vivian stood to start the motor. *Time to get the boy out of here—away from this place with its ghosts.* "Okay. I'm…"

The next words never left her throat as the river erupted. An enormous creature arched out of the water with an explosion of spray and launched at the bow. With a massive shudder, the boat tipped sharply on its end. Vivian's muscles contracted involuntarily as she fought to regain her footing on the slippery tin floor. Then another crash resounded as the boat was hit again. She stumbled backward with a cry. Ned leaped from the seat and grabbed her arm with pinching fingers. But he was only a gangly teenager, not strong enough to maintain the hold as the creature rammed the boat again. This time, she had no hope. Her head snapped sideways, her torso twisted in an arc, and she toppled over the side, sprawling face down into the river.

For a moment, all went black—suffocating blackness. Blood pounded in her ears as she frantically kicked upwards to the surface. With a grunt, she burst out of the water, floundered for a moment, then gargled and coughed as she tried to breathe. Once air began to trickle into her lungs, Vivian forced herself to calm down. The boat bobbed erratically, though thankfully hadn't capsized. She treaded water and strained to see what had hit the boat. When Ned shouted frantically, "Swim, Viv, swim!" panic flared through her.

Not far away was the biggest saltwater crocodile she'd ever seen.

With desperate strokes, she swam for the bank. It took less than twenty seconds for her feet to hit the bottom. Only when she was up to her thighs in the mud-choked water did she dare turn to look. Ned was poised at the front of the boat, screaming incoherently as he jabbed an oar at the scaled back. Ten metres from her now, the crocodile moved forward aggressively. Fear caused a sick lurch in her stomach. She could taste the sourness. She knew she'd never make it up the bank. In the failing light, the dead man floated under the spindly branches that hung in a veil of silvery-grey.

With a do-or-die effort, she lunged forward to grasp his pants and her fingers latched on to the belt around his waist. She pulled hard to propel the cadaver towards the crocodile. The belt came off in her hand as the body shot forward. It was the only thing between her and the giant salty. Her nerves shrieking, she shrank back against the roots. They were so close the creature's head was clearly defined—the yellow eyes hooded by double lids—the pocked, scaly ridges down the centre to the snout—the heavy jaw lined with teeth. And the eyes were fixed squarely on her. Vivian began to pray.

Then the miracle happened. As quickly as it had materialised, the monster vanished. In a split second, the massive jaws snapped over the bloated chest of the corpse. With a thrashing swirl, both disappeared from sight. She didn't hesitate, striking out for the boat that Ned had brought in closer. With a cry of relief, she pulled herself over the side, the dead man's belt still clutched in her hand. Awkwardly she flopped to the floor, cradling her knees to her chest as she fought to breathe.

Ned looked strained and pale, a tear leaked over his lid as he embraced her. "I was afraid you were a goner."

Vivian could only manage a semblance of a smile. "Me too. I guess he thought we were taking his dinner. Damn he was a big mongrel, wasn't he? Come on—let's get the hell out of here before he comes back."

The first pull of the rope produced an unsettling hiss. She jerked it once, twice, and by the third attempt sweat trickled down her face. Not only from exertion but fear too. She wiped her face clean with rough swipes. It would be dark soon, so she had to hurry. Vivian was careful to compose her next words when Ned began to whimper. He needed to be calmed down—she knew blind panic when she saw it. The lad was terrified. "She must have got wet. Hand me the rag over there and I'll try to get some of the moisture off."

She worked quickly, with an ear alert for a telltale sound of something swimming close by. It didn't come. All she could hear were the croak of frogs, the buzz of insects, the beat of her heart, the breath coming in and out of her lungs. Ned had fallen silent as if his voice might somehow call the creature back.

Satisfied at last, she flung the oilcloth back in the toolbox. "That should do it. I'll give it another go."

With this pull, the outboard motor purred into life. The fishing boat surged out into the middle of the channel to begin its journey home as the last rays of the sun petered out over the western mountain range. The water darkened to a deep purple. Vivian switched on the spotlight, though she knew they wouldn't need it for long. Tonight was a full moon, its glow already visible seaward. It crept steadily over the marshes and soon there would be enough silvery light to navigate home.

Consumed with their own thoughts, and content to watch the mangroves pass by, they wound along the labyrinth of river canals. Half an hour later, speckled lights from the three houses on the bluff appeared in the distance nearer the main branch to the sea.

"Are you going to see the police tonight, Viv?"

Vivian nodded. "I guess I should, though there's not much point. They'll never find the poor bloke now. He'll be in the belly of the croc. Here, take the tiller and I'll have a look at that belt."

Vivian picked it up off the floor and turned it over curiously in her hands.

Ned leaned forward as he strained to look. "What is it?"

"Just a leather belt, though it's got a fancy buckle. There's quite a big pouch attached to it."

"Anything in it?"

"I'll have a look. We'd better not tamper with it too much. I'll have to give it to the police."

With the release of the zip, Vivian hissed. The pouch, apart from a slip of paper tucked into the side, bulged with fifty-and one-hundred-dollar notes. She glanced quickly at Ned. From the look on his face, the boy had caught sight of the cash. He turned wide, unblinking eyes to her. "That's a lot of dough." His face tightened into a calculating expression. "Will we keep some of it?"

Vivian shook her head. "No way, Ned, we'll hand it in. It's not ours to keep nor do I want it. We were lucky to escape with our lives so let's not ruin it." Pensive, she stared at the tangle of trees and rocks on the banks and then at the river behind them.

Black clouds rolled in from the east to swallow the moon. The countryside retreated into darkness, closing in on the small boat like a cloak. The gloom was enough to take them out of the physical reality and back into their imaginations.

CHAPTER TWO

To Vivian's relief, Ned seemed in relatively good spirits when she dropped him off home. She gave his mother a wave when she appeared at the door. Mary Graham was a small wiry woman, the reddish gold of her hair already turning a light grey although she was not much past forty. The climate, hard work and worry had taken its toll. Four years ago, she had lost her commercial fisherman-husband at sea, leaving her with three children to rear.

"Hi Viv. Back already?"

"Hello Mary. No fish tonight, unfortunately. We had a run-in with a croc—Ned will tell you the story. I've got something to do." Vivian smiled with genuine warmth. Mary had come to her in desperation earlier in the year, asking if she would give her son a job to get him off the streets after school finished. Vivian agreed to take him some weekends and during the school holidays. Over the months, she had grown fond of the lad. He wasn't a bad kid, just one of those who had too much sting. Resilient too. She had no doubt he would describe the ordeal with enthusiasm to his mates tomorrow.

She checked her watch—half past seven. Now she would have to disturb the sergeant at home. Joe Hamilton was a good country cop, but with only one constable to share the workload, there had to be a good reason to call on him officially at night. The four hundred and eighty-six permanent residents of Ashton Bay knew the rules—only in an emergency. Desperate to scrub the putrid odour of decay off her body, her first instinct was to go home for a long shower. And her hair was coated with so much mud that the strands were clumped together in thick wads. But a dead body needed to be reported as soon as possible. By the time she went out to her house and returned it would be very late.

Her mind eased when she saw the light on at the police station. The sergeant's residence stood next door so she was glad she didn't have to go there. It wouldn't do to have to face Dee Hamilton in her present state. The police officer's wife was definitely more of a force to be reckoned with than her more liberal husband. Vivian climbed the six stairs and rapped on the door of the small building. She couldn't remember seeing the sergeant so well groomed—in this isolated place, the dress code was definitely casual. Whoever was inside must be important.

Hamilton looked at her in surprise. "Viv, just the person I want. I've been trying to get you all afternoon. There's a guide job going and I recommended you if you're interested. They're paying well." His florid face became even redder as he sniffed. "Damn you smell foul. Where have you been?"

"Fishing, Joe. I wouldn't have come in looking like this, but I found a body in the river. I figured I should report it tonight."

The policeman became alert. "A body? Who was it?"

She shrugged. "Nobody from around here, or at least I don't think so. A bit hard to tell. It was a man…I'd say in his thirties or forties. Ned and I found him in the mangroves. He'd been there for quite a few days by the look. Then when I pulled it out with the grappling iron, a croc hit the boat. He was coming back for it."

"How'd you get so filthy?"

Vivian gave a shudder, with no attempt to keep the tremble out of her voice she continued. "I fell overboard. I don't mind telling you I got the fright of my life when I thought I was going to be his next feed. Then he grabbed the corpse and disappeared. It was the biggest croc I've even seen."

"I heard there was a big 'un out there." Hamilton looked at her with sympathy and tossed his head in the direction of his office. "I've got a couple of secret service people inside. They've spent all afternoon snooping about looking for a missing man. Your corpse could just be him."

"He was too bloated and damaged to be recognizable. But maybe the photos will be good enough for them to see if it's the bloke they're after." She handed him the belt, stepping back self-consciously after she had done so. "I pulled this off him. That's the main reason I came here tonight instead of ringing. We can't do much for the poor guy now, but you'd better take a look inside the leather pouch. It's loaded with money."

Hamilton whistled when he unzipped the flap. "Come on in and take a seat. I'll have a word with them before I bring you in."

With a dubious glance down at her clothes, Vivian shook her head. "I'm not in any fit state to see visitors. I should go home for a shower. You can have my phone with the pictures."

A sly smile crossed his face. "You show them. It won't hurt these two. The bloke's a bit pushy."

"All right, but warn them."

After he disappeared into the office, Vivian sat gingerly on the wooden bench against the wall. She hoped the smell wouldn't linger, though didn't hold out much hope. The foyer was small, a counter separating the cramped visitors' space from the receptionist's section. That part was filled with a desk, chair, a photocopy machine and an instant camera machine for license photographs. Utilitarian austerity. The walls were decorated with police paraphernalia: photographs of wanted criminals, missing persons' pictures and a few public notices.

When Hamilton appeared fifteen minutes later, Viv's clothes had stiffened, dried hard in the air-con. "Come on in," he said with a jerk of his head.

Vivian was sure she creaked as she walked into the room. A man and a woman turned to study her while she sheepishly shuffled to a seat as far away as possible. The office was a good deal larger than the foyer, but from their audible gasps it was obvious that they'd smelt her. After a cursory glance at the woman who sat shadowed in the corner, Vivian turned her full attention to the man. Automatically, her training clicked in and she did a quick appraisal. Short haircut, fit body and though he wore casual summer clothes, the labels were more upmarket than the local attire. As well, the slight bulge under the shirt signalled his shoulder holster. A member of some enforcement agency, though not a cop.

When the sergeant made the introductions, the man, Ross Hansen, hung back without offering a handshake. Like her companion, the woman, Claire Walker, was dressed casually, though lacked his arrogant air. She gave Vivian a pleasant smile but didn't extend her hand either. Not that Vivian blamed them, but it irritated her nevertheless.

Hansen eyed her dispassionately, tipped his head and said, "You found a body?"

By the set of his mouth, Vivian knew he found her distasteful. Her voice was hoarse from coughing up the muddy water and she rasped, "Yes?"

"And you were there fishing?"

"Yes I was."

"And you claim a crocodile ate it?"

"That's right."

"Why didn't you ring first before you came here?"

"I was just uptown so it was easier to call in. We're not into formalities in this place," she said, puzzled by his aggression.

"You didn't…ah…think it advisable to clean up first?"

A harder edge was in his voice, which made her hackles rise. He reminded her unpleasantly of a senior officer who had plagued her unnecessarily after an incident early in her career. "No. I live out of town."

"Tell us what happened and where exactly you found him." He stabbed a finger as he enunciated the words.

Anger swept through Vivian. His tone smacked of interrogation. *Arrogant bastard.* "I will when you speak to me civilly," she snapped.

"I asked you a question."

"It was a fair way up a tributary of the river. He's been dead for a while when I found him. The croc would have taken him and then stashed him somewhere. They do that if they've already eaten, but mostly because they prefer their flesh to be softer. It comes off the bone easier."

"I don't want a wildlife lesson."

She narrowed her eyes and said in a flat voice. "Get over yourself. I'm off home."

A feminine voice interrupted in a soft tone. "I'll take it from here, Ross. I'm sorry we put you through that, but we wanted to see how you would react. You see, we need your help and we want someone who can handle stressful situations."

Vivian turned her head to look at her. "What help, Ms Walker?"

"It's Claire, Vivian," the woman said, walking over with an outstretched hand and a friendly smile.

"Whoa…don't come too close. I'm not in any fit state to shake anyone's hand."

Claire ignored the remark and clasped her hand. Then she pulled a chair up to sit close; far away enough not to invade Vivian's space, but near enough to make the conversation intimate. Vivian had to give her top marks for not flinching— the smell was atrocious. "Sergeant Hamilton recommended you as a guide. We're looking for something we believe is up in these parts somewhere." Claire reached into her coat pocket and pulled out a photograph. "Was it this man you saw in the mangroves?"

Vivian peered at the snap of a young man in his early twenties and shook her head. "No. The dead bloke had a moustache and a beaked nose. I'd say he was Middle Eastern or Mediterranean, though it's just a guess. He was a mess." She fished the phone out of her pocket and tapped. A picture appeared on the screen. "Here he is."

Claire visibly relaxed as she studied the image. "No, he's definitely not the man we're searching for, but we can't ignore your find, especially since he was carrying so much money.

Sergeant counted nearly seventy-five thousand dollars in the pouch. It could very well have something to do with our case. We want to offer you a position as our guide for two weeks, but the timeline will depend on what we find. A fortnight should be ample. Our employer is prepared to pay three thousand dollars a week for your services. There won't be any time off once we start. The sergeant recommended you as the best person for the job."

Vivian leaned back in the chair to study her before she answered. Claire Walker was of average height, with a comely body and an earnest attractive face. Her hair, nearly dead white, was plaited into a long braid halfway down her back. As she spoke, she flicked away a loose strand a couple of times without a thought, which seemed more of a habit than a necessity. Her eyes were an unusually pale blue, like a bleached patch of sky. She wore tailored pants with a V-necked green top, sensible heels and little makeup. Estimated age, late twenties or early thirties. At first glance, she didn't look particularly strong, but on closer inspection, Vivian could see the subtle muscles rippling across her shoulders and down her arms. There was a hidden strength there, and it would be a mistake to take her lightly. She held herself with confidence and poise, though not overbearingly.

"Who is the young man you're looking for?" Vivian asked.

"That information is highly confidential, so before I can tell you anything, can I assume you're interested?"

"No, I'm not. Sorry. Now if you'll excuse me, I'll be on my way."

Claire Walker showed no dismay but merely smiled. She had a set of perfectly white teeth in her full-lipped mouth. "We can up the ante if you like. How does another five hundred a week thrown in sound to you?" She accompanied the words with a light touch on Vivian's arm.

She's good. Classic technique. For a second Vivian studied the finger then gave just a hint of a smile. "Sorry. Sarge can give you two or three names of blokes who would be more than willing to do the job." She looked over at Hamilton and said mildly, "Bruiser or Thom might help these folk, Joe. What do you think?"

"I'm sure they would take leave from their jobs for that amount of money."

Claire gave her a frankly appraising look. "Is there anything that really bothers you about the offer, Vivian? If so, I think we could come to some agreement in the terms of the contract."

Damn. Can't the woman take no for an answer? Vivian forced a note of brusque finality as she reeled off her stock answer. "I'm not interested. I'm too busy at the moment."

"I'm sure we can arrange someone to assist you. What exactly do you do for a living?"

Vivian made a defensive gesture. The woman was an expert as she herded her into a corner. "I have a market garden."

"Good. It shouldn't be too difficult to get someone to help you."

"I prefer to take care of my own business."

"Come now. We will make sure a competent person is put in charge of it." She chuckled. "At least you're not a brain surgeon. Now *that* would be more difficult."

Vivian glowered. Walker was unflappable, using a level pleasant tone as she whittled away at her. She had been trained well in the art of persuasion. And underneath the beguiling inflections, Vivian caught a hint of intractability. This woman was going to be as hard to shed as a tick on a dog. At this rate she'd never get home—she desperately needed to chill out with a cold beer and a long shower. The crocodile drama had caught up with her. "Look, I don't want to be rude but I really am very tired. We can take this conversation up tomorrow, but don't expect me to change my mind."

Claire's face broke into a charming grin. "I'll be there at eight tomorrow morning on the dot, Vivian."

Vivian grunted as she rose to take her leave, well aware she had deftly been manoeuvred into giving an interview. When she reached the door, she turned her head quickly to look back at the woman. The congenial smile had gone and in its place was a measured expression.

As Vivian made her way back to her truck, she couldn't suppress her curiosity. Who the hell was Claire Walker? She was certainly no amateur in the cloak-and-dagger stakes. And who was the mysterious dead man in the mangroves? For two agents, one showing all the signs of an interrogation expert, to be sniffing around made the case very important. But even if Vivian went with them, there was no doubt they wouldn't be telling her the true reason for whatever it was that they were here for. She dipped her hand in her pocket to satisfy herself that the small piece of paper with the phone number from the belt wallet was still there.

She understood secrets. She'd recognized the number immediately.

* * *

Claire thoughtfully watched Vivian depart before she flashed Hamilton a smile. "Thank you for your help today, Sergeant. We'll go back to the hotel now and see you in the morning."

"So he wasn't the fellow you were looking for?"

"No. However, the fact the dead man turned up close to our investigations suggests he may have some connection. Could we have the belt to examine overnight?"

Hamilton eyed her for a moment before his face firmed. "Sorry, a corpse is a police matter. The belt and contents have to be kept as evidence until my superintendent releases it. You may come tomorrow to study it here since I've been instructed to give you any help you require. Now if you'll excuse me, I'll lock this money in the safe and file my report. Show yourselves out…I'll shut the door when I leave."

Claire dipped her head in acknowledgment. Her estimation of his capabilities went up a notch. He was a man who knew his duty and intended to do it. Somewhere down the track when they found out exactly what they were dealing with, it would be advisable to seek his aid. She turned to her companion. "Come on. Let's get back to our rooms."

Less than half a kilometre from the station, the town's only hotel was a sturdy brick building, re-enforced to withstand the cyclones that plagued the far north coast in the wet season.

Once inside her room, Claire threw the file on the table and gestured to the chair. Senior Agent Ross Hansen was a solid man, with a square burly face and hair cropped short at his temples. A hardnosed agent with many years in the field, he wasn't particularly likable but a good man to have at her back.

Hansen frowned at her, obviously put out. "Why insist on Ms Crocodile Dundee as our guide. She's nothing out of the ordinary, in fact, I thought her boorish and ignorant."

Claire eyed him in surprise. It wasn't often someone got under his thick skin. "I'm certain there's much more to Vivian Andrews than meets the eye. My gut feeling tells me she'll be a good person to have in a tight situation. The way she held herself suggested she wasn't the average market gardener—she was remarkably in control after a traumatic experience. She's honest too. Seventy-five thousand dollars was a lot to hand in. Since the body was never going to be found, it would have been easy to pocket the money with nobody any the wiser. And she wasn't fooled at all by me. I could see in her eyes she knew very well I was trying to coerce her."

"She agreed to see you tomorrow though."

Amusement twinkled in Claire's eyes. "Only because she was tired. There's no doubt she'll try her best to fob me off when I go out. I'll have to give her something to interest her into taking the job."

"It's up to you. So, do we go to the site in the mangroves?"

She shook her head. "Not by boat. I've booked a plane to survey the area from the air tomorrow afternoon at two. The pilot who brought us here agreed to the charter. Have a look around the town while I'm out at the market garden?"

"I'll go with you tomorrow."

"No. I'm going alone."

Hansen shook his head emphatically. "We have to stick together."

"If you're there, Andrews won't take the job."

"Rubbish. How do you know?"

Claire tilted her head with a frown. "It's what I'm trained for, Ross. I am, after all, a behavioural scientist. If I can't read an average person, how can I possibly find Dane Ahmed and persuade him to go home?"

"Do you think that dead guy could be something to do with our case?"

"Very likely," said Claire. "Too much of coincidence not to be."

CHAPTER THREE

With yesterday's drama still indelible in her mind, Vivian pushed damp wisps of hair back from her face as she walked to the bathroom. The near-death experience had tormented her dreams, though she wouldn't have a chance to put the memory away just yet, not with Claire Walker due in a couple of hours. Under the shower, she ran her fingers over the scar tissue on her abdomen. The wound was still tender even after five years, though it didn't burn anymore when touched. The feeling had thankfully faded with time. She dressed carefully, paying more attention to her appearance than usual. Somehow, the thought that the agent may see her as a country bumpkin grated.

A dog's bark outside the front door brought a smile to her face as she headed to the kitchen for breakfast. At least someone was happy. A small Australian terrier, his hair slick with dew, bounced into the house as she opened the door. When Vivian gave him the usual scratch and scruff, he squirmed in her grasp and licked her face with a warm tongue. She stroked him fondly—Toby was the only one she truly loved here. With a sigh, she filled up her coffee cup before she went to sit out on the front deck. This morning she felt more unsettled than usual, aware how increasingly difficult it was becoming to come to terms with her loneliness. Her self-imposed exile was now a heavy weight, though she had no recourse other than to wear it. Her bridges were burnt behind her.

Not that she missed her former life with Beverly. Far from it. When Vivian arrived back from the hospital in Germany to find the house empty, she had experienced an initial burst of grief at the abandonment and then guilty relief. Though nothing was said, they both knew their relationship was already on the rocks when Vivian left for that last assignment in Somalia.

Four years they had lived together, but like a broken-down modern appliance, there was no point tinkering with the mechanics to try to fix it. Their emotional bond hadn't been built to last. Vivian wondered if there ever had been a real connection between them. Sexual attraction, but unconditional, selfless love? *No.* When the first six months of passion eased into everyday life, things began to go stale even then. It seemed easier to let the connection falter, rather than spend time trying to keep it intact. They had been too wrapped up in their careers to worry they were drifting apart until there was nothing left to salvage.

But before its expiry date, the relationship had accrued affection, and Beverly had obviously decided to disappear rather than let their time together deteriorate into recriminations. The only correspondence Vivian received from her afterward was through solicitors when their house in Sydney was sold. Vivian's shoulders sagged a few centimetres. Would she ever know the kind of love that she could never do without? With an irritated shrug, she put aside her thoughts to get ready for the day. There were things to do before Walker arrived.

The air was spicy with a cloying fruity scent as she made her way through the orchard to the vegetable plots. Cane toads squatted under the trees, their numbers thicker now the rains were imminent. She grimaced—ugly little invasive suckers, with their dull brown, warty skin and protruding eyes. Her irrigated garden and orchard was the ideal environment for them. They didn't have to live near water to survive, for they absorbed water through the skin on their bellies. At night, she had no trouble distinguishing their calls from other frog and toad species. The cane toad had a high-pitched broken *brrr brrr*, like the sound of a motor running.

She brushed past the banana trees to the beds beyond. The summer plantings had been finished last week: the Asian greens, zucchinis, snake beans, cucumbers and sweet corn spread out in long rows. Her first year's gardening had been a hard lesson when she had tried a variety of cooler climate seedlings. Everything had bolted into seed, been devoured by bugs or simply rotted at the centre.

At the creek bank, she filled the fuel tank of the small engine, primed the pump and gave the rope a pull. The stream had shrunk to a trickle, but soon it would be a healthy flow again when the rains came. The irrigation system sprang into life. Jets of water squirted across the vegetable section in a soaking spray. Hopefully, she wouldn't have to do this much longer.

Vivian hurried back to the house to open her computer. She edged her chair closer and tapped in her password. When the Google page popped up, she typed in *Claire Walker*, sifted through to the right person, and the woman's particulars blinked onto the screen. Claire was born in Adelaide, aged thirty-one, and had a double degree in Behavioural Science and Science (Animal Studies) from Flinders University. Her first position was with the Federal Police in the missing person's bureau. She stayed there for four years, but where she went to after that wasn't recorded no matter how many sites Vivian trolled. She swung backward in her chair, consumed with curiosity. In what covert organization was Claire? Not only was it off limits to the public, but also to the more selective sites Vivian was able to access.

The rumble of an engine in the driveway made her glance at the clock on the wall. Eight o'clock—punctual to a fault. Vivian wasn't surprised. Everything about the agent reeked of efficiency. Toby beat her out the door when Claire stepped out of the Jeep. Not that Vivian minded that her dog was the welcoming committee. He was an icebreaker. Claire wasn't an exception, clearly enchanted with the terrier when he leaped onto her leg to beg for attention. She gave a cry of delight as she reached down to ruffle his head.

"Down Toby," Vivian called out half-heartedly, though experiencing a flush of pleasure at the sight.

"He's a cutie," said Claire with a grin.

Vivian slid her hands into her pockets, tightening her lips. *Damn. I've turned into a sentimental fool.* "Come in, Ms Walker. I'll listen to what you've got to say, but I have to warn you my answer will be the same."

A dimple appeared in Claire's cheek. "I told you to call me Claire, Vivian. I'd love to come in. Your home looks interesting."

Vivian hunched her shoulders. By the sound of that statement, there was no way she was going to get rid of the woman easily. She may as well show her through the house and be done with it. She led the way through the hallway to the downstairs area. "I built it when I came here five years ago. Come on through and I'll give you a tour. The timber's been locally milled and it's designed with this open-air plan for the tropical climate and natural lighting. Cyclone proofed, of course, and the electricity comes from a solar plant on the roof. It's completely self-sufficient, with an environmental waste disposal unit for anything biodegradable."

As they walked through, Vivian studied her guest. Claire seemed more at ease without the other agent. She was dressed casually, jeans and shirt, but if she were going to stay, she'd be wiser to put on lighter clothes. The heat would wear her down. Her hair, still in a long plait, looked even whiter in the sunlight and her pale skin conveyed a hint of vulnerability. Vivian, who topped her by about three centimetres and tanned to a golden colour, felt awkward and graceless. She found herself at one stage about to place her hand on Claire's back to usher her through a doorway, before she realized what she was doing and jerked her arm back. After that, she was careful to keep her distance, content to watch her guest examine the house.

Vivian was proud of her home. It blended perfectly into the landscape, the interior functional and comfortable. The huge living area combined the kitchen, dining section and lounge. The outer walls were made up of long panels of glass to let in the sunlight, which made an attractive reflection off the polished wood floors. An overstuffed lounge suite flanked a low coffee table carved from red cedar. The dining table and chairs, as well as a bookcase in the corner of the lounge area, were also made from the same timber.

"It's lovely, Vivian, and so practical. I bet you had fun designing it."

Vivian was pleased with her reaction. She didn't have many visitors and it was a pleasure to show her creation, especially to someone from the city. "Come and have a look at the back garden." She was proud of it too. It was a mass of exotic blooms.

"What a gorgeous display!" said Claire as she stepped out on the back landing. "And no neighbours behind either." She looked over the back fence at the wall of rain forest, which continued unbroken to the range of mountains in the distance. "Do you ever go in there?"

"Rarely. Although there are tracks in, the vegetation's dense and too many things that bite hide in there. I prefer to bushwalk along the coastal areas which are much more user-friendly."

"I don't blame you. It looks like a jungle."

Her good humour restored, Vivian gazed warmly at the agent. It wasn't such a chore to entertain Claire, though she was still determined not to accept the position. "Sit down and I'll make us a cup of something. Tea, coffee or something cold?"

"Tea please. You live alone?"

For some reason she couldn't explain, Vivian was thrown off balance by the question. She frowned. "Yes. Why do you ask?"

A touch of pink stole over Claire's cheeks. "Forgive me. That was rude. It's none of my business."

"So Claire, let's put our cards on the table. What do you know about me, and why are you so adamant that I be your guide?"

"The sergeant assured us you were the best one for the job. He said you are an avid bushwalker and been on every trail in the district. Also, you are self-employed, and this time of year is your slack season."

Vivian brought the cups to the table and sat down on the chair opposite. "Come now. That doesn't explain why you're so persistent after I declined the position. Many locals would be more than adequate for the job and can take time off. You picked me for a reason. What is it?"

"We need someone discreet, who doesn't panic under pressure."

"And you think that's me? Damn, you don't know anything about me."

Claire lowered her voice and lightly touched her arm. Vivian looked down at the hand. It was exquisite, the fingers long and narrow like a musician's, with delicate blue veins under the surface of the skin. Though from the handshake the previous day, Vivian knew there was a surprising strength in the fingers. Her voice was equally charming, throaty and articulated. "It's what I'm trained to do. Read people. I sense you know how to look after yourself and will be handy in a sticky situation. And you're honest. We need someone like that. Would you help us… me?"

Vivian felt a pang to destroy the intimacy of the moment. The agent was very persuasive. "Sorry. No can do. This heroic, larger-than-life figure that you're trying to portray me as is rubbish."

The pale eyes widened in surprise then narrowed. "So, what will it take to persuade you?"

"Nothing."

"You don't look like a person who'd be content to miss an opportunity for a little adventure and different company. It must be lonely living alone in such isolation."

Vivian bristled. *How dare the woman judge me.* "You think I'm incarcerated in this place? It's my own business how and where I choose to live."

Claire fiddled with the spoon on the saucer. "Sorry. I didn't mean to upset you. It was only an observation."

"Huh! I'm beginning to think nothing you say is a mere *observation*. You're not going to change my mind so give it up," said Vivian in a firm voice, but underneath the veneer, she knew Claire was right. She wasn't satisfied with being alone anymore.

Claire eyed her for a moment with a thoughtful expression, as though she was measuring the percentages. "Then I shall have to give you something to make you interested," she murmured.

"Don't you ever give up?"

A sunny smile broke out on the agent's face. "Not if I want something. Now, I'm going to tell you who we are looking for. I expect you to keep it confidential. Agreed?"

"Whoa! If you start telling secrets, I'll be under an obligation to help. You can begin by being truthful about why you want me. When you looked me up on the Internet, what did you find?"

For the first time, Claire looked disconcerted. "You know very well I found nothing. You haven't a profile anywhere. No Facebook, no Twitter, nothing."

"But…?"

"Okay. I made a phone call to my boss when I got back to my room last night. You're Vivian Rathbone, ex-Australian Secret Intelligence Service officer. You were wounded in a covert operation five years ago and retired from the service for medical reasons."

Vivian's skin goose bumped. Claire's chief must be a hell of an important person. Vivian's details were top secret, especially now she'd left ASIS. Everyone she knew, including Beverly, thought she was a regular officer of the Australian military and wounded in Afghanistan. "That's highly classified information. Who do *you* work for?"

"Let's just say my organization isn't on anyone's radar."

"So, what brings you hugger-muggers up here?"

"We're looking for that young man I showed you in the picture. We know he was seen in Port Douglas three weeks ago. He told a backpacker he was coming up here somewhere."

"To this town?"

"No, somewhere just outside."

"What on earth for?"

"We suspect there may be a terrorist training camp hidden in the hills and he's been recruited," said Claire with a grimace.

Surprised and intrigued, Vivian stared at her. "Where did you get that information? I've seen nothing to suggest there's a foreign base in these parts. How would they get in and out without anyone seeing them? Hell, the damn grapevine would have them nailed within two days. In the winter, it's a bit different. We get a few grey nomads in their caravans making a detour here, though mostly they stay on the established routes. There's no mobile phone coverage, which tends to put people off from staying for long. And in the wet summer, it's only the local population."

"But there is an Internet service."

"Yes, satellite broadband. You have to pay through the nose for the usage."

Claire smiled. "Sounds a good place to disappear to."

"I suspect that a few in the town are escaping from something."

"Like you?" Claire toned down the statement with a smile.

Vivian nodded reluctantly. "Like me, I'm afraid. Now who's this person you're looking for?"

"Dane Ahmed, son of Senator Basil Ahmed."

Vivian leaned forward with heightened interest. "Ah…I remember Dane was in the news a couple of years ago. He used his father's government credit card to rack up thirty thousand bucks shouting his mates' grog, trips to the races, online gambling and callgirls. So how long has he been missing?"

"Three months. My organization's been called in to find him."

"Why? Young people often go holidaying without touching home base. There's a lot more to it than that, isn't there? If I were to take a stab, I'd say it would be something to do with his father being a person of interest."

Claire rapped a tattoo with her fingernails on the top of the table. Straightening, she stated firmly, "If I say any more you're in, whether you like it or not. Do you want me to go on?"

"First, I have to ask why you're hell-bent on trusting me. I could be a part of whatever organization is up here. As you know, I'm not your average gardener."

"Let's just say I've got on good authority your credentials are impeccable and you're fiercely loyal to your country. When the police sergeant recommended you as a guide, it was simply just to do that. But now we know who you are, I have the authority to share certain particulars with you. This business could be a major security alert and I've been assured you're a good person to have behind my back."

Vivian got up, walked to the window and pressed her fingers against the glass. She looked with pride across to her orchard and the gardens. It had taken over four years to get to this point. Did she want to get involved? She could be throwing it all away. Her life now was stress-free. There was no more looking over her shoulder, or worrying if the next bullet had her name on it. Yet, though she had found peace and security, she hadn't attained the most important ingredient: happiness. What did she want to do with the rest of her life? She certainly didn't want to be put into a niche, or to be under orders again. But she knew those were negatives. Wistfully she looked at her land and knew that whatever would fulfill her from now on couldn't be found here. She was already struggling against her own restlessness. It was time to go further afield.

She turned to study the agent. Claire eyed her steadily. Vivian knew if she declined this time, it would be the last of the matter. But she also knew as sure as there were stars in the sky, that she would regret it. And there was something about the agent, something that made Vivian desire to know her better. "If I say yes, when do I start?" Vivian asked.

"As soon as possible. You'll do it then?"

Vivian wiped her palms on her shorts, smiled wryly and thrust out her hand. "I will. I've moved past my issues now and as much as there are no pressures in my life, I can't throw off the feeling I'm just treading water. And have been for months. Do you know what I mean?"

Claire clasped her hand. "It's not surprising after your former life. Your mind and body have healed, so this…" she waved her free hand in the air, "all this isn't enough anymore."

Vivian looked down, surprised how welcoming the handshake felt. It had been a long time since she had experienced anything so comforting and she felt a slight reluctance to release it. "Okay, now tell me what you can."

CHAPTER FOUR

Claire pulled a photograph out of her bag and handed it over. It was a snapshot of Senator Ahmed with three men of Middle Eastern ethnicity. While Vivian examined it, Claire travelled her eyes over the ex-agent. Cleaned up, Vivian was a different woman. Her body was honed by physical work, her sleeveless shirt showing off well-muscled arms and wide shoulders. Yet for all the masculine overtones, she retained a definite aura of femininity. And the way she held herself suggested she was comfortable in her own skin and completely in control. No surprises there. She must have enormous inner strength and capability to have spent so many years as a deep undercover agent.

Her features were strong and prepossessing, though her brown hair hung untidily over her ears as if she had hacked at it herself. Her nose was straight, her cheekbones clearly defined, her mouth generous and her firm chin had a defined cleft. A scar over her left eyebrow added a hint of intrigue. Claire hummed with appreciation and then turned her head guiltily when she realized she had lingered too long.

Vivian's personal information in the dossier had been thin on the ground. Thirty-three when she was medically discharged, which would make her thirty-eight now. At the time of her last assignment, she had been in a relationship with a woman, though nothing further had been added. Claire wondered what that story was.

When Vivian noticed her scrutiny, Claire focused back on the immediate problem. "We've got some particulars on two of the men. They have ties to the Islamic militants in Syria."

"Where was it taken?" asked Vivian, peering at the photo.

"The Australian National Security force told us it was somewhere in Switzerland. The senator was there last August for a trade convention."

"Who took the photo?"

"We haven't been supplied with that information. I presume it came from someone undercover."

"But all the same," said Vivian, "they must have something else on Ahmed. But being seen with suspected terrorists isn't proof he's in collusion with them. Or that it's a conspiracy to perform a terrorist act."

"Last year he had to front an investigative hearing regarding some of his larger holdings and coal gas investments which he sold. This certainly isn't common knowledge, but the authorities suspect it may have been to fund Islamic State."

"I see. So, what kind of man is he? What's his profile?"

Claire shrugged. "He seemed to be liked by his parliamentary colleagues, popular in his electorate though he is outspoken on the floor. He's a Muslim and a good family man. But our main concern is Dane Ahmed. We haven't been employed to investigate the senator, we've been assigned to look for his son."

"So what's your organization?"

A ghost of a smile flittered on Claire's lips. "Ah…that's classified."

"Okay. So why are you trying to find Dane. What exactly has he done?"

"He's suspected of being in an ISIS training camp here somewhere. Find the son, and the father can be nailed. That's their theory. So far satellite surveillance has found nothing, which leaves us no option but to track him by land."

"Hmmm. It's a bit sketchy. So how long have you been looking for him?" asked Vivian.

"A month."

"It took you *that* long to discover he was here?"

Claire flushed at the tone. "He covered his tracks like an expert. He was either smart or had help. We got a tip he came north, and it took a lot of legwork to find that backpacker in Port Douglas. Dane hasn't been using his credit card or contacting anyone."

"Does he have any trade or profession?"

"He's got a Wildlife Science degree," said Claire. "Just through last year and hasn't a job yet."

"Have you any concrete proof he actually intended to hide. Lots of young backpackers vanish for a period then resurface somewhere else."

"The feds have been keeping tabs on the family for quite a while. Dane's been keeping a low profile since the credit card incident."

"Do you think the corpse in the mangroves could be tied up with him?" asked Vivian.

"A dead stranger with a considerable amount of cash on him certainly isn't an ordinary occurrence. From the photos you took, he seemed to have a darkish complexion, though from the state he was in, it was a bit hard to tell." She paused to take a long sip from her cup before continuing. "There should be some fingerprints on the money. We're lucky the belt pouch was waterproof."

"That in itself tells us something," mused Vivian. "The body had been in the channel for days by the look of it, yet water hadn't seeped into the money. It was obviously no ordinary pouch. The owner must have expected to go places where the contents had to be protected from the elements."

"Yes. And that begs the question. How did the dead guy get so far inland? You did say it took you a while to get to the fishing spot?"

Vivian nodded. "Yes…a long way from the shoreline, so it's hardly likely he fell off a passing ship out to sea. Sharks or crocs would have taken him before he was washed too far. You don't swim in the sea here. The only way inland up the river estuary is by boat. It would be virtually impossible to hike in that terrain. The mangroves and surrounding scrub are much too thick. But if he did come upriver, someone must have taken him there because there was no boat in sight."

"Or he could have been thrown out of a plane or helicopter," added Claire.

"That's an option as well." Vivian looked at her expectantly. "What do you want me to do, and where do you to plan to start?"

"We've hired a plane this afternoon to do a sweep over the area so I want you to come," Claire answered, her voice now businesslike. "We'll have to rely on you after that. You know the area and we'll formulate a strategy from there. We can look at local maps tomorrow. Since it's now Thursday, you can have the weekend to organize someone to look after your business and we can start on Monday. How does that sound?"

Vivian smiled but looked hesitant. "That's fine, but does your partner know my history? I have a feeling Hansen is going to resent me giving orders."

"No, I haven't shared that information with him. I'm in charge of the operation and I was given your particulars in strict confidence. But don't worry about Ross…he's a professional," said Claire with a dismissive wave.

Vivian looked at her dubiously though didn't comment further. When Claire made to rise from the table, Vivian reached across and touched her arm. "Would you…um…like to see the gardens?"

"I'd love to," said Claire, pleased and surprised. The diffident woman was thawing out. There was something appealing in how Vivian suddenly looked so shy. "I've never been so far north. Actually, I haven't been further than Townsville and I'm finding this a really beautiful part of the country."

"North from Ingham I think is the one of the prettiest parts of Australia. Mind you, it is also the wettest. We've had a dry spell for a while, but the clouds are rolling in so I expect that's going to change. It may hamper our search if the rains start. Now come on, I'll show you around."

Claire followed Vivian across the lawn, appreciating how pretty the scenery was, with tropical lush vegetation as far as the eye could see. An immodest green, almost too vibrant to be true. And somehow surreal: there was something fundamentally incompatible between the crowded city and the isolation of the bush. In the orchard, she stepped gingerly to avoid the toads beneath the trees. As she moved through, the smell of damp earth brought back the memories, sending a shiver down her spine. A familiar ache filled her chest. Then her mind snapped to the present when something squelched under her foot. She grimaced. "Yuck! I just stood on a toad. How do you put up with them?"

Vivian rolled one over with a stick and held it in place with another. "Ugly little bugger, isn't it? There is very little we can do. They thrive in these tropic conditions and their offspring can reach adult size within a year. They have no specific predators or diseases that can control them. Some of the birds flip them over to eat their stomachs, but the rest of the animals learn to leave them alone." She pointed to a raised lump on the toad's shoulder. "See here…they're poisonous glands. I don't take much notice of them anymore."

Claire didn't comment again, though was extra careful where she walked as they wound their way past the paw-paw trees and the bananas to the space beyond. Strips of vegetables filled the sizable plot. She found something comforting about the well-tended garden, warmed by fingers of sunshine peeking through the clouds. She could easily understand why Vivian had chosen this life. It was a safe haven, undisturbed by the foibles of civilization: no conflict, no self-righteous asses telling you what to do. But Claire also knew that eventually it would never be enough for someone like her. The sanctuary would become a cage once Vivian was healed.

Vivian explained the plantings, the marketing strategies and the intricacies of the irrigation system. The former ASIS officer had to be admired. Claire knew she had sustained life-threatening injuries, yet she hadn't coddled her affliction. Instead, she had gone on with life.

"Are there any lingering effects from your abdominal injuries?" Claire asked and immediately regretted her words. She had just let the woman know she had more than just a passing knowledge of her service record.

Thankfully, Vivian didn't comment. "It took a while, but I'm healed now, body and soul. In the beginning, it was hard, but eventually, I went cold turkey on the medication."

"I'm sorry for asking," said Claire, impulsively grasping her arm. "You are a brave woman."

Vivian smiled, though it was laced with a little bitterness. "Sheer obstinacy is far more durable than courage. You'll learn that one day."

"Oh, I know that well enough. We all have our demons to contend with," muttered Claire.

Although Vivian looked at her enquiringly, she didn't offer anything more. "So what about your colleague…do you work together all the time?" Vivian asked.

"Ross and I have been on many assignments. He's solid and capable."

"Is this what you do…find people?"

"Mainly." She swung round to face Vivian as they turned back towards the house. "Now that's all I'm going to tell you, so no more probing."

"Fair enough, though you can't blame me for trying. I love a good mystery."

Claire mirrored Vivian's friendly smile, though she was well aware not to make a mistake in front of this woman. She had better be careful her easy companionship didn't cause a slip of her tongue. Vivian Rathbone, AKA Andrews, should be kept at arm's length for she had considerable experience in espionage. But strangely, Claire didn't want to keep an impersonal distance. The woman intrigued her.

"A plane's booked for two this afternoon. Can you come?"

"Sure. Who's the pilot?"

"Gaby Hillman. Do you know her?"

"Very well."

"Okay, I'll be off then." Claire lightly scratched the top of the terrier's head before she pulled open the car door. As she turned the wheel to drive onto the main road, she adjusted the rear vision mirror to catch the last glimpse of Vivian in front of her house. A sense of satisfaction settled over her. The morning had gone extremely well. Claire had no doubt the ex-agent would be invaluable in their search, but as well as that, she found she was looking forward to sharing more time with her. Vivian was an interesting woman, personally as well as professionally.

CHAPTER FIVE

Vivian reached the airport ten minutes before they were due to depart. At the end of the strip near a six-seater Cessna plane a tall woman stood with one hip against the rail of the steps, her arms crossed.

"Well, well…look who the cat dragged in," said Gaby in a low drawl. "Looking for a ride?"

Vivian settled her sunglasses firmly over her nose, more to hide her eyes rather than to protect them from the glare. Gaby's brash good looks, intense blue eyes and sporty physique always made her feel like a country cousin. True to form today, Gaby was a bewitching poster girl. Her short dark hair was arranged into a tousled windswept look, her shirt fit firmly across her chest and the uniform pants sat snugly over her tapered thighs. Her scuffed brown boots were designer. Next to her, Vivian's dress sense defined the word nondescript. "I'm going with the people who hired you this afternoon."

"Oh? What's up?"

"Haven't they told you where you have to go?" asked Vivian.

"I'm to do a sweep of the inland areas, starting with the mouth of the river. They said they'd fill me in when they got here."

"I'm to show them where I went fishing yesterday and then it's a general look around."

"What are they looking for?"

"Sorry Gaby, I'm not at liberty to discuss it. You'll have to ask Claire when she gets here."

Gaby had a definite gleam in her eye when she said, "I flew them up yesterday but didn't get to say much to her. She's a hottie, isn't she?"

"And straight," retorted Vivian sharply.

Gaby chuckled. "We'll see about that."

Vivian's hackles rose. "You'd…" She bit back the next words at the sound of crunching gravel. Self-consciously, she smoothed away the creases in her shirt before moving to greet the two agents.

Claire smiled in welcome, though Ross only gave a curt nod. Gaby flashed her trademark grin as she indicated the plane was ready for boarding. Vivian was pleased to note Claire only acknowledged Gaby casually before she handed Vivian a chart. "I'd appreciate if you would point out the places we see on this map. We both have a copy so just call out when we're over a particular site. It'll give us more of an idea of the lie of the land." She turned back to the pilot. "We're doing a survey of the river catchment and surrounding mountains, Ms Hillman. Go as low as you can. On the way home we can have a look at the shoreline."

"Will do. Just call out when you want me to change direction." She lowered her voice to a murmur. "And call me Gaby. Would you like to sit up front with me?"

For a second Claire held Gaby's gaze. From her expression, Vivian could see that the agent was no stranger to the attentions of women, as well as men. Claire gave Gaby a dismissive shake of her head. "Ross can keep you company."

Not completely able to quash down the spurt of satisfaction, Vivian gave Gaby a fleeting wink as she climbed into the plane.

Once they were belted into their seats, the engines began to hum and then the plane was taxiing down the runway. The seats were comfortable though hardly roomy, and as soon as Vivian sat down, she was aware of how firmly Claire's warm thigh pressed against her leg. She didn't analyse why it was so disconcerting but edged closer to the window side of her seat to put space between them.

Not that it did any good. Once they were in the air Claire continuously leaned over to look out the window, and brushed her breast against Vivian's arm. Each time, the delightful scent of spring flowers swirled around her. The perfume, coupled with the touch, sent tingles of pleasure through Vivian's body. It was something she hadn't felt for a very long time. With an effort, she divorced her mind from the sensations and concentrated on the job at hand. Even so, it worried her to be so hypersensitive to someone's touch. Her reaction to Claire was a puzzle and Vivian had no idea why she was responding to her as she was. It was completely out of character. She had even asked her to view her gardens without a thought, something she rarely invited any visitor to do, and never one she hardly knew.

Ruthlessly, she forced away all the disturbing thoughts as she looked down at the bay. The trawler grounded by yesterday's ebbing tide was no longer there. "The entrance to the river is just around the headland," she said, tilting forward to scan the area.

A bell-shaped basin filled with mud and salt flats came into view. As she turned the plane to follow the delta, Gaby called out, "Which channel, Viv?"

Vivian projected her voice to be heard over the steady thrum of the engines. "Go to Hurley's Bend then veer to the right. It took us just under an hour to get there in the boat." When she estimated they were over the site, she arched even further in her seat. "It was around about here. Do a couple of runs over it."

The Cessna banked in an arc and skimmed the vegetation. There wasn't a sign of anything untoward—just the interminable mangroves. Though she hadn't expected to see anything, Vivian still felt a prick of disappointment. It was as if the crocodile drama had never happened. Claire must have sensed she was a little troubled because she touched her arm. "Remembering?"

Vivian twitched irritably at her seat belt. "I'm not dwelling on it. It's just that Ned and I could have been the croc's next meal and nobody would ever have known."

"I'm afraid I've been unfeeling," murmured Claire. "You had a traumatic experience and needed to de-stress."

Vivian sensed the woman was genuinely concerned. She patted her hand to reassure her. "I've been in a lot of shitty situations in my lifetime, so don't worry about me." Then she couldn't help smiling. "Though that animal was by far the worst badass boy I've ever come across."

"I've never seen one in the wild," said Claire. "One thing's puzzling me though. You were a fair way up the channel. I know it's tidal, but I imagine, especially in the wet season, it would be mostly freshwater where you were. I thought saltwater crocodiles only lived in seawater."

"No, contrary to their name, they're just as happy in freshwater. Here they live in the rain forest swamps and delta channels. They don't like fast-running streams."

Claire wrinkled her nose in distaste. "Are there very many? I hope we don't happen to meet one on a dark night."

"The place is full of them, especially in the brackish water along the coastline, so don't go swimming unless it's in a house pool. The saltwater croc has the strongest bite of any animal living today, so you wouldn't have a chance." She looked at her solemnly, but with a definite gleam in her eye. "Especially a tasty morsel like you."

When Claire raised her eyebrows and murmured, "Really?" Vivian realized what she had said. *Damn, now she'll think I'm flirting with her.*

Claire gave her a friendly poke in the ribs. "Come on. Let's get back to the job at hand, though it's probably a waste of time. The trees are so thick down there, it'll be virtually impossible to see anything under their canopies."

"You're right. Unless the training camp is built in a clearing, it wouldn't be seen from the air. Any fair dinkum terrorist organization would hardly be so stupid as to have their base visible from the air, not with the ease it can be camouflaged in the rain forest. The hope of finding human activity by air will be slim, but this will be a good exercise to show you the terrain and where, if there is indeed a camp, it would most likely be situated."

After another hour, she knew she was right. No sign of buildings or tents, except for a communications tower on top of one of the higher mountains. They'd flown over the tower site, which was too isolated to be accessed except by helicopter, and seen nothing suspicious. During the search, Vivian had indicated various points of possible interest. Most of the rain forest and mountains would be too inaccessible to be a realistic site, which narrowed down the field.

After it left the mountains, the plane did a few low sweeps over the bay. Even though she had flown many times down the coast, Vivian was still enchanted by the colours of the water. The pristine white beach sand created a vibrant edge to the tapestry of emerald greens and azure blues of the ocean.

After a final run, Gaby swung the plane towards the landing strip. With barely a shudder the Cessna touched down and taxied to the hangar. At the bottom of the steps, Claire turned to Vivian with an easy smile. "Would you like to join us at the hotel for dinner? It'll save you having to cook and I don't know about you, but I'm hungry."

Although she had intended to go straight home, Vivian accepted without a second thought, "Sounds good."

Gaby, catching the invitation as she climbed out of the cockpit, looked enquiringly at Claire. "I'm staying at the pub. Do you mind if I join you?"

"Please do."

"Could I catch a lift into town with you, Viv?" asked Gaby. "You can clean up in my room if you like." Not waiting for an answer, she threaded an arm over Vivian's shoulders with the familiarity of good friends.

Vivian paused only briefly before she replied, "Okay. We'll see you there, Claire." As she turned to the parking lot, she moved out of the grasp. Damn Gaby. It was going to take more than a friendly hug to get back into her good books.

"Are you cranky with me?" asked Gaby as they climbed into the utility.

Vivian jammed the key in the lock then turned abruptly in the seat. "What's with you? I thought you were with that physiotherapist. Now you're trying to get on to Claire."

"She's old news. If you came down to Cairns more often, you would have known that. You've become a hermit."

"I know. I can't seem to get myself motivated. But be careful with Claire. She's given no indication she's gay, and the man with her is quite protective," said Vivian, though she doubted the warning would get through to her friend. Once Gaby had her eye on a woman, she was tenacious.

"Don't worry about me. I can handle myself." She looked at Vivian with a curious expression. "What exactly are they looking for and why are you mixed up with them?"

"I'm going to be their guide for a while, but other than that, I can't say."

"Okay, I know it's hush-hush, but I find it hard to believe that anything world-shattering would happen in this frigging backwoods place. If they're looking for someone, he or she couldn't remain hidden here for long."

Vivian didn't comment further. Gaby was right. Anyone new would be noticed immediately. And that could only mean one thing—if there indeed were a camp nearby, they would have to be helped by a local person, or persons. She thought about the town's residents, aware that given the right motivation, some people were capable of any subterfuge. But this was a close-knit community, mostly fishermen. Tonnes of coral trout and Spanish mackerel were shipped to the southern markets from these waters.

She couldn't think of anyone here who would commit an act of violence against the country. Perhaps, though, searching for someone in the town with past ties to the Islamic world, or a grudge against the government, could be a starting point.

* * *

The two agents were already seated by the time Vivian and Gaby arrived in the hotel lounge. All vestiges of fatigue disappeared and Vivian's pulse quickened when she saw Claire across the table. Her silk shirt brought out her gentle curves, the blue complementing her eyes perfectly. She wondered if Claire had anyone at home waiting for her, then concluded reluctantly she must have. No one who looked like her, and with her personality, would be alone. Vivian felt a pang of envy. It would be wonderful to come home to a lover. She had forgotten what it felt like to open her door to anyone other than the cold welcome of her empty house with only a dog for company.

Still in her day clothes, Vivian took a seat at the table, feeling out of sorts. All eyes were fixed on Gaby who looked like a sporty supermodel in a fresh outfit, casual but elegant, tight pants and revealing top. With a shrug, Vivian reached in her wallet for her credit card. "I'll get the drinks. What'll you have?"

"Our shout tonight—we have an expense account so Ross will sort it," said Claire with a wave of her hand.

Vivian tucked her card back. "Sounds good. I'll have a Bacardi and Coke."

"And I'll have a white wine. What about you, Gaby?" asked Claire.

"A beer please," said Gaby, and lowered her voice to a murmur as she leaned over the table. "You look great tonight, Claire."

Ross, who was eyeing Gaby warily, muttered, "Yes, she does."

Gaby watched him slide his chair closer to his colleague. When he left for the bar, she shifted her own seat nearer to Claire and asked. "Are you two an item?"

After an awkward pause, Claire answered in an annoyed tone. "That's hardly any of your business."

"Sorry…no offense. I always manage to put my foot into it."

As she watched from the sideline, Vivian held back a cynical snort. Gaby rarely made a wrong move. The smile accompanying her words was a combination of innocence and temptation.

She'd seen her friend in action too many times for Vivian to be impressed. But it seemed to work every time.

"No offense taken. But just so you know, Gaby, I don't play for your team," said Claire, her gaze fixed steadily on the pilot.

At those words, Vivian felt an inexplicable sense of loss. Gaby, though, took it in her stride as she flashed her teeth in a wide, white smile. "Now that's a challenge, honey."

Claire's only answer was to arch her eyebrows, and then Ross was back with the drinks.

As they talked, Vivian had to admire Claire for the way she handled Gaby's flirting with so little effort. At first Vivian was amused, but in the end, it got under her skin. "For shit sake," she snapped at Gaby, "leave Claire alone. You're making a fool of yourself."

"It's only a bit of lighthearted banter and I think I'm quite capable of handling the situation," said Claire with a frown. "There's no need to put your ten cent's worth in."

Vivian gave her a long, level stare, her temper ignited by a spark of anger at the dismissive words. "Maybe. But it's really irritating. It might be entertaining to you, but I came to have a nice, peaceful meal."

Spots of red tinged Claire's cheeks. Her jaw tightened. "Well, we don't want to upset you, do we?"

"Problem with that?"

"It depends," Claire said, curling her fingers tightly around the stem of her glass.

"On what?"

"On whether you…" Claire stopped abruptly and brushed a strand of hair off her face. She gave a rueful shake of her head. "Sorry, you're right. I should have nipped this in the bud much earlier." She looked at Gaby. "I'm not available, so please, knock it off."

"No worries," said Gaby quickly. "I was only having a bit of fun." She turned to Vivian with a gleam in her eye. "I think it's about time you had a night out. You've lost your sense of humour and you're getting crotchety. What about coming with me to Cairns on Saturday night? I fly to Cooktown tomorrow morning for a couple of charters, so I'll pick you up on the way through on Saturday afternoon. Be at the airport at five."

Even though Vivian could think of nothing worse than a big night out before what promised to be a gruelling couple of weeks, she *was* pleased to receive the invitation. She needed to go to Cairns, though not for the reason Gaby suggested. But she may as well kill two birds with one stone. After the way she had just overreacted, the pleasure of a woman's company was probably what she needed. She should have been able to sit back and enjoy Claire's efforts to fend off a suitor, but she hadn't thought it comical. In fact, she'd been overcome with an unwelcome feeling that had felt a little like jealousy, though she knew that couldn't be right. She hardly knew Claire and the woman was neither gay nor unattached.

With a nod, she said lightly, "I'll take you up on that offer. As long as you get me back by Sunday afternoon, I'd like to go."

Gaby smiled. "I'm sure Madeline will be happy to see you."

Vivian ignored the remark. "Anyone like another drink?"

"Shall we order our meal? I don't want a late night," said Claire.

"Good idea," chipped in Gaby. "I'm famished."

An hour later, Claire pushed the empty plate to the side and for a second held Vivian's gaze. "It's time I went to bed. I'll see you at the police station in the morning at eight."

Ross rose as well. "I'm off to the front bar for an hour."

Vivian watched them exit the room before she turned to Gaby. "Why did you mention Madeline? You know I'm not interested."

Gaby skimmed a finger down the side of her beer bottle and pulled absently at the label. "But you like Claire, don't you?"

"What gave you that impression?"

"Come off it. It was written all over your face. I would suggest you don't get too wrapped up there. She's way out of the league of a small-town market gardener."

Gaby had Vivian's full attention now. She studied her friend. She had subtly taken on another persona, one Vivian hadn't seen before. More serious, more…she groped for the words in her mind…more calculating. Why was she warning her off the agent? Vivian knew instinctively it had nothing to do sex, or attraction or whatever the hell Gaby thought Vivian was feeling. No—this was about Claire's reason for being here. But what had it to do with her? With a forced smile, she reached over and gave Gaby's arm a squeeze. "You've got a one-track mind. What you're seeing on my face is probably indigestion after that big meal. Now I'd better be off as well."

"I'll see you Saturday then," said Gaby as they rose from the table together, seemingly content not to pursue the matter.

After Gaby disappeared up the stairs to her room, Vivian took a deep breath, lost in thought. Idly she fingered the slip of paper tucked in her pocket. The planned night out in Cairns couldn't have come at a more opportune time. Madeline had some explaining to do. Why her phone number was in the dead man's pouch would be a good place to start.

CHAPTER SIX

Claire woke with a start, her heart pounding, her gut churning. Wet with perspiration, she slipped her hand over her stomach to ease her nausea. Roughly, she wiped her face with the sheet as she grappled to get her bearings. Lost in the dark unfamiliar surroundings, she tossed off the covers. Disoriented, she stepped towards what she thought was the bathroom, only to kick her toe on a chair. She hopped and cursed in pain. Why hadn't she left a gap between the curtains? It was pitch black.

She groped blindly along the wall until she found a light switch. The long fluorescent bulb above the bench lit up. She made her way into the bathroom, but even as she splashed water on her face, a remnant of the dream lingered. She shuddered. The smell of sickly decay mixed with damp earth seemed to fill the room, along with the sound of the mother's sobs, the father's accusations. Tears swirled in her eyes. She forced them away, anger replacing the desire to weep. *The same fucking dream! Why has it resurfaced again?*

Coffee helped chase away the demons and put her in a better frame of mind. Daylight was beginning to creep over the horizon when she stepped outside to embrace the cool air. At least rising at dawn meant she could relax for a while before the heat ramped up. Overhead a few clouds floated in the sky, which reminded her of Vivian's prediction of rain. Seated on a balcony chair, bits and pieces of the previous day flew through her mind in no particular order.

As much as she tried to be objective, somehow her thoughts swung back to Vivian. What was it about the woman that got under her skin? Claire had met far more attractive and eligible women, yet none had made such an impression, or unsettled her like the reticent ex-covert officer managed to do.

A flicker of guilt niggled. Even though it had been none of their business last night, she hadn't wanted to deny her sexuality. For years, she had compartmentalized that part of her life away from her profession. It wasn't as if she was actually in the closet. Her friends and family knew, but she had deliberately not mentioned it at work. Working with alpha men, it just wasn't worth the effort. The place was swimming in testosterone. She had enough to contend with as a female in a male-dominated organization without having to put up with digs about her sexual orientation. And between assignments, she didn't have to go out in public to seek company. Ruby was very happy to take her to bed to help her de-stress.

Another wave of self-reproach hit. Claire didn't enjoy their sex much anymore—had she ever really found it that exciting? Before she left this time, she had hinted she was no longer happy, but she hadn't been able to make the final break. Although they both had agreed their occasional liaisons came with the label "no-strings-attached," Claire sensed Ruby was becoming serious. The attractive marketing CEO with her soft feminine looks and her love of designer clothes was the opposite of Vivian, but the type of professional woman Claire had always thought attractive. She grimaced. If she were honest with herself, Ruby was really the kind of partner that everyone *expected* her to find appealing.

Irritated, she stared over the street at the sea in the distance. The sun was a bowl of glowing light on the horizon, mirroring the emotion rising within her. Professional women in power suits really didn't excite her. And Gaby's style, with unabashed androgynous good looks and bold charm did nothing for her either. But Vivian…well…she was one of the most appealing women she had ever met. Strong, quiet and slightly rough around the edges. God, her mother would have a fit if she brought her home. Camilla Walker was okay with her daughter being a lesbian, as long as Claire's partner had social standing. Not that there were any worries on that score. Vivian didn't seem overly impressed with her.

The coffee cup empty, Claire rose to get dressed. She had to put away all personal thoughts—this was work, not happy hour. The assignment was too important to be distracted. But as she soaped herself under the shower, a question, and a smidgeon of jealousy, nibbled in the back of her mind.

Who exactly was Madeline?

* * *

Ross arrived at the breakfast table with a mumbled "Hello," and bleary-eyed, flopped down with a grunt.

"How did you get on?" Claire asked. "It must have been a good night by the look of you."

He grinned. "They sure can drink up this way."

"Anything to report?"

"Yes and no. The boys at the bar hadn't seen anybody new in the town except for a few grey nomads. There's only a basic council park, so they usually only camp for a day or two and move on. Unless they're interested in fishing, they never stay."

"Any backpackers?"

"One or two came through in the winter, but none recently. There's no hostel so they don't tend to stay either…this isn't exactly an adventure seeker's utopia. Off the beaten track for any action. Cairns and Port Douglas are the trendy places."

Claire growled in frustration. "We didn't think it was going to be easy. So what's the *yes* part?"

"There *was* something the blokes noticed. Occasionally a trawler comes into the bay and anchors off the beach for a day or two, then disappears again."

"Does the crew ever come into town?" asked Claire.

"No, they don't. It sounds a bit promising, doesn't it? A boat would be the ideal way to bring supplies in for a camp. A truck would be noticed."

"You're right. They could ferry stuff to a deserted part of the beach then carry it inland. But still," she mused, "there would be lots of big items having to be brought in for a camp housing a lot of men. Someone is sure to have seen something. Did they say when the vessel was last in the bay?"

"Only a few days ago, unfortunately. That means it probably won't be back for a while."

"Do they know what it's called?"

He reached into his pocket for a pen and scribbled three names on the serviette.

"But that's three different boats."

Ross nodded. "The locals all know it's the same trawler, even though the owner changes the name. He, or she, doesn't go to much trouble to renew the paint work."

As her mind whirled Claire absently reached for the butter. "Maybe Joe Hamilton has more information on the vessel," she said. "When we've finished eating, we're going over to the police station. Joe has maps of the area and he and Vivian can plan where we should be looking."

* * *

Vivian bustled in half an hour late to the station. "Sorry, I hope I didn't hold you up. I asked a friend to give me a better haircut now I'm going out this weekend, and she took her time. I've been cutting it myself lately as you no doubt noticed."

Claire tried to ignore her twitch of attraction. The super short cut, layered over her cheekbones and tousled on top, made Vivian look sexy as hell. "Being shorter it'll be much easier to handle in the places we're going," she replied in a matter-of-fact voice. "Now come over here and have a look at these maps and mark the possible routes to the mountains. I've got your sites from yesterday's plane trip, so we can go from there." When she caught Vivian's disappointed look, she added more kindly, "Your hair looks fantastic."

Vivian shoved her hand in her pocket with a little cough. "Thanks. It certainly feels much better now it doesn't flop over my eyes."

Claire couldn't help tilting her head and smiling. Vivian looked disarmingly vulnerable, totally unself-conscious in her slightly rumpled shirt and faded shorts. Then aware she was staring, she moved quickly over to allow Vivian a place in front of the table. She turned to the sergeant. "There is one thing we want to ask you, Joe. Do you know anything about the fishing trawler that comes periodically into the bay?"

He scratched his head. "Which one? Most people make their living from fishing here."

"Apparently this one doesn't belong to a local. It only stays a night or two and the crew never come to town. Our source told us it goes by these three names." She handed over the list: Blue Moon, Miss Millie and Lucky Catch.

"I've seen it. I haven't any idea why the owner changes the name, but it's the same boat, all right."

"You've never investigated it?"

"There were no indications the crew was doing anything illegal. In fact, they caused no disruptions in the town. They just kept to themselves. I presumed the owner was a businessman who went fishing when he could get away. The boat's not the kind used by foreign fishermen."

"You didn't think it odd that the vessel has a few names?" asked Ross sharply.

Joe studied him for a moment before he said firmly with finality. "People can be strange, but they're entitled to do what they like with their own property. Unless they break a law in my town, I can't go out and arrest them for calling their boat something different every time they take it out. For your information, a hull ID number is required for registration, not a name. Now let's get on with it." He signalled for Vivian to come closer and pointed at the map spread out on the laminated top. "I've marked with a red pen the likely places for a camp. See what you think."

As they examined the maps, the door opened and middle-aged woman carrying a biscuit tin entered the room.

"Dee. Weren't you going shopping?" asked Hamilton.

She set the tray on the end of the desk. "I thought I'd make some biscuits for morning tea since you've got company. We can't let visitors go without showing them some Bay hospitality."

"No indeed."

During the introductions, Claire watched the interaction between the couple. Dee Hamilton was a short, plump woman, with a warm friendly face and wavy brown hair speckled with grey. Claire surmised by the way Joe snapped to attention when she entered the room that Dee wore the pants in the relationship.

Dee gave them a wave of her hand. "Go ahead and continue what you're doing. I'll put on the kettle."

She stayed all morning, cheerily topping up their cups, and by noon, they had finished. The possible sites and routes in mountains were plotted until they were reasonably happy they had covered every scenario. The lists of supplies, vehicles, medical kits and tracking aids were finalized. The weekend was left free for the two agents to do more investigations in the community.

"Right," said Vivian. She stood and stretched the cricks out of her neck. "That'll have to do me. I've work to do at home. Thanks for the help, Dee." She turned to face Claire. "Would you like to come over to my place for dinner tonight? That is, if you haven't any plans. I can throw some streaks on the barbie."

Claire looked at her in surprise. She instinctively knew the invitation didn't include Ross, though Vivian had left it open-ended if she preferred he accompany her. She was saved embarrassment when he said, "I'm going for a drink with Joe."

"Then I'd love to come. I'm sure the men will have a better time without me." She smiled at Ross. "I trust you won't need the Jeep tonight?"

"I can pick you up and take you home," offered Vivian.

"You can have the car," said Ross firmly.

She nodded to her colleague. "Thanks. Then I'll see you at say…six-thirty, Vivian."

"Right. I'll be off then."

As Claire watched her walk away, she couldn't help feeling a rush of warmth mixed with anticipation. It was only dinner between colleagues, but all the same, it did oddly feel like a date.

Dee watched on from across the room.

CHAPTER SEVEN

"Where's my shoe, Toby? I swear I'll get you for this, you little mongrel."

On her hands and knees, Vivian peered underneath the bed. As the terrier darted just out of reach, she swore sometimes the dog could understand every word she said. Resigned to the fact they were her old loafers, she gave up. There was only half an hour left to slip through the shower, dress and prepare the salad before her guest arrived. Typically, the irrigation pump had played up just when it mattered. Toby ducked off downstairs to wait by his dinner bowl in the kitchen as she stripped.

Vivian had given up wondering why she had asked Claire to dinner. The invitation had just sprung out of her mouth without a thought. Not that she regretted her spontaneity. She hadn't felt this excited to be seeing someone for years and had to remind herself it wasn't a date. Claire wasn't available, nor was she a lesbian. A part of her accepted that, but the other half didn't care or damper her enthusiasm. Tonight she was going to have dinner with a fascinating, attractive woman, something she hadn't done for years.

After she shuffled through her uninspiring wardrobe, she chose what she considered the best of a bad lot. Black jeans and a deep purple top, with a silver neck chain and belt to add some colour. She assessed her reflection critically in the mirror. The outfit seemed too severe, but with a glance at her watch, she left the clothes on. They'd have to do.

With a dash to the kitchen, Vivian poured dog biscuits into the bowl, grabbed two coral trout fillets from the freezer, put a chardonnay in the fridge and began to tackle a Caesar salad. As she was putting the sprigs of parsley on top, the doorbell rang. She opened the door to find Claire on the porch, a bottle of wine clutched in her hand. Vivian was unable to keep the admiration out of her voice. "Hi there. You look really great!"

A damn sight more than great! You're a knockout.

Claire wore a colourful summer frock, her long hair, free of its usual braid, was gathered loosely into a scarf at the end. Vivian knew she was staring, but found it hard to look away. With an effort, she pulled herself together enough to wave her fingers. "Come on in."

Claire, who had been gazing at her with a bemused expression, blinked then smiled. "You look very nice too."

Vivian made a huffing sound, a mixture of amusement and scepticism. "You've put me to shame. I need to update my wardrobe."

"Oh, I don't know about that. The outfit kinda suits you." Claire waggled her eyebrows. "You know…big bad sexy secret agent. Haven't the lesbians around here got a pulse?"

Vivian tossed back her head with a laugh and threw her arm over Claire's shoulder good-naturedly as they made their way inside. "You're good for the soul, missy. Now come on in and I'll put that bottle on ice. Would you like a glass now or something else to start with? I'm having a Corona."

"A beer will be fine. It's a lovely evening, isn't it?"

Vivian screwed the bottle top off with a quick twist. "The nights are really pleasant this time of year. The barbeque is out on the patio—I've hung a bug lantern for the mozzies. Take a seat while I throw on a couple of steaks. There's lemon on the bench if you want to put a piece in your beer."

"Thanks. But there's no hurry to eat, is there? I'd like to talk for a while to get to know you. We'll be spending a lot of time together so I really would love to find out what makes you tick."

"Ah," whispered Vivian, "always on the job."

Claire relaxed back in the padded outdoor chair. When she crossed her legs, a hint of thigh flashed before the fabric settled back down. "I guess I am, but that doesn't mean I don't personally want to get to know you. Where are you from originally?"

"I was brought up in Toowoomba."

"That's a lovely town. I went to see the festival of flowers once."

"It's a pretty place with a pleasant climate."

"Are your parents still there?"

"My father died young, leaving mum to raise two daughters." Vivian's throat went dry. A memory of laughter filling the air came, but then it was gone. Unwanted images seeped in—her mother's hands only bones and veins, the coffin being lowered into the ground, her sister's sobs beside her. She forced herself to continue. "When I was twenty-two she died of bowel cancer. I had already joined the service by then." Too abrupt she knew, but couldn't bring herself to elaborate. Chemo and cancer—talking about them still brought a feeling of devastating loss.

Claire was silent a moment before she asked softly, "Do you ever see your sister?"

"Barbara lives in England with her husband and their three children. It's only Christmas cards now. I used to see them occasionally between assignments, but after the injury…well…I figured I needed to get away by myself to heal properly."

"She could have helped you?"

"Barb and I have always been close, but it wouldn't have been fair for her to have to look after me as well as her own family. I was pretty messed up for a while."

Claire reached over and softly stroked her arm. "You did have a battle, didn't you?"

"I've managed."

"Didn't you have anybody close to turn to? A partner?"

Even though her failed relationship with Beverly was old news and hardly traumatic, Claire's probing tone hit a nerve.

She thinks I'm a damn charity case. That assumption really hurt. Vivian jerked her arm away. "I didn't tell you my history to be pitied. I just wanted you to know where I'm coming from. I look after myself and don't expect any favours. I'm completely self-sufficient and expect my privacy to be respected. You have to understand I dislike people who pry."

"Okay, point taken," replied Claire, outwardly unfazed by Vivian's outburst, but her fingers trembled on the neck of her bottle. "Would you like me to share some of my life now, or do we get onto safer, less personal topics? Perhaps the weather?"

Mortified she had overreacted, Vivian sniffed. "Yeah… well…I guess I was a bit touchy and a little rude." She bent down to run her hand through Toby's hair to help calm her nerves. *A highly trained operative and I reacted like a total amateur. What is it about this woman?*

"So…you haven't answered my question."

Vivian raised her eyes and their gazes locked. Eventually, Vivian was the one to break contact. She realized in that moment that she was afraid of Claire. Not physically, but for the power she had to disrupt her life. And it wasn't about sexual attraction. It was about the very core of her existence: her beliefs, her needs, her plans for the future. "I have to be honest with you, Claire. I acknowledge I was out of order just then, but it's taken me a long time to get where I am today and people have disappointed me. I've learned the hard way that what I do with my life is up to me to make it happen."

"Then you're to be envied. So many of us are burdened with responsibilities, our lives aren't our own."

"But *you* don't envy me, do you? You think I'm a cop-out."

"You'll have to answer that one yourself, Viv. But be prepared—self-analysis, though rewarding, can be painful."

Vivian frowned—she was losing this encounter. The only way to get back on an equal footing was to trivialize and divide, so she chuckled. "Damn it, Claire, you're good…really good. You had me going there for a while. Now get off your high horse and let's have a good few drinks and a nice meal without being so intense." She took the empty bottle out of the agent's hands. "Stay there while I get you another drink. We'll have that wine you brought while I cook the steaks, and then over dinner we'll finish off the other bottle I've got in the fridge." She gave her a wink. "And while I'm cooking, you can tell me all about that man you've got waiting for you at home."

Claire's chagrined look was worth every bit of the uncomfortable time preceding it. Vivian guessed she was not often outfoxed. Claire accepted the glass with a nod but remained silent while Vivian clicked on the gas. After the fish was on the hot plate, she turned to Claire. "Come on. What's he like?"

"I doubt you'd be interested."

"Try me."

"Well, he's...he's nice. Quite tall...rugged. Now that's all I'm going to say on the matter. Do you want me to set the table?"

"Uh-oh! Me thinks thou dost play games," Vivian murmured. "I don't think you're being truthful. You haven't a steady guy waiting for you, have you?"

Claire blushed. "How did you...okay, you're right. I haven't. I often use that defence mechanism. Being attached stops unwanted attentions, something I can do without. Satisfied now?"

"Tit for tat, I'd say," said Vivian with a satisfied gleam in her eye. "So, let's eat and you can tell me the movies you like and what music you listen to."

"Okay, but don't open that second bottle of wine. I'm driving."

Time passed as they talked on into the night, just like two people on a first date. But no matter how much Vivian wanted it to be, she knew it wasn't, just two new friends having dinner. "So what are you doing tomorrow?" she asked.

"Computer work. Actually, we should have done it before we arrived, but we didn't know where Dane was until two days ago. We're going to investigate the locals to see if we can pick something up online. Someone may be friends with someone suspicious, or one of our 'persons of interest.' Interpol supplied us with a list of suspected of terrorists and those having ties to them."

"So how will you start?"

Claire chuckled. "Facebook and Twitter, of course. They're the best source to find out who's who."

Vivian nodded. "Never a truer word was spoken. We're kidding ourselves if we think we've got privacy anymore. Big Brother *is* watching us. Your computer records everything you access in its database."

"Is that why you haven't a profile anywhere?"

"Yes. I think social media can be dangerous. While the Internet has plenty of benefits, there's a dark side we've yet to see properly. Stephen Hawking called the Internet a 'command centre for criminals and terrorists' and I think he's right. As far as I'm concerned, we're too reliant on it."

"It's the way the world works so we have to manage it properly," said Claire firmly. "We can't put our heads in the sand."

"Like me?"

"No, I didn't mean that. You are very aware of the pitfalls. It's people like you who don't use it, who will try to keep the rest of us safe." She looked at her watch. "Oh…I didn't realize it was so late. If I'm going to function at all tomorrow, I'd better get some sleep. And you have another late night tomorrow."

If Vivian didn't know better, she would have sworn Claire sounded a bit peevish about the trip to Cairns. She gave an exaggerated yawn. "Yes. The Cairns ladies are real party animals."

Claire didn't comment, but instead rose to her feet. "I'll be off then. It's been a lovely night. We'll be packing up the car on Sunday afternoon so I'll see you about four at the hotel."

"I'll be there. Put in a good pair of hiking boots. You'll need 'em." As she walked Claire to her car, Vivian thought how much they had in common and how their intellects were in tune. She couldn't remember when she had enjoyed someone's company quite so much, and she sensed Claire felt the same.

At the door of her vehicle, instead of a casual peck on the cheek to say good-bye, Claire pulled her into a hug. Vivian savoured the feel of her soft curves against her body, enjoying the moment. God, she had better watch her heart with this woman.

CHAPTER EIGHT

Claire typed the next name on the keyboard then lost concentration again. However much it seemed an exercise in futility, this was the real investigative work. Time-consuming and methodical, but a necessity. Today, though, her mind kept wandering back to the previous night. When Vivian had opened the door, Claire had nearly dropped the bottle of wine. She had thought Vivian attractive before, but dressed in that dark edgy outfit, the woman had some serious sex appeal.

Claire ran her hands over her brow, recalling with embarrassment how she had baited her almost immediately. She couldn't explain why she had wanted to get under Vivian's skin, to get a reaction, but regardless of the motivation, it had backfired. Vivian had adroitly cut her off at the pass. But after that initial tussle of wills, the night had gone extra well. She couldn't remember when she had been so entertained or felt so comfortable with someone.

"Any luck?" She was brought back abruptly from her musings by Ross's question. He was on another laptop at the end of the table with the N to Z list, but now was looking at her expectantly.

"Nope. I'm up to G, and haven't found anything remotely suss." She irritably scrolled down the page. "Why do people put so much shit on Facebook? Don't they know the whole world has access to everything they enter?"

"I don't think they give it much thought. We can be thankful this isn't going to take all day. It's such a small population." He suddenly froze the finger on the mouse and peered at the screen. "Hang on. I think I've found something. Francine Stavros's son, Ben, has posted some photos of his trip to the Middle East."

"What countries?"

"Jordan. Most are shots of Petra, but some are of Amman as well. Do people still go there with all the fighting over the border?"

"Wait a minute and I'll Google it." With a few clicks she brought up the site and skimmed through the information. "The government hasn't forbidden travel to Jordan, merely advised exercising a high degree of caution. I imagine tourism would have nearly dried up being so near Syria and Iraq. Guided tours won't go near hot spots, so he'll either be travelling alone or with friends." Claire rummaged through the stack of name files until she found the one on Francine Stavros. It was only a bare summary. "She and her husband own the only café in the Bay. They have three children, but none lives here. Ben's a twenty-four-year-old electrician."

Ross swivelled round to look at her. "What do you reckon? Should we have a chat with his parents?"

"I'll go over to their shop for lunch. The interview will have to be very low-key. I don't want to tip off the town we're snooping around."

"Yeah."

"It's way past time we let drop our cover story. They must be wondering who we are. I'll tell Francine Stavros and the grapevine should do the rest." She flexed her fingers. "Come on…back to the grindstone."

Two hours later, she swung back in her chair and snapped down the laptop lid. "That's it for me. I didn't find anything. You finished?"

"In just a sec. I was waylaid for a while. Apparently, there is a bow hunter's club here, and when I went to the site there are lots of pictures of their kills."

"I really don't know what anyone gets out of killing animals for sport," said Claire, wrinkling her nose in distaste. "And they'd better watch out…it's all over the news after that lion was killed in Africa."

"You go on and get something to eat," said Ross. "I'll grab a sandwich when I finish."

"Okay. I'll get lunch at the café and work out a way to have a talk with Mrs Stavros."

Painted a vibrant turquoise, with a bright striped awning supported by two Grecian columns, the Olympia café stood out like a beacon in an otherwise nondescript main street. The building occupied a site between an oil-stained garage and a tired public ablution block. Claire found the inside of the shop, contrary to the garish outside, was surprisingly tasteful: comfortable padded chairs, gingham tablecloths on the solid polished wood tables, and two colourful mosaics on the walls that offered splashes of colour. The ordering counter was back in the room, with none of the greasy fried food common to fast-food venues. Instead, there was an assortment of delicious-looking cakes, gourmet pies, quiches and pieces of lasagne inside a long glass container.

As she automatically did a swift assessment of the other customers, she saw Vivian with her head buried in a newspaper at a corner table. Without hesitation, she walked over, not even attempting to keep the pleasure out of her voice. "Care for some company?"

The reading glasses slipped down her nose when Vivian's head jerked up. "Well, well. This is a nice surprise. Sit down." She grinned and handed her the menu. "I've already ordered."

"What do you recommend?"

"You can't go wrong with the fish here. It'll be freshly caught. And the calamari is wonderful. If you're looking for something lighter, cakes and salads are on the counter."

"Calamari and salad sound good to me. And a decent cup of coffee. I was getting sick of that instant stuff at the police station."

"How true," said Vivian with a laugh. "Dee does the ordering. Poor old Joe and his constable have to make do with the cheap brews."

"Where's the constable? I haven't sighted another cop."

"She went on three weeks leave yesterday. There are only two permanent police here. The Cairns's station sends up a couple of officers every so often to do a breathalyser blitz. They also help out with difficult cases, or if Joe needs to shift someone out of the lockup."

"So how's your organizing going?"

"All done. A mate of mine is going to look after the place. I'm fortunate that everything's been planted so it's simply a matter of maintaining things until the vegetables reach maturity. Mainly keeping the weeds and pests out. With luck, we'll probably get some rain soon, which will eliminate the need to water. Another friend is going to take Toby for the duration," said Vivian and folded away her paper to make room for the coffee mug.

Claire leaned her head on one side to appraise the waitress as she took her order. From her looks and age, Claire guessed this was probably Francine Stavros. After she returned to the kitchen, Claire asked quietly, "Francine Stavros, I presume?" When Vivian nodded, she continued, "Can you introduce me when you get back, please? What's the name of one of her daughters?"

Vivian looked at her curiously. "Alexis. What do you want to know that for?"

"I need an opening to start up a conversation. What does she do?"

"She's a computer tech lecturer at James Cook Uni."

"Married?"

"No, but engaged to a guy who owns a sports shop."

"Good. That sounds ideal. Now before she comes back, will you tell me everything you know about Alexis and her brother Ben?"

Vivian hurried through the recital. Claire formed her hands in a steeple as she listened intently. Then when Francine appeared with the drinks, she asked brightly, "You wouldn't be Alexis Stavros's mother by any chance?"

A look of pleasure flittered over the woman's face. "You know my daughter?"

"I met her at a university function in Townsville. I'm interested in computer technology as well. My name's Claire."

"It's very nice to meet you. Please, call me Francine, and I see you already know Vivian."

Claire reached over and patted Vivian's hand with affection, letting the contact linger a little. "We're childhood friends. I looked her up as soon as we arrived. That's part of the reason I chose the Bay as a base."

"I heard there were two new people in town. I won't be prying if I ask why you are here, will I?"

"Of course not," said Claire. "Our consultancy group has been employed by the Queensland government to investigate the tourism potential north of Mossman. Vivian has kindly offered to show us around your area and Sergeant Hamilton has given us access to maps in his office. We've already viewed the countryside by air, so now we intend doing a few treks along the coastline and inland. Have you time to have a quick drink with us? I'd like to pick your brains as the owner of the only café in town."

Francine cast her eyes around the room. Only two other tables were occupied. "I think I can manage a few minutes. My husband is cooking your meals and the other customers have been served. I'll fetch your coffee and we can have a chat."

After she disappeared to the espresso machine, Vivian whispered, "You nearly had me believing that story. You could sell ice blocks to Eskimos."

Instead of a smile, Claire's mouth drooped. "I don't like having to lie. It's the part of the job that I find demeaning, but a necessity. When one has to make up stories often enough, reality becomes blurred. Do you know what I mean?"

Vivian gave a harsh grunt. "You're asking *me* that? I lived undercover for long periods and had so my aliases, sometimes I forgot who exactly I was. And I'm still going by a false name."

"Sorry. I was preaching to the converted. Does it worry you now?"

"Yes and no," said Vivian with a shrug. "I feel I've lost my identity, my family roots. But there are pluses amongst the minuses. I don't get bothered by anyone from the past. Only my former boss knows I'm here." She eyed Claire thoughtfully. "And now you."

"What about your sister? You must have…" She quickly broke off the sentence as she spied Francine heading towards their table carrying two cups.

Francine took a seat. "Here you go. I'm having one as well. Now, what would you like to know about the Bay?"

When Claire began to pepper her with questions about the tourism potential of the area, she found Francine had a good grasp of the industry, with many ideas how to attract visitors to the town. As they talked, Claire suffered pangs of guilt. It seemed downright fraudulent to lead her on—the woman genuinely cared not only for her business but for her community as well. Claire pushed aside self-reproach, and when there was a lull, angled the conversation back to Francine's family. "You really have been a great help, Francine. It's most appreciated. Have you or anyone in your family travelled overseas?"

"I've never been out of Australia, but my daughters have, and my son, Ben, is backpacking at the moment."

"Oh? What part of the world?"

Francine gave a nervous little laugh. "He and a mate are in Jordan, much to my horror I might add. I don't know why they didn't go somewhere safer."

"I sympathise with you, but young people think they're invulnerable," Claire said and added casually, "Does Ben's friend come from that part of the world?"

"Heavens no…far from it. His parents own a property north of Julia Creek. He and Ben were at boarding school together and both are country lads, so naturally I worry. They're going back into Israel tomorrow, which will be a relief. They wanted to see the old city of Petra before they left the area."

The sound of the door opening brought Francine to her feet. "Duty calls. You'll have to bring Claire back for a real chat before she goes, Viv."

"Will do."

"My colleague is a fishing buff and hopes to get some in before we leave, so we'll be around for a while yet," Claire added.

As Francine walked away, Claire mulled over the conversation. She had no doubt that the café proprietor had spoken the truth. Even if her son had some hidden desire to fight with the Islamic States, (which wasn't entirely out of the question but would seem highly unlikely), his mother didn't know anything about it. Claire suddenly felt dejected. The investigation was going nowhere fast. There wasn't even a sniff of terrorist activity in the wind. Maybe the whole business was just smoke and mirrors. But she was sure the Port Douglas backpacker had spoken the truth when he said Dane had come here. She knew she had read him correctly. At the sound of a cough, she brought her gaze back to eye level to find Vivian regarding her quizzically. "Well, that's that," Claire muttered, not bothering to hide her frustration.

"I could have told you Ben wouldn't be caught up in terrorism, or his parents."

"It's the only lead we found in all the morning's work."

"Have you questioned that there is definitely a terrorist training outfit here?" asked Vivian. "By what you told me, it's only a supposition. And it seems so unlikely."

"Yes, but that's the theory we've been given, so we've got to roll with it. Have you any ideas what else Dane could be doing up here?"

"Hiding out from someone?"

"From whom and where?"

Vivian threw her hands in the air. "Don't ask me. I'm just along for the ride."

Claire almost laughed aloud. She couldn't imagine Vivian ever being satisfied with being left out of the loop. "I guess the big boys must have a pretty good idea about why he's here. As I said, our only job is to find the lad."

"Getting off that subject…are there any fingerprints on that belt?"

"Joe's sent it away to the state forensic lab. He hasn't heard back yet."

"Then we can only hope the dead man is someone on a police database," Vivian said as she arranged the cutlery for the plate Francine was coming back with.

They were mostly silent while they ate, though Claire was acutely aware of Vivian's presence. She was unsure why Vivian had such a soothing effect on her, but knowing she was coming with them made Claire less overwhelmed by the daunting task ahead. She also knew that if anyone could help figure out the mystery and get the young man back safely, it was this enigmatic woman.

When the last mouthful was finished, Claire put down her knife and fork with a contented sigh. She had rarely enjoyed a meal as much. Vivian was right—the calamari was delicious. She stole a glance at the ex-agent, noting how relaxed she looked as she ate. Without a thought, Claire reached over with her napkin and wiped away a spot of mayonnaise on Vivian's chin. She pulled back, embarrassed, as Vivian's eyes widened at the intimate gesture.

Claire cleared her throat then muttered, "Sorry…force of habit. My best friend has two young children."

Vivian smiled. "That's putting me in my place. I'll have to watch how I eat in future. Now I guess I'd better be off. I have a few things left to do before hitting Cairns."

"I'll see you on Sunday. Have fun tonight."

"Will do," said Vivian, and then she was gone.

As Claire watched until she disappeared from sight, she wondered why the friendly warmth had vanished with her. She gave herself a mental shake. This unexpected distraction had to be put aside. She had a job to do. Daydreaming was out. The mission could turn dangerous.

CHAPTER NINE

Images that hadn't surfaced for a long time preoccupied Vivian as she packed clothes into her overnight bag. Somehow, Claire made her think of Beverly, though they were hardly alike. Her ex had been ambitious and charming, traits that had drawn the younger Vivian to her like a moth to a flame.

Vivian had never agonized over the fact that she preferred women as lovers. It just was. She didn't give a damn about labels and expected the rest of the world to accept what she was with as much equanimity. She had been flattered when Beverly expressed interest in her at a mutual friend's party. In retrospect, she thought the word best to describe Beverly would be *Princess*, but that would suggest a fairy tale, with a happy-ever-after ending. Their life together had hardly been that. Even though their relationship had worked in a fashion, she knew it had been more of a convenience for them both. Guilt niggled as Vivian closed her bag. She had casually dismissed the four years they had had together as mostly forgettable.

But now after meeting Claire, a suppressed excitement hovered under her skin. It was as if she was emerging from a state of limbo, like a butterfly from a cocoon. With a shrug, she pushed aside the thoughts and concentrated on the night ahead. She hadn't been to Cairns for months, and not from Madeline's lack of trying to get her to visit. They'd had a brief fling two years ago, but before it could develop into something more permanent, Vivian had called it quits. While the boutique owner was a passionate and alluring woman, that special spark had been missing. After Beverly, Vivian knew it was pointless settling for someone for the sake of having a partner. She had long since resigned to being alone.

She puffed out a frustrated breath as she swung the bag over her shoulder. Just her luck. Finally, someone had come along who interested her and she was as straight as a proverbial arrow. On the outside landing, she tucked Toby under one arm and his food and bed under the other before she locked the front door. Satisfied everything was in order after a quick scan, she walked out to the truck in the garage. At the door, she took a moment to sniff the air. Moisture hung in the atmosphere—she could smell it. After she dropped Toby off to Ned, light raindrops began to splatter the windscreen. Vivian flicked on the wipers with a little whoop.

At the airport, it wasn't long before she heard the buzz of an aircraft in the north and caught a glimpse of silver as it began to descend through the layer of clouds. As it taxied towards her, she couldn't help feel a surge of excitement. It had been too long since she'd had a night out in the company of women.

Gaby gave her a wave as she climbed out of the plane. "Ready?"

"All packed."

"Stow your bag and hop in while I top up the fuel. I won't be long. We want to get there before dark."

Vivian settled into the co-pilot seat, sank back into the leather and closed her eyes. She must have dozed off, for the next thing she knew, Gaby was talking next to her in the cockpit. "Want one of my shirts? Yours is a bit on the sober side."

"Hardly. I'm quite happy how I am, thank you very much."

"You're such a stuffed shirt."

Vivian rolled her eyes. "Come on…get this crate in the air."

After the initial turbulence during takeoff the flight was smooth, and the layer of clouds had disappeared by the time they made a turn to approach the Cairns airstrip. The sun was low in the west, though there was still enough daylight for the plane to land without the runway lights.

"Right," Gaby said as they walked to the terminal. "We'll drop our gear off at my flat before we go. Do you want to do anything first?"

"Nope. I'm ready for a drink. I don't know about you."

Gaby's eyes sparkled. "You bet. We'll pick up some beer and wine at Dan Murphy's on the way."

* * *

"Viv, darling, it's about time you came again to one of my little get-togethers. You've been hiding for months in that little backwater." The low husky voice floated around her ear as Vivian was enveloped into a long hug. The familiar scent of the subtle French perfume, enchanting and alluring, tickled her nose. A breath warmed her cheek. Without hesitation, she returned the greeting with enthusiasm. Madeline's soft body was a delightful place to rest for a moment. She had been too long without the touch of a woman.

Madeline kept her hands on her waist as she chided with a pout, "Why have you stayed away so long?"

Out of habit, Vivian quickly roamed her eyes over the room before she focused back on her friend. She looked striking. Her honey blond hair spilled in waves over her shoulder, and her long red dress dripped over her flaring hips like a silken waterfall. The bodice was scooped very low, with an ornate blue sapphire on a gold chain resting on top of her cleavage. *Oh, yeah! Way to go, Maddy.* Madeline always said that if you have it, flaunt it, and she certainly had ample, not artificial either. She was fairly bursting out of the dress. "You know me, Maddy, not one for the social scene," answered Vivian, then added by way of apology, "but I am sorry I haven't come to see you sooner. It was rude of me."

Madeline smiled, apparently mollified by her words. "I know what you're like. Well, you're here now, so make sure you enjoy yourself." She nodded to the pilot. "It's lovely to see you too, Gaby. You needn't have brought drinks, you know that. But thank you. Go into the bar and get yourselves something. I'll join you shortly."

After she twisted the top off a beer, Vivian walked out on the balcony, leaving Gaby to catch up with friends. The house was huge, built on the side of a hill overlooking the city. It was surrounded by a lush, tailored garden, with a good-sized swimming pool in the front. Vivian viewed it with a suspicious eye tonight. The whole place reeked of money. She had never questioned how Madeline supported this lifestyle. The consensus was that she had been left money by her grandparents, though she hadn't any idea whether this was true. Madeline seemed to have plenty, for she certainly didn't stint on the monthly parties that were the social hub of the lesbian community. Strictly invitation only, her guests were mostly professional women, but members of her sorority could invite their friends to the soirees.

Her beer finished, Vivian moved from the comfort of the shadows to enter the lounge. The room was packed with women. Tempting finger foods were set on a table in the corner, which she headed straight for. Her rumbling stomach demanded to be fed. While she chewed on a spicy chicken leg, she surveyed the other guests. God, she felt so out of place. Many of the younger crowd sported spray tans, some with eyeliner so thickly applied they looked like extras from *The Addams Family*. There were sprinklings also of Gaby's type—wild poster girls in designer jeans and Edward Mellar boots, mostly free of makeup but with carefully arranged hairstyles.

Vivian felt nostalgic. The partygoers were every shape and size, all ages, but having one very essential thing in common: they all loved women.

As was the custom, dancers were relegated to an adjoining room so as not to disturb those who came to chat. She could hear the strains of an ABBA song wafting out from behind the closed door. When someone opened it, Vivian could see the enthusiasts jumping and swaying in abandon.

She was searching for a place to put her chicken bone when something popped loudly behind her. She froze, for an awful moment transported back to Iraq. Beads of sweat burst out of her pores. She yanked at her collar to ease the sudden tightness in her throat and the two top buttons of her shirt shot off like tiddlywinks. A woman waving a bottle, smiled at her when she spun around. A groan gurgled out from deep inside Vivian. Just a damn champagne cork. And so much for decorum. She now looked a little slutty.

She suddenly wished she were home. It was hard to fit in any longer, not that she ever really had.

"Viv…what a lovely surprise. You should have told me you were coming."

At the sound of the familiar voice, Vivian's cloak of insecurity vanished in a flash. Elaine Harrington regarded her with delight, with arms outstretched. Vivian fell into them, hugging her tenderly. She was one of the kindest people Vivian had ever met and a good friend. In her early fifties, Elaine had a pretty face, framed by bouncy curls, but due to a constant struggle with her weight, suffered from low self-esteem. Married to a prominent barrister, she was caught in a place she no longer wanted to be. Even though her children were grown up and had left the family home, she had never gathered the courage to leave him. These parties were her escape from her otherwise unsatisfactory existence. In the past, she and Vivian had spent many hours discussing world affairs and politics while others partied around them. She also had a clever wit and one person Vivian was sorry about not seeing on a regular basis. She regretted it was over four months since she had come to Cairns, for she had very few real friends as it was.

"Great to see you too, Ely. And might I say you look blooming tonight."

"Things have changed since I last saw you."

"Oh? Do tell."

"I'm separated."

"You mean you've finally left him? Good for you."

A tinkling laugh burst from Elaine. "No, he left me three months ago…for a woman half his age. Now he's the big bad wolf and I can do anything I like. Isn't it delightful?" She tugged shyly at Vivian's arm. "Come with me. I want you to meet someone."

A tall handsome woman in faded jeans, leather jacket and long black boots, somewhere in her forties, looked up as they approached. From the blush on Elaine's face, she guessed this woman meant more than just a passing fancy. "Meet Robyn Burton. This is Vivian Andrews, a dear friend of mine, Robyn."

Vivian blinked, somewhat shocked. She'd seen lots of things in life but this one took the cake. Refined Elaine had hooked up with a bikie. Robyn clasped her hand in a solid shake and threw her arm possessively around Elaine's shoulders. With a smile, Elaine announced proudly, "I'm a HOG now too. That's an acronym for Harley's Owners Group."

"Yes, I know."

"We ride tandem," added Elaine. "Have you a motorbike?"

"I own a Kawasaki Ninja One Thousand…not as flash as a Harley, but I enjoy taking it out for a spin."

That announcement was just what was needed to break the ice. Robyn immediately looked more comfortable, and as they talked, Vivian studied them closely with a little concern. Elaine deserved to be treated well. Her fears were soon allayed. Robyn, an owner of a security firm, was obviously smitten and quite protective. She also conversed with intelligence and humour, which solved the puzzle of the unlikely coupling. They had all been chatting for half an hour when two arms circled Vivian's waist from behind. The well-known perfume drifted over her shoulder. "Hi Maddy," she said without turning around.

A chin nuzzled her shoulder. "I think it's time I spirited you away, Vivvie."

Vivian caught Robyn's stare of surprise and Elaine's roll of the eyes and grinned. "I guess that's my cue, folks. I'll catch up later." Then she allowed herself to be led away down a passageway to a room at the back of the house. She knew it well: the master bedroom. It was a huge handsome room, with a plate glass front overlooking the city, and a king-size bed covered with a rich embroidered quilt that matched the drapes.

Madeline sat down on the bed and patted the space beside her. She wriggled the dress up her legs until the fabric collected into sensuous little folds around her knees. "Come and sit here. We've got a lot of catching up to do."

"Ah…no…I don't think so." Vivian reached for her hand. "I want to have a talk with you, so let's go out on the balcony."

"Really?" Madeline squirmed in a successful impersonation of a vamp waiting to be ravished, causing Vivian's libido to give an involuntary hitch.

"Yes…really. Now up with you."

A little laugh puffed from Madeline. "You always did play hard to get. Go out and I'll get a bottle of champagne. I won't be a sec."

The air was warm and balmy outside, with a faint scent of spring flowers in the air. The moon was a butterball in the sky, the stars bright as fireflies. When a hand caressed her shoulder, Vivian looked up quickly, catching a sparkle of tears in the green eyes. The moisture was blinked away quickly. Realization what it meant hit with a jolt. Madeline really cared for her. Vivian watched as the flutes were filled, and accepted hers with a nod. "Thanks. It's lovely out here, isn't it?"

"It is. I often sit here at night. It gives me peace."

Vivian spun the stem in her hand, watching the bubbles rise to the surface. "You know, Maddy. I've often wondered what you see in me."

"You haven't a clue, have you?"

"What do you mean?"

"That's one reason why I like you so much. You're so unself-conscious. I think you're the sexiest woman here tonight, and I know a few others share the opinion."

Vivian laughed. "Come off it. I'm socially awkward with little dress sense."

"Babe, that's window dressing. You've got *it*…that elusive something you can't buy off a rack."

For a moment, Vivian was at a loss for words, not knowing how to reply. She had thought the few times they had made love had been a dalliance for Madeline, an amusement. Now she wasn't so sure. She leaned forward to cup her chin. "We're better off as friends. I'll never fit into this world, nor do I want to."

"I realize that," said Madeline sadly. "I've always known you're different, and I've always suspected you're not who you make out to be."

"No, my life up here is a far cry from what it was."

"Would you like to tell me why you chose to live in the Bay? We've never really had a frank discussion about our pasts."

"No," said Vivian. "I've got secrets, as I suspect you have as well, and I really can't share them with you."

Madeline tipped her head to the side and peered at her intently. "That scar on your stomach. It wasn't from a car accident, was it?"

"It wasn't, but that's all I'm going to say on the subject. That part of my life is history. Now I've…ah…got something I want to ask you." Vivian stopped, overcome with reluctance to continue. It might be the end of their friendship, something she didn't want to lose. She was extremely fond of Madeline.

"That sounds ominous," said Madeline lightly, but Vivian caught the quiver in her voice.

"I found a dead man in the mangroves a few days ago when I was fishing. He had a large amount of money in his belt pouch and a slip of paper with your phone number on it."

Madeline became still, and the silence stretched out uncomfortably until she eventually asked, "Oh? Who was he?"

"We don't know. He wasn't from around the Bay area. A croc took his body so the police can't identify him." Vivian intently eyed Madeline, who was shifting from side to side in the seat. "He was swarthy with a moustache, which is about all I can tell you about him. Would you have any idea who he is?"

Madeline visibly drew herself together. She looked subdued. "I haven't a clue. Will…will the police be paying me a visit in the near future?"

"No, I kept it to myself. I wanted you to tell me before I decide what I'll do. And I need the truth. No bullshit. This could get you into a lot of trouble. There are agents sniffing around up there."

Madeline looked at her, eyes pleading. "I suppose there's not a proviso on that information."

"None…it's either me or the police. I'll keep it to myself unless…" Vivian paused, glowering sternly, "unless it's something connected to terrorism, then that promise is off."

With a sudden bounce, Madeline was on her feet, her eyes wide as they tended to be when she was upset. She put her hands on her hips and glared. "Terrorism! Really Viv, what kind of person do you think I am?"

Vivian gave a sharp wave of her hand. "Calm down. If I honestly thought you were a traitor, we wouldn't be having this conversation. Now tell me who he was and why he had your number."

Madeline brushed at her dress fabric with a nervous flick before she resumed her seat. Her face sagged as she said with an obvious effort, "Okay. I'll tell you everything. I haven't a clue who he was, but it's probably connected to a scheme two friends and I have going on. It's to do with visas."

"Visas?"

"You got to understand that this doesn't involve refugees, but people from overseas who seek residency. As you know, if anyone wants to remain in the country they have to be sponsored after two years. Government channels take months, without the guarantee at the end that they can stay in Australia, especially if they don't fit into the occupations that have residency status. So that's what we do. We get sponsors for them for a price and fast-track the system. We have some…um…connections."

Vivian frowned. "How much do they have to pay you?"

"It's not cheap. Fifty thousand. Even going through normal channels can cost the applicant up to twenty thousand dollars. We're not really doing anything illegal per se, just manipulating things a little."

"That's debatable," remarked Vivian with a sense of dismay. Madeline was making money by ripping off the system. "I can't say I approve, but I won't dob you in. It's none of my business. But there still remains the conundrum of why a dead man in a remote part of the country virtually inaccessible except by boat had your phone number."

"He must have had another agenda as well." Madeline reached over to lace their fingers together. "You've got to believe me, babe. I know nothing else and we aren't hurting anyone. Our clients are mostly from Europe and the UK."

"I never thought you capable of causing suffering. That's why I didn't give the police that slip of paper. I'm just disappointed in you." Vivian gave a long sigh. "But then again, who am I to judge anyone. If I were you, I'd cease your activity, at least for the time being. There's something afoot up there and if the shit hits the fan, there's going to be a widespread investigation. The north will be crawling with cops and reporters."

Madeline swallowed and her face paled. "I will." She turned away to stare into the distance. "I know this has put a strain between us, but I don't want you to go away and never come back. I...I value your friendship."

Vivian pulled her back around to face her. "It won't ruin anything. I've seen some shocking things in my life, been in some awful places. Whether or not what you are doing is acceptable by law, at least you're helping someone achieve a dream. So come on, let's go back to the party."

"Would you kiss me before we go? For old times' sake if nothing else."

Without another word, Vivian gently took her into an embrace and captured her mouth. At the first touch, Madeline spooned even closer until their bodies were pressed tightly together. Vivian felt the rise and fall of her breasts, yet nothing stirred inside. Softer than velvet, Madeline's lips were exquisite, and the seductive pressure of her tongue was an invitation to take it further. As the kiss became more insistent, Vivian, without meaning to, began to imagine she was in another place, in another woman's arms. But when she couldn't feel the long plait down the arched back, she stepped back. She shrugged helplessly, aware her world had shifted in some fundamental way and she was powerless to halt the progression.

She opened her eyes to find Madeline looking at her sadly. "I have a feeling that kiss was the last one I'm going to get. You seem different now."

Dismay was so evident in her eyes that Vivian didn't even try to deny it. "I guess I have. And it was so sudden I didn't see it coming. One minute I was pottering around in my safe little veggie patch and then…" She stopped abruptly, unable to voice something she was uncertain of herself.

"Ah…if I didn't know better, I'd say you've met someone."

Vivian felt the heat rise to her cheeks. Denial was the only option, for Madeline would persist otherwise, and whatever she was beginning to feel for Claire would never be reciprocated. "No, I haven't. And what's with that 'if I didn't know better' remark?"

"Oh babe, you're the most unapproachable woman I've ever met. Many women have tried to get your attention, but you've been completely oblivious to their charms. It took me a year to get you into my bed and then you skipped away after three nights leaving me dangling for more."

"God you carry on. You would have been bored silly with me after six months and you know it. Now let's go back to the party and you can give some lucky woman a night to remember in those lovin' arms of yours." Even as she said the words, Vivian felt a tinge of guilt for being so flippant. She knew she had hurt Madeline.

As she followed her back down the hallway, Vivian realized she'd lost her urge to party. She figured it best to catch up briefly with people she knew and then disappear quietly to Gaby's flat. The coming week was the only thing that interested her now. Then as the image of Claire floated into her thoughts, anticipation stirred.

CHAPTER TEN

Satisfied she had included all the necessary gear, Claire shouldered the backpack. It was different from one she had humped around Europe ten years ago. This was a tactical army rucksack, jungle-camouflaged with extra storage. She had been ruthless with the clothes she'd stowed—the lighter the better in the tropical heat. She didn't relish the hike, but those were the breaks in this job. It wasn't all hotel living. She hoped she'd be able to keep up. Not having worked out for a while, she was nowhere near as fit as she should be. Ross was a powerhouse, and Vivian looked like she could trot all day and not raise a sweat.

When she reached the car park Ross was stacking the back of the Jeep. "I've made up three parcels of dried food to last a fortnight," he said. They're basic army rations so shouldn't be too heavy. Put one in your knapsack. I can carry the medical kit. We should have everything we'll need."

"Right. Did you give Sergeant Hamilton our two-way set?" He would be their main lifeline now. Because the area had no mobile coverage, it would be their only avenue of communication. It was also imperative that Hamilton keep an eye open for any unexpected activity and defuse anything dangerous. The enemy may well put two and two together.

"Yep."

"What about the maps from the police station?"

"I've got them when I dropped off the set, so as soon as Vivian gets here we'll go to the bar."

As she thought about the next phase of the operation, Claire took the food and absently tucked it away into the separate front pocket. It was time to cement their cover story, and the Sunday session at the pub was an ideal place to get the word out in the small community.

"I could do with a cold drink. This damn heat is a bit wearing." She had no more uttered the words when Vivian's pickup truck came round the corner. Claire eyed her admiringly as she strolled over with her rucksack. She didn't look tired, in fact, seemed remarkably rested. Maybe she hadn't had a late night. This observation gave Claire's spirits a little boost. She didn't stop to analyse why, but the thought of Vivian in another woman's arms actually turned her stomach. Claire quashed the feeling of annoyance. It was disconcerting.

"Hi there," Vivian said with a smile as she handed over her pack. "I should have everything. I found some superlight climbing rope in the shed, so I brought it along as well. What time are we heading off in the morning?"

"O seven-hundred. That should give us enough time to search the shoreline, shouldn't it?" asked Claire.

"Yes. If you know where to go, it's easy enough. As I said at the briefing, any route into the hills from the sea will probably be somewhere in the bay. The cliffs past the northern headland are too steep for a passage from the beach and you've seen the river delta to the south. No hope there."

"Good. Now everything's in the back of the Jeep, we're going to the pub to mix with the locals. By this time, they should have heard our cover story from Francine. I want to drop a few more snippets of information now we'll be on the move. I'd like you to join us unless you're too tired from your night out."

Vivian rubbed her palms together then straightened her shirt. "Count me in. I'm as fresh as a daisy."

As they walked to the hotel door, Claire bumped her lightly with her shoulder. "I thought you'd be worn out from partying all night. I bet Gaby is."

Vivian looked at her with a definite gleam in her eyes. "I'm nothing like Gaby. I thought you knew that."

Claire held her gaze for a moment, then turned without another comment and entered the bar. As they snagged seats around one of the tables, she watched Vivian assess the area. She did it quickly and unobtrusively, but Claire was in no doubt she knew who was there and had prepared an exit strategy if needed. She did her own scan. They seemed a friendly bunch. Many had acknowledged Vivian when she walked in. By the smiles she received as well, it was obvious that Francine had passed on the news that they were old friends. After Ross left to get the drinks, she asked, "Do you know everyone here, Viv?"

"They're all from the Bay except for the Japanese couple in the corner. They're staying with friends for a week."

Ross arrived with the drinks tray and a plate of hot nibbles. "These will help us keep sober," he said and stuffed a meatball into his mouth.

Claire gave a dreamy sigh of pleasure as she attacked a piece of battered fish. "Oh my, this tastes good."

They weren't alone for long as people began to drift over to talk. Claire made sure the message was loud and clear why they were in town, and that Vivian was to be their guide. People came over to socialize briefly, but two men, Thom and Bruiser, settled in for the session with them. After half an hour, Claire wished they would go away. Not only were they already half drunk, their attentions towards her boardered on obnoxious. Plus the cloying musty smell of zealously applied aftershave was turning her stomach. They didn't seem to have the wit to realize she wasn't interested. To make matters worse, the others seemed to think it was amusing. When they went off for a toilet break, she snapped, "Come on, you two. I could do with a little help here."

Vivian's thumb danced over the rim of her glass. "Oh, I don't know. I thought you were handling them quite well. Lighten up…they're harmless. They must have heard there was a good-looking woman in town because they're spruced up more than normal."

Claire narrowed her eyes and slapped her arm. "When Dumb and Dumber come back, you better get them off my back or you'll be sorry. Now I'm going to the loo too."

She arrived back to find them monopolizing the conversation again, this time about pig chasing. When she sat down, Vivian edged her stool closer until their thighs touched. She smiled serenely, reaching over to fiddle with the back of Claire's neck. "How's your drink going, honey?"

Surprised, Claire threw her a cautious glance. When she caught the amused expression on Ross's face, she exhaled heavily. *Okay…if they want to be funny, then who am I to ruin things?* She edged even closer to Vivian with a sultry smile. "I'd love another one, thanks sweetie."

Thom's face dissolved into a scowl. "I think we're all ready for another."

Vivian held out her empty glass. "Your shout, Bruiser. Make it light beer this time. I want to go easy."

Claire watched him as he collected the rest of the empties. He was a tall man with a full beard, and hair tied in a ponytail hanging well past his shoulders. Judging by his weather-beaten body, she guessed he spent most of his time outdoors. His faded jeans hung loosely over his hips, and his T-shirt had *Cowboys* splashed across the front. As he reached for a can, she saw the thumb and index finger were missing from his right hand. She estimated his age somewhere around the early to mid-thirties.

When he trudged off to the bar, Thom flashed a toothy grin. "You interested in a ride to the beach to see the sunset, Claire?"

She made a point of staring at his beefy hand on her arm until he removed it. He was a solid man, with strong masculine features and a bodybuilder's biceps. She would have considered him handsome, except his large jaw made him look bulldoggish. A couple of day's growth of beard on skin textured with pockmarks did nothing for his looks. He looked to be in his thirties as well. He was easy to slot into a stereotype—she'd seen enough of his type over the years. A male chauvinist—he would be affronted if she displayed more interest in Vivian than in him.

So you think he's harmless, Viv. Well, we'll see. Claire curled a hand around Vivian's upper arm, gave a squeeze and drawled, "You want to tell him I'm off limits, sweetie?"

"She's not interested," stated Vivian smugly.

"No. I'm perfectly satisfied," Claire purred, sliding the tip of a finger lightly down her arm. When Vivian trembled, Claire felt a flush of satisfaction. She liked that she could eke out a response from this contained woman. Then she snapped back to attention. Vivian wasn't the only one affected. Thom had stiffened, his gaze fixed darkly on Vivian. He didn't appear a harmless provincial now. The good-ole-country-boy look had been replaced by something quite repugnant. Her senses went into overdrive. Rarely had she experienced a reaction so acute.

Then in a blink, it was gone, but it was too late for Thom. She had twigged there was something definitely *off* about him. Suddenly the bar seemed gloomy, the smell of beer nauseating. With a concerted effort, she pulled away from Vivian. But because she was so het up, the loss of the warm safe body was overwhelming.

When Bruiser arrived with the drinks, Claire hastily downed hers. At the first lull in the conversation she announced, "I've had enough to drink. Any more and I won't be functional tomorrow. We've got a big day ahead of us." When Ross made motions to get up as well, she shook her head. "You stay. Vivian promised to show me some of the town highlights at dusk, so we'd better go before it gets dark." She turned to Thom and Bruiser, concealing her aversion as she said politely, "We might catch up again before we leave the area."

Vivian rose to join her without argument, though her eyes held questions. At the door, Claire looked back over the room and shivered. A saying came to mind as she tried to ignore her disquiet: *Something wicked this way comes.*

Vivian didn't say a word until they reached her truck, then asked in a tight whisper, "What happened in there? I thought you were going to freak out."

Claire jerked open the car door and hurriedly got in. "Come on. Let's get out of here."

"Where to?"

"Can we grab some fish and chips and go down to the beach. I need fresh air."

"Okay. The café has takeaway seafood."

Claire leaned against the bonnet of the truck while Vivian went inside the Olympia to order. With her heart rate and breathing settled back to normal, she tried to figure out what had just happened. It wasn't as if she hadn't had to deal with criminals before. But for a moment in there, every fibre in her body had screamed a warning. And when Thom had looked at Vivian as if he wanted to kill her, Claire's hackles had risen. She'd nearly thrown her drink in his face. *Damn, I'd better get a bit more control.*

The sun was only a pinkish glow over the far ranges when Vivian pulled up at the dunes. They were silent while they climbed to the top, and after they sank down on the sand, Vivian spread back the paper off the food. She handed over a Coke before she said with no preamble, "Now tell me what happened in there."

"Okay," Claire muttered, "I'm a behavioural scientist, which simply means I read people. I've done a lot of training on the subject and seem to have a natural aptitude for the job."

"Are you always accurate in your assessments?"

"Most of the time." Claire wriggled self-consciously. "For a second there when Thom realized we were…um…together, his expression changed. It was a fleeting thing, but in that moment, I just *knew*. My inbuilt polygraph antenna went off the chart. He's not who he makes out he is. I know it sounds stupid, but you have to believe me. There's a bad streak in that man."

Vivian snapped back the tab on the can, her mouth curved in a cold smile. "And I thought it was only my distrustful nature. I've never liked those two, though I had no cause to suspect they were doing anything illegal. But what sent you into a spin?"

Claire shivered. "When he looked at me, I could see he *knew* I saw through his act. And he glared at you with such hatred. You've got an enemy there."

"I can handle myself, so don't worry," said Vivian firmly. She turned her head a fraction to meet Claire's gaze. "This week has been a real revelation for me. The Bay has been a boring little place where nothing ever happened. Nothing interesting anyhow. Now it appears I'm in the middle of a John Le Carre book, or maybe it's a Dean Koontz. And the plot continues to thicken."

Claire shivered. "For a second there, the bar in the hotel reminded me of a movie I once saw. *Dust to Dawn*, I think it was called. Halfway through, nearly everyone turned into damn vampires."

Vivian snorted and gave Claire's braid a playful tug. "Good lord, woman, you have a vivid imagination. Come on...let's forget about things for a while and get into the fish and chips before they get cold." Without another word, she squeezed a tickle of lemon over a piece of fish.

As they ate, Claire gazed out to sea, the air warm against her flesh. The landscape, which had darkened at nightfall, was changing again with the rising moon. A line of light formed where the sky met the ocean, and the headlands, indistinct only a few moments ago, gradually came back into view. The only sounds were the lapping of the water on the beach and the screech of a solitary seagull overhead. Claire became calm again, happy to share the intimacy of the lonely spot with Vivian. Over the short period she had known her, the ex-agent had won her respect. It was easy to put her faith in someone so solid and dependable. On impulse, she reached over and touched her hand. "I'm really pleased you're coming with us."

"I am too."

"So no regrets I persuaded you to come?"

"No. I'm looking forward to the challenge," said Vivian with a wry smile. "Though I suspect my life is never going to be the same again. My sleepy little retreat may well turn out to be a den of inequity."

"I hope it doesn't. I'd hate it to disrupt your life in the future."

"Oh, you've already done that."

Claire turned sharply at the ambiguity of the words. Vivian's expression couldn't quite be read, her face still shadowed by the darkness. Claire nearly answered with an off-handed remark, but bit it back as her emotions soared at the thought that maybe Vivian wasn't so unaware of her as a woman. Then Claire forced herself to be more objective. The surreal setting of endless space was having an effect on them both, like a scene glimpsed through a warm fuzzy veil. Nevertheless, she experienced a thrill when her fingers brushed Vivian's knuckles as she withdrew her hand. They remained silent for a while, and as the sky lightened under the glow of the full moon, she saw Vivian was studying her with unreadable eyes.

Claire returned her gaze unflinchingly, and at last, she nodded in acknowledgment. Whatever was happening between them was better left unsaid. "I think we should call it a night," she said.

CHAPTER ELEVEN

Through her bedroom window early the next morning, Vivian watched smoke spiral in powdery wisps from the tip of the northern headland. She guessed the old pensioner living out there was burning off near his favourite fishing spot. He did it every year to give a clear access to the water's edge, for snakes were too plentiful to be walking through long grass. At the thought of the impending trek through the rain forest, she felt a moment's unease. There'd be plenty of snakes lurking there too. It wasn't going to be a Sunday stroll, and she hoped Claire was tough enough. At some stage, they would have to make their way through thick undergrowth, which would tax the hardiest hiker.

She pulled on her gear, slathered on a thick coat of sunscreen and walked to the kitchen. Relaxed in a chair on the deck with a cup of coffee, Vivian felt tingles of excitement. Finally, she had some action. She hadn't realized how much she missed it. Eyes alive at the thought of the thrill of the hunt, she padded back into the kitchen to cook a substantial breakfast before they came to collect her. It wasn't long after she had washed up that she heard the hum of their car engine in the distance.

"Hi," called out Claire with a welcoming smile as the Jeep pulled up. "All ready?"

Ross handed her two instruments. "Keep these on your person at all times."

Vivian only gave the GPS a cursory glance before she put it in her top pocket, but the two-way handset she turned over in her hand. "This looks flash."

"It is," said Ross. "It's the latest in radio technology, a Bower and Wilkins Diamond system. Far more powerful and harder to pirate than the police radio communication network, which outside of Brisbane isn't digitally encrypted." He handed her a packet. "These are extra long-life batteries for both. There's enough charge to last at least three weeks. Now are you ready to go?"

"Yep." Vivian gave one last sweeping glance around the house before she climbed into the backseat and clipped on her seat belt.

"Do you want the front seat to navigate, Viv?" Claire asked.

"No, I can do it from here. There're not many roads. I thought you might get a better view of the place from the front."

"Which way do you want us to go first?" asked Ross.

"Go back to the main street and turn left. We'll take the road to the lagoon where the fishing boats are moored. It's a natural inlet further along the beach."

"So nearly everybody makes their living from fishing here?" asked Claire.

"Yep. It's a half a day's sail to the main reef and the fish are still in abundance out there. Supplies haven't being depleted like further south."

"Are you interested in fishing?" queried Ross.

"I occasionally go out with a friend to the reef, but mainly I go up river. It's a shorter trip and the delta and tributaries are full of barramundi and mangrove jacks. Plenty of flathead, grunters and cod as well."

"Sounds like a good life," remarked Ross.

"It is. I can organize a trip to the reef with a friend of mine if you're back this way after this is over."

He glanced over with a smile. "Thanks. I'd like that."

Vivian smothered a grin. He was a tough egg to crack, but was definitely thawing. She knew Claire would be much happier if they got on. Before long, they had crested a hill and branched off to a road that wound its way through tunnels of overhanging trees to a lagoon at the bottom. Coconut palms circled the water's edge. The sea was joined by a channel running through crescents of pale sand backed by small dunes. Swaying on water ruffled by the breeze, eight trawlers were anchored in the cove. Claire announced breathlessly, "Oh my…it's drop-dead gorgeous."

Vivian agreed with her. She never ceased to be in awe of the beauty every time she came here. "It's one of nature's more magnificent creations."

"It's a perfect swimming spot."

Vivian gave her a sharp look. "Don't try it unless you're wearing a stinger suit. This time of year the box jellyfish are out and a few come in with the tide."

"What a pity," muttered Claire. "The water looks so inviting."

"Yeah well—nature is a harsh mistress up here." She wound down the window and pointed. "Park the Jeep over there near the jetty, Ross, and we can have a look around. There probably won't be anything unusual. The only route in and out is this road. Afterward, we can hike to the top and see if we can pick up tracks heading towards the hills."

"You don't think this is the place they'd land?" he asked.

"It's too well used. If I were bringing in contraband, I'd go further round the bay and bring it in from a trawler by dinghy. Because the ocean beach is protected by an inner reef, there're virtually no waves to hinder them. But we should eliminate this site first."

"Fair enough," said Ross as he eased the vehicle to a standstill beside the wooden jetty.

Vivian's conjecture proved correct. There were no fresh tracks leading off from the lagoon or from the hill above it. By midafternoon, they had driven most of the rutted gravel roads that crisscrossed the land surrounding the bay, and hiked along a good proportion of its shoreline. Vivian silently cursed—they were running out of options. The only place left that would be a reasonable landing spot away from prying eyes was a small inlet between two huge jutting rocks near the far northern end of the bay.

After giving directions, she stared out the windows at the backdrop of the ocean. It looked peaceful, the only activity a tanker on the horizon in the shipping channel. Then without warning as they were cruising along a straight stretch, the vehicle took a sharp nosedive. As it jerked and bucked, Ross fought to control the wheel. He lost the battle. The Jeep cleared the ditch, skidded and rammed sideways into a tree on the road fringe. The windscreen disappeared into an explosion of glass fragments, and the front airbags inflated with a whoosh.

"Shit!" yelled Ross as he flailed at the nylon cushion with a hand. "Where did that frigging hole come from? I didn't even see it."

Vivian slipped off her seat belt. She forced herself to take a deep breath. Her right breast had been caught hard by the belt and was on fire. With a grimace, she swallowed back the salty taste of blood, and gingerly felt the tear in her inner cheek with her tongue. A tooth had split the tender skin. With as much speed as she could muster, she reached over to haul the now partly deflated bag off Claire's face. The door was jammed against her. "Are you all right?" she asked anxiously.

When the only response was a grunt, she moved forward to get a better view. "Hold on a minute and I'll work out the best way to get you out."

For a heart-stopping moment when there was no reply, she feared Claire was hurt, but then there was a muffled groan. "Define *best*. I feel like I'm in a damn sardine can with the lid on."

"Are you hurt?"

"I don't think so, but I'll have to count my fingers and toes when I get out. That bloody airbag going off was one scary experience." She struggled upright and with Vivian's help from the backseat, pushed away the nylon material. Claire turned and let out a gasp. She followed her gaze. Ross was out the door, nursing his arm and hunched in pain.

"Are you all right?" asked Claire anxiously.

"My damn elbow hit something. The door handle I think. It hurts like frigging hell."

Vivian quickly reefed open her door. "I'll have a look at it."

The strangled moan that escaped from the agent as she gently prodded the tissue around the elbow suggested this was serious. A tough man like Ross would be conditioned to take a great deal of pain.

"How badly does it hurt?" asked Vivian sympathetically.

Sweat dribbled down his face as he struggled with the words. "A hell of a lot."

"Okay. Sit down over there on that log. I'll get Claire out then get the first aid kit for some painkillers. We'll immobilize the arm. There should be a sling in the pack."

Vivian eased Claire over the centre console to exit. "I'll attend to Ross, and then we'll see what the damage is to the Jeep. The front passenger door took the brunt of the impact. We can only hope the vehicle is still drivable."

Claire for once looked dishevelled, her immaculate cargo pants and once perfectly ironed shirt rumpled and streaked with sweat. At least there was no blood. "How are you both feeling? Does everything move the way it's supposed to?" Vivian asked.

Claire answered in a decidedly testy tone. "Apart from the fact I had a fucking crappy encounter with an airbag and a door, I'm fine."

Vivian fought to contain her grin. Underneath that calm exterior, the agent obviously had a temper. "Are you sure you don't want me to examine you?"

When Claire merely curled her lips, Vivian couldn't stop the little bubble of laughter. "I guess that means *no*."

Claire turned to Ross. "Is the pain easing any?"

"Some. Get me those tablets and I'll be of more use."

"Stop there," said Vivian. "Don't put any pressure on that arm until we find out what's happening with the elbow."

"Just get me that sling so I can have a look at the car."

"I'll do that. But we could all do with a rest first. The car can wait until we settle down."

Once the arm was in a sling, Vivian stepped back and gave Ross a wry grimace. "God knows what you've done. Hopefully it's not fractured, and just badly bruised. Time will tell."

Twenty minutes later, she announced her verdict on the state of the Jeep. "It should be drivable. The underneath's fine. The passenger door and side copped the brunt of the impact. The engine's intact, which is the main concern."

"Then we'll stop for the day," said Claire. "First thing, we'd better get to the cove you've been talking about. We'll camp there the night."

Vivian was only half listening as she glanced back at the road. It was only a rough track, but there seemed to be something unusual about that hole. She walked over and nudged the branches away with the toe of her boot. Ignoring the twinge in her chest, she squatted down to examine the now gaping ditch. Lightly, she carefully brushed away leaves and sticks until the edges were free of debris. For a moment, she could only stare at the shiny surface marks. This wasn't a natural washout; the road had been dug out and then deliberately hidden with branches. *Hell!*

"Come over here and have a look," she called out. "This whole business is beginning to stink. This was a booby trap. There are fresh shovel marks on the sides, which means someone wanted to stop us going further along this road."

The muscle twitched along the side of Ross's jaw as he studied the road. "Bastards! We could have been seriously hurt. They dug it deep enough." He swept his eyes around the encroaching trees. "At least we landed on the right side. The trees are too thick to be able to drive around it. Is there another way out of the cove once we get there?"

"There's another track closer to the headland. It's not used much. It goes through the grasslands further inland."

"Come on then. The Jeep needs to be clear of the tree before I try to start it."

The effort to move the vehicle nearly proved too much for Vivian. Her chest had settled to a steady ache, but heaving against the solid weight caused the pain to flare up again. The blood was roaring in her ears when eventually they managed to free the wheels from the tree trunk and roll the Jeep back onto the road. She felt herself quivering like an old woman as she sank down to rest. Concerned, Claire immediately knelt by her side. "Are you all right?"

Vivian tried to sound cheerful but only managed to croak out, "The seat belt caught me hard across the chest. I'm a little bruised but it'll settle down by tomorrow."

"Damn…I'm so sorry. I never thought that you might have been hurt. When we get there I'll have a look at you."

Vivian blushed. Injured or not, there was no way she was going to let Claire look at her breasts. "There's no need to fuss. I'll get over it."

Claire reached over and stroked her arm. "I'd be happier if you let me have a look. Stay there for a minute to get your breath while I fetch some painkillers."

By the time Claire came back with the tablets, Vivian was at the truck door. Dutifully, she gulped them down before she slid into the driver's seat. Ross and Claire climbed into the back. The vehicle surprisingly purred along without a hiccup, a constant rattle from the passenger front door the only sound disrupting the drive. There were no further surprises as they made their way down to a small cove surrounded on either side by jutting black rocks. It was another extraordinary spot, with a small beach of smooth white sand lapped by sparkling clear water.

A perfect place to camp. No need for tents tonight—they were far enough away from the trees where snakes and other crawlies lurked. A liberal spray of citronella should keep away the mozzies.

She watched Claire gaze around appreciatively. The cove seemed to have acquired even more of a charm since Vivian had been here last, but she had been by herself then. Such beauty could only be really admired by sharing it with others. She swallowed back a feeling of regret. She had been alone far too long.

CHAPTER TWELVE

Claire was pleased to see Vivian was her old self again as they parked their backpacks between boulders not far from the water's edge. To give them privacy, Ross bedded down further up the beach. After some cajoling, Vivian opened her top. An ugly bruise streaked in a puffy purple line from the top of her shoulder, disappearing over the swell of her right breast. Claire idly traced it lightly with her fingertip, pulling back quickly when she heard Vivian suck in a breath. "Sorry. It must hurt," Claire murmured, conscious her touch had been a little inappropriate.

A faint blush of pink stole over Vivian's cheeks. She hurriedly buttoned up her shirt. "It'll be okay by morning. There's a small stream at the end of the line of palm trees over there. The water's always cold coming from the mountains, so I'll soak for a while to bring down the swelling. You'll be able to enjoy a dip tonight."

Claire watched her reflectively as she disappeared over the dunes and struggled with the realization that the coming trip into the mountains could become emotionally difficult.

She kicked her toe irritably into the sand. *Damn!* As if she didn't have enough problems with the physical aspect, without having to cope with a growing attraction to a woman she was never likely to see again after the assignment was over. As yet the feelings were fledgling and easy enough to quash. But the pull towards Vivian was increasing the more time they spent together, stronger than anything Claire had ever experienced before. She resolved to be more ruthless in the future when they were together. To form an emotional attachment in the field was a definite no-no.

She walked over to join Ross. He was seated in the shade of a palm tree and she sank down beside him. "How's the arm?"

"Fine…if I don't move it."

She reached for the bottle of Paracetamol in her pocket. "Take two more."

With a half-hearted nod, he took the medication. "Thanks. This is a real bummer."

"It's happened so we shall have to deal with it. We'll see how you are in the morning." A sharp wave of unease swept through as she thought about the coming weeks. Ross's injury put a huge spanner in the works. Would he be fit enough for an extended hike? But if he wasn't, where would that leave them? She met Ross's gaze. His eyes mirrored her concern. "What do you think we should do if you're not able to go with us?" she asked.

"If my elbow's not right in the morning we can't go in. An injured party in that jungle would be dangerous for the three of us. We'll have to wait until I'm on deck again, or failing that, get someone else up here to replace me."

"That would be the logical thing to do, but…" She let her voice trail away.

He looked at her with a frown. "But what?"

Claire turned her gaze to the mountains, knowing her gut feeling was right. "This may be our only chance to find Dane if he's here. That hole in the road was meant to stop us getting to this cove. They're on to us, or at least worried about us. I have no doubt tomorrow we will find a used track into the hills from here. The guilty parties in town will be in contact with whoever is up there, but they still have to get out. If we leave it even a couple of days, we've lost the boy. Vivian and I shall have to go it alone."

"Nonsense. I can't let you do that," said Ross flatly.

Claire groaned. "I wish. But we've no option."

As she watched Ross struggle with the dilemma, he reminded her of a teddy bear having the stuffing slowly pulled out of its insides. By the time he accepted the inevitable, he looked totally deflated. "It's against my better judgment, but I guess I'll have to agree. At least Vivian is an expert hiker and looks like she can handle herself."

Claire stared at him surprised and pleased he seemed to have lost his antagonism towards her. "The boss thinks so. He told me to get her for the job."

"You didn't tell me that."

"Sorry. Her history is confidential, but I can say she is really suited for this operation and will look after me, so don't worry."

He peered at her for a moment before rolling his shoulders to concede defeat. "Then I'll have to let you two go it alone on the condition that if you sense there is any danger whatsoever you get out."

"Of course."

"I mean it, Claire. If there is a camp in there, just go. No heroics."

"Okay…okay. But first, though, we still have to establish there are actually people up there, or if it's not all a…"

"There are." They spun round at the words. Vivian was behind them, her hair wet, a towel draped over her shoulder. "There're wheel tracks on the other side of the stream. Recent ones, in fact, there's been a lot of traffic."

"Then that's settled—we go in at first light," said Claire. "It'll only be you and me going, Viv, unless Ross is fit by the morning. We can't take the risk otherwise. Do you have a problem with that? If you have, don't be afraid to say so. It's a lot to spring on you at the last moment."

"I've been expecting something of the sort. But it's going to be a more physical slog with just the two of us."

"If we don't go now we've lost him." She looked at Ross thoughtfully. "It might actually suit our cause if you go back without us. Nobody would dream you would leave two women to go into the forest alone. Tell them at the pub that when the car hit the ditch you hurt your elbow so Vivian and I stayed for…um…a camping holiday."

For a second it looked like Vivian was going to argue, but instead she shrugged. "You're in charge."

"There's a pot of stew in the esky," said Ross.

* * *

By the time Vivian followed Claire to their bed site, it was well after ten. She let Claire go first to change then quickly stripped while Claire disappeared to clean her teeth. Dinner had put them all in a mellow mood, and the conversation around the campfire topped off a pleasant night. Ross had interacted quietly, though at times looked uncomfortable. After he was settled for the night, Vivian spread out her sleeping mat on the ground, and blew air into the stem. It puffed up into the size of a single bed mattress. She gave a chuckle as she stretched out— it beat her old square blanket. The hiking outfit she had been issued was much more high tech than her own well-worn gear. Everything was lightweight and serviceable: from the insulated inflatable tent for wet weather to the compact hydration bladder attached to the rucksack.

Claire sat cross-legged on her mat and began to brush her hair. Vivian couldn't look away. The sight of the silvery white hair fanning Claire's face in delicate strands was not only appealing, it was mesmerizing. A bolt of heat shot straight to Vivian's centre as Claire stroked down over the curve of her breasts. She swallowed, trying to school her expression into indifference. She didn't succeed. The arousal was too strong. As if she sensed her regard, Claire turned to her with an intense gaze, her pale eyes bright. "What's the matter?" she murmured.

With a quick jab, Vivian pumped her inflated pillow with a fist. "Nothing. I'm just trying to get comfortable."

"Oh, is that all? You looked in pain. Is your chest still hurting?"

Vivian dropped her head. "The cold water did the trick. It's hardly sore anymore."

"I guess we'd better get some sleep then," said Claire as she tucked away her brush. "We have to be up at dawn."

"Don't forget to put some mozzie spray on."

Vivian rolled over, determined not to look at Claire spread out under the thin sheet. A leg poked out—the smooth skin glowed in the moonlight. Vivian was worked up enough as it was without having to look at that sight. Sleep took a long time coming. She couldn't divorce her thoughts from the woman just a metre away, or ignore her interest. She drifted off eventually, only to be jerked awake with a start. Confused she sat upright. What time was it and what had woken her? She clicked her watch light on—ten to two. Then came a snuffle, followed by an agonizing sob. Claire was writhing on the bed, the sheet tangled in her legs. For a few moments Vivian watched, but when the cries became more persistent, she slipped over to the bed.

Gently, she placed her arms around Claire's shoulders and pulled her close. "Shush, sweetie, shush. It's only a dream."

The thrashing subsided immediately, but Claire continued to whimper like a wounded fawn. Sweat slicked her skin, and her chest heaved under her light cotton top. When she eventually settled down without waking, Vivian went back to her own bed, too unsettled to sleep.

An hour later, an agonizing cry came from Claire. "Please, Ruby, please. Make me forget," she whimpered. Moments later, a soft snore echoed in the night.

Flat on her back, Vivian stared up at the stars. She wriggled restlessly, desperate to relax. But the questions kept churning repeatedly. Who was Ruby and why had Claire called out a woman's name?

CHAPTER THIRTEEN

"Morning," Claire called as she rubbed the sleep out of her eyes. The first glow of dawn was on the horizon—time to get up. Already washed, dressed and her bedding stowed away in her backpack, Vivian stood facing the sea. She looked imposing in army jungle fatigues. Claire, who had opted for a plain khaki outfit, remarked with approval, "You look the part."

Vivian smiled. "The uniform is a relic from my op days. I dug it out of the cupboard and found it still fitted. I've got another one in the pack."

"You look a little tired. Didn't you sleep well?"

Vivian coloured and dropped her eyes. "I woke about three and couldn't go back to sleep. Once I have breakfast I'll come good. Lack of sleep seldom slows me down."

"Well, I feel great and ready for the road."

"Then I'll sort out the billy and leave you to dress." As Claire wandered off to the creek, she wondered why Vivian had seemed embarrassed about not being able to sleep. She dismissed the puzzle as one of the woman's quirks. Once she was dressed and her hair plaited, she went to eat. Vivian handed her a bowl of muesli when she joined them.

Ross caught her eye, pre-empting her question by saying, "The swelling hasn't gone down, and I still can't bend the arm. I guess I'm out for the count."

"Then that's that. Vivian and I will go in alone."

Though Ross's manner still held a hint of concern, he seemed to have accepted the situation when he nodded. "Be careful and don't do anything rash. I'll take the radio base set back to the hotel room. Make sure you call in twice a day."

"Get it x-rayed," said Claire sternly.

"I won't be leaving my post," said Ross gruffly.

"It could be fractured."

"I'll get someone to look at it if it gets any worse."

"Will you be able to drive?" queried Vivian. "The tracks are rough."

"It's an automatic so I'll only need one hand."

"You sure you're up to it?" asked Claire.

"Hell Claire. I've been in worse pain than this and in tighter spots. You know that."

Claire didn't offer a further comment, knowing any argument from her would be water off a duck's back. He would do what he thought best, and they really had no other option. After going over the plans one last time while they ate, she felt ready to face whatever she had to.

It was easy enough to follow the car tracks. They began at the edge of the beach, wound across a lightly timbered sandy flat and then through a sea of grass to the edge of the rain forest. Vivian drove with caution but met no obstacles. By the time the wheel ruts petered out and a walking track began, the sun was already well up in the sky, throwing heat like a griddle iron over the countryside.

Claire took her knapsack from the boot, hoisted it onto her back and waited while Vivian secured hers. Now they had found the track in, she was itching to be gone. The trees afforded more cover. Where the Jeep was parked was exposed and she couldn't discard the feeling that danger wasn't too far away. To a casual observer, Vivian would have appeared relaxed, but Claire knew by the way her eyes scanned continuously that she too sensed something and was on high alert.

"Ross, this track will eventually get you back to town. I've driven it a couple of times. Be careful," said Vivian. "They may have booby-trapped this one, but I doubt it. Nobody would have expected us to get over the first hole. It was only luck we cleared it."

"Will do." Then as soon as Ross gingerly hit the accelerator, they began their walk.

"Why did you think we should go north, Viv?"

"Just a hunch. It's only logical to keep as far away from the town as possible, so it's as good a place to start as any."

"Do any of the locals come here?" asked Claire, peering through the trees.

"The only people who come here are members of the bow hunters' club. That's why there are some tracks."

"Are they likely to be in here now?"

Vivian shook her head. "No. It's State Forest. Their hunting season is the winter months. They're only allowed to hunt feral animals like cats, foxes and pigs—all native animals are protected." She stood up. "Come on. We better keep going but be vigilant. Whoever set that snare might be nearby, and we don't know whether they're relevant or not."

The flat path heading north was easy going at first, as the forest outskirts were ringed sparsely with ferns, small trees and woody plants. As they moved in deeper, the trees became taller and thicker, spiralling upwards to great heights. Vines snaked up the trunks, and lichen dotted the bark. Lush flowers blossomed on glossy bushes, while exotic orchids and stag-horn ferns hung from the trees.

Sweat trickled in little rivulets down Claire's skin. Even though under the leafy canopy the temperature was considerably cooler than in the open country, the humidity was taxing. Vivian led the way with an even, constant pace and at noon, she called a halt for lunch in a tiny clearing. Claire pulled the pack off her back, sank to the ground and sprawled against an old log. "Ahhh…that feels good. It's like a sauna."

"You'll get used to it," said Vivian, plopping down beside her. "Just make sure you drink plenty of water."

"When can we fill up again?"

"There're plenty of little streams in the lowlands. I've hiked in this rain forest a couple of times, though nearer the town. The coordinates of the three major waterways are on my GPS. One of the maps from the police station had them marked. Tonight we'll camp beside a waterfall another four or five kilometres from here. Once we get higher up, it'll be different vegetation and not so thick. There are plenty of springs up there on the map. We'll need water whatever way we go." Vivian unzipped a front pocket of her pack and brought out a packet of sandwiches. She handed one to Claire. "Here, I packed us a lunch. We won't have to start on the dried stuff until tonight."

Claire stretched out her legs, content to eat in silence. All the different shades of green were so peaceful. The floor was inches deep with leaves and mulch, while brightly coloured butterflies fluttered in the sunbeams that filtered down through the branches. Strange fungi and carpets of moss covered the rocks and tree trunks, and the air smelt damp and earthy. It was an ancient place. She closed her eyes, listening to the trills of the birds. Somewhere in the underbrush came a thumping noise, which she thought was probably a wallaby. She had seen a few on the trail this morning. She closed her eyes, and the next thing she knew Vivian was nudging her with her elbow. "Time to go," she said.

A spider scurried past Claire's hand. She stared at it, fascinated. It was huge. As it ducked into a hole, Vivian said, "It's a wolf spider. They're common here. You didn't jump, so I assume you aren't afraid of them."

"They don't worry me. I read there weren't any poisonous ones up here."

"No, they're all harmless. Is there anything you have a particular aversion to?"

"Snakes. I hate 'em."

Vivian chuckled. "Me too. If you see one, give it a wide berth. They are plenty of venomous ones around. I carry this thick stick with me in case I'm cornered, so get one too."

With a stab of disquiet, Claire picked up a sturdy stick. She vowed to be more alert in future. As she heaved the pack onto her back, Vivian had already strode off. The path deteriorated into an animal track further into the forest. It was hard going, brushing through bushes and large fern fronds. Dark sweat stains blossomed under Claire's arms.

Suddenly Vivian stopped dead. She moved back a few paces, squatted down and scanned the ground.

"What's wrong?" whispered Claire, craning over her shoulder.

"See there?" Vivian pointed at the ground. Claire had to squint to catch the silvery gleam of a wire across the track. They followed it through the bushes to a small snare tied to the root of a silky oak tree. Inside was a lizard. Vivian pulled it free.

"Careful, he might bite."

"Nah...it's a pink-tongued skink. They're docile and make great pets," said Vivian as she placed it on the root. "I wonder who wanted to catch this little fellow. He hasn't been here long."

"Maybe it's an environmentalist doing some kind of study."

"I don't think so. I haven't heard there's anyone around like that." Vivian tilted her head. "To be quite honest I can't even hazard a guess. But we know now someone's in here."

"They could be some hikers."

"It's not open to tourists and, quite frankly, there are friendlier places to walk. And the weather isn't exactly conducive to a pleasant hike."

Claire glanced around at the surrounding vegetation. Her heart gave a little hitch at the realization that this was proof that someone *was* in the rain forest, but were they just chasing an animal lover? When Vivian began again, Claire wriggled her backpack to a more comfortable position and followed with renewed enthusiasm. They walked another two kilometres in single file without another word, though Claire wasn't uncomfortable with the silence. It saved energy, for the humidity was taking its toll. Her legs ached and she felt increasingly light-headed.

Vivian must have noticed she was feeling the strain because she called a halt every half an hour as the afternoon wore on. Finally, a baritone hum could be heard in the distance, like a faint rumble of a train. "You hear that?" she asked.

"What is it?"

"You'll see."

The sound accelerated the further they trekked until it was a roar. Suddenly the forest fell away and a great chute of water came into view. It tumbled in an explosion of white spray to a large pool in front of them. Sunbeams danced over the flume, forming a rainbow in the mist. Claire halted in her tracks. "Bloody hell. It's awesome, in the true sense of the word!" she gasped.

"It is indeed." Vivian turned with a smile. "I think we've earned a swim tonight. Stay here, and I'll have a look around before we set up camp. I want to make sure we're alone." She dumped her pack down and silently melted into the trees.

Claire slid her hands over the surface of one of the boulders, smooth as polished mahogany, lining the edge of the pool. She sank down against it, relishing its coolness. Despite her fatigue, her mind was alert. She strained to listen for noise of anyone nearby, but it was impossible to hear much over the thunder of the waterfall. Ten minutes later, Vivian reappeared, her eyes sparkling. "No one has been around here for a while. There was an old campfire site, but it hadn't been used for months. Come on…let's go for a swim." She rummaged in her pack, coming out with a cake of soap. "This will help. It's biodegradable, environmentally friendly. I make the soap myself out of vegetables."

"You beaut," Claire cried, but then gaped when Vivian stripped off her clothes. Claire stared at her sleek, muscular back as Viv ran into the pool. Arousal flushed through her. Completely overwhelmed by the unexpected intensity of her physical response, she froze. Indecisive, she was in two minds what to do, but then chastised herself. This certainly wasn't the place to be prudish. They were both mature adults as well as professionals. Vivian would hardly expect her to behave like a blushing maiden, though Claire was still relieved when Vivian turned her back to allow her to undress in private. Hurriedly, she peeled off her clothes and took a running jump into the pool.

The cold water hit with a jolt, forcing Claire to gasp out loud. Vivian turned with a grin. "This will get the juices flowing."

At the analogy, Claire inwardly groaned. Now she had enough flowing. With an effort, she kept her eyes locked on Vivian's face, refusing to sneak a peek at the gentle swell of her breasts with the hint of nipples. "Ummm…it certainly is refreshing." She pulled her hair free of its braid. "Pass over the soap when you're finished."

Vivian made a circle with her finger. "Turn around and I'll wash your back."

Claire forced herself to relax. "Okay. I feel a total grunge after sweating all day."

After Vivian slathered on the soap, she began to massage Claire's shoulders. "I'll get all these knots out for you. It'll help you carry the pack tomorrow."

"Thanks." Claire couldn't help the groan of pleasure as the fingers worked their way into the muscles. "Oh God, that's divine."

"It's advisable to do this every night. The climate can sap everything out of you. I've learned in the field that your body health is extremely important. And keep up the fluids, otherwise, cramps will cripple you. I've got some magnesium tablets to ward them off too, so take a couple each night."

"Your turn," said Claire when Vivian eventually pulled away.

"I'll be all right. I'm used to the heat."

"Nonsense. Turn around," ordered Claire. For a second she thought Vivian would refuse, but slowly she swivelled. Vivian shuddered as Claire began to soap her back. As Claire slid her fingers over the rippling muscles in a steady rhythm, her hips unconsciously began to undulate in time with her strokes. The cool air cut across her nipples, sending little tingles to the valley between her legs. She was so consumed with the feeling, she moved too close. Their bodies brushed together. Vivian stiffened. Unnerved, Claire pulled back and dropped her hands. Overcome with embarrassment, all she could do was give Vivian's shoulder a pat and mutter, "That should do it." Then in a flurry of strokes, she fled to the other side of the rock pool.

Treading water under the spray of the fall, she tried to calm down. Her behaviour brought a wave of remorse.

CHAPTER FOURTEEN

It took a few minutes before Vivian settled down. The feel of Claire's naked body swaying against hers had sent her feelings rocketing. She was still twitching. Cripes, she had to get a grip on her emotions. As she watched Claire float beside the waterfall, Vivian began to get annoyed. What was she playing at? There were some proprieties a straight woman had to observe when near a lesbian. But the anger soon passed as she remembered the full-on hormonal rush that had exploded through her at the touch of the exquisitely soft skin. The sensation had been incredible. And Vivian knew she'd brought it on herself when she insisted on the massage. With a groan, she exited the water and put on her clothes.

Dinner was a subdued affair and they retired immediately after cleaning up. Vivian didn't know when she actually made the transition to sleep. There was a period when her thoughts were so busy she thought she'd never drift off. To her surprise when she opened her tent flap, the sun was shining brightly. She couldn't remember the last time she hadn't woken at daybreak. When Claire smiled at her and said, "Hi there", any awkwardness of the evening before melted away.

Vivian glanced at her watch. "Hell, is it eight already?"

"You must have needed the sleep. Your muesli's there. I've already eaten."

"I'll have a wash and change first before I eat."

To give her privacy Claire sat down with her back to the water. "While you do that, I'll write up the diary, and touch base with Ross on the two-way."

By the time Claire had finished these chores, Vivian had eaten, packed up and was sitting with a map spread out on the ground. "Come over here and we'll plan where we're going today." She pointed to a spot with her index finger. "We're here. I've been giving this a lot of thought. I really don't think a camp will be too high in the mountains. It's too steep and they'll need running water for a contingent of people. I believe we should turn southwest. I found an old track heading that way at the end of the pool."

"Have you got a place you want to reach by tonight?"

Vivian stabbed the map with her index finger. "Here. A stream is marked on the map, so we'll have water and a bath."

"Okay. That sounds fine to me."

As Claire rose, Vivian grasped her arm. "We have to be more careful today and try to be quieter. I've a feeling we're getting close. We don't want to advertise our presence. How's Ross's elbow?"

"Much better apparently. He's in the hotel room with the two-way base now, and will be there most of the time. I'm to call at eight each morning and six at night. When he has to go out for food et cetera, he'll avoid those times and be as fast as possible." Claire got to her feet and pulled on her pack. "Right, lead on Macduff."

And they were off again.

* * *

Claire's mood deteriorated as the morning wore on. Even though the path they followed wasn't as hard to navigate as the one the previous afternoon, the air was even more humid. Light rain started to fall by lunchtime, which brought some relief. She sank down on the ground with a sigh when Vivian called a halt. As she was chewing a protein bar, she felt a sharp prick. With an irritable hiss, she whacked a big mosquito that was feeding on her neck. The dab of dark red blood merged with the globules of sweat leaking down her skin. She rummaged in her bag for the repellent. "The mozzies are bad," she said in a low, cross voice.

"The misty rain is bringing them out," replied Vivian, though she didn't seem too concerned.

"Want some spray?"

"I put some citronella oil on this morning. I find that does the job. They don't bite me much."

"Well, they like my damn blood."

They both fell silent, content to conserve energy. As she sat quietly, Claire thought over her earlier conversation with Ross on the two-way. Everything was quiet in the town, and from all accounts, his elbow was on the mend though he still couldn't bend his arm. At the news that there was proof someone was indeed in the rain forest, he vented his frustration at not being with her. She felt a flare of anger. As if she hadn't enough to contend with, without having to soothe his male ego. At least Vivian didn't go on with that rot.

As her companion sat back with her eyes closed Claire studied her quietly. The woman seemed at home here. She felt envious. The heat didn't affect her, she was tireless and very little fazed her. It was no wonder she had been such an effective undercover operative. "Why did you choose to retire to a tropical area, Viv?"

"I like heat and rain. Too many operations in the Middle East put me off the desert."

They fell back into silence again and when Vivian rose ten minutes later, Claire mopped her face and reluctantly got to her feet. As they moved along, Vivian seemed more cautious. She constantly stopped to scan the track and peer through the trees. By midafternoon, Claire felt thoroughly spooked.

They were progressing at a steady pace when Vivian halted abruptly at a blue ginger shrub across the path. Without a thought, Claire moved past her to see what had caught her interest. She pulled at a branch for a better look.

"Don't!" Vivian snapped urgently.

But it was too late. The fragile calm shattered.

A swarm of red wasps flew out of the lush foliage. Caught unawares, Claire brushed them away in fright, which only served to infuriate them more. She stumbled backward, fighting to contain the scream that rose in her throat. They stung her face, her arms, her fingers—she was on fire with pain. Frantically she swatted at them as they zipped in a flurry around her. Not able to stop herself any longer, she gave a loud piercing cry. Panicked, she began to run blindly, mindless of the sharp branches that scraped her skin. A hazy blur filmed her eyes as she ran like a deer.

In less than a minute, Vivian caught her. She clutched her arm like a vise, forcing her to a halt. "Claire, stop! They're gone." She hauled off her rucksack and pulled out the medicine pack. "Here…quickly…take two antihistamines."

While Claire swallowed them with a mouthful of water from her pouch, Vivian opened a tube of ointment. "Where did they sting you?"

Claire groaned. "On my face and arms, and one got me on the stomach through the shirt."

Vivian looked at her anxiously. "You're not allergic to bees or wasps, are you?"

"No…no." She started to shiver, tears blossoming in her eyes. She clawed at her face and arms. "Oh, fuckityfuck! I'm hurting like hell. They were vicious little shits."

"Calm down. Take off your shirt and I'll put on some antiseptic ointment. It contains an analgesic as well, which will deaden some of the pain." She patted Claire's shoulders with sympathy. "I want you to sit down here for at least ten minutes. The tablets should stop the swelling, but if you have any trouble breathing, I'm going to give you a shot with the EpiPen."

Without hesitation, Claire ripped off her shirt to allow Vivian to slather on the thick salve. "From now on, stick close to me. The stream isn't too far off where we'll stop for the night."

"There're no worries about that," muttered Claire. "I'll be grafted to you like glue from now on."

Vivian's eyes twinkled though she didn't reply.

Claire eyed her curiously. "Why have you been so on edge all afternoon?"

"Because there were signs that people, two maybe three, had been in this part of the forest not long ago. Not fresh, but only a day or two ago at the most. The place reeked of them. Bent twigs, broken spiderwebs, and I even saw a few very faint boot marks. And that track…it led us straight to that ginger shrub. Whoever made the detour was good, but not clever enough."

Fifteen minutes later, though there was localized swelling, she pronounced Claire fit to proceed. The going became more difficult when Vivian left the narrow track to wind through the towering trees. It was a haphazard route and she was periodically forced to skirt areas of tangled undergrowth. Every now and then, she stopped to consult the small GPS she carried in her pocket. True to her word, Claire stayed right on her heels. Suddenly Vivian pulled up at a huge curtain fig and peered between the long roots. "There's something dead in there. I can smell it."

Claire followed her gaze. What looked like rotting chicken lay there in a pile. A rancid smell of decay hung in the air. Vivian picked up a stick and prodded the heap apart.

"What is it?" asked Claire.

"Remains of pythons. They've been skinned."

Claire examined the flesh more closely with interest. "That's a bit sick. Why would anyone do that?"

"To make handbags."

Claire winced. She wasn't a raging environmentalist, but taking skins for handbags seemed an outrage. "The poor old pythons. They aren't poisonous, are they?"

"No, but the amethystine and the carpet pythons grow big up here."

"I hope not as large as anacondas."

Vivian laughed. "You've been watching too many movies. I can assure you they won't hurt you. They're harmless."

"Why do they skin them and not ship them out alive."

"Too much trouble to transport them considering their size. Come on, we'll keep going. We're almost there."

This watercourse was nowhere near as spectacular as the one the night before, but Claire still thought it delightful. It was a lovely little creek, which meandered in a bubbling stream through tunnels of overhanging vegetation. They walked a little way upstream until they came to a small clearing where they could set up camp.

"This should be ideal. Let's have a soak," said Vivian, already pulling off her shoes.

Claire chewed at her lip. Was it going to be a repeat of yesterday? "You go first. I'll unpack."

Vivian reddened to her hairline but didn't drop her eyes. "I think we need to talk about this, Claire. We're on an assignment in dangerous territory, and we have to be together for days yet. Modesty can't come into the equation. We're professionals so let's get the job done. I know you're wary about my sexual orientation, but I can assure you I wouldn't do anything to embarrass you."

It was Claire's turn to blush. "You're right. I really didn't mean...well...oh, shit...I'm making a hash of this. You took me the wrong way. I just thought you would prefer some privacy. For the record, I've never ever considered you would take advantage of me."

"Of course, I wouldn't." She studied Claire with a frown. "You must have been out in the field with men lots of times. How did you handle them?"

"It has never been a problem. They know my boundaries and the organization has strict behaviour protocols."

Vivian gave a snort. "Rules are made to be broken. Have you never been attracted to someone you've been partnered with?"

"No. Now let's have that bath." Claire rose to indicate the conversation was over.

But much to her chagrin, Vivian persisted. "I find that hard to believe. An agency like yours would have lots of virile, good-looking men. You must have felt something for someone."

"You're annoying me now. I said I never have, so drop the subject. It's none of your business."

"No, it's not. But I can't understand why you're behaving like I'm a threat. I'm a little offended, that's all."

Claire put her hands on her hips and glared at her. "Honestly, for a woman of the world you're pretty thick. I don't have any problem with men because I prefer women in my bed. Now I'm going for a dip in my birthday suit, so you may join me if you like."

CHAPTER FIFTEEN

Vivian remained perfectly still. "I see," she said finally, the words coming out as a taut sigh. She averted her eyes while Claire undressed and went down to the water. She was in two minds what to do, but not wanting to appear childish, peeled off her clothes. Her heart thumped as she self-consciously sidled into the water. Though the stream wasn't wide, it was relatively deep in places. Claire, who was humming a tune as she soaped herself, ignored Vivian who sank under the water until only her head showed. She tried not to look in Claire's direction, but couldn't help sneaking a few peeks. When Claire lifted her arms above her head and ran her hands through her hair to spread it out, Vivian couldn't look away. As if aware of her scrutiny, Claire flashed a sultry glance over at her.

Vivian ducked her head—she hated feeling so insecure. Claire now being available, at least in theory, changed everything. Annoyed with herself for stealing yet another glance, she called out gruffly, "Throw over the soap when you're finished."

With a few lazy swimming strokes, Claire was by her side. "Do I get a massage again, honey?"

"Turn around," Vivian ordered, ignoring the exaggerated batting of the eyelashes.

A tinkling laugh burst from Claire. "I'm sorry. I couldn't resist. There's no need for us to be awkward with each other. Just because we're both lesbians doesn't automatically mean there's an attraction. I enjoy your company, so let's be friends."

"Of course. I'm glad we've cleared that up. We have to work together. Tension would only compromise the operation. Now, you really should let me give you a massage. It's the third day tomorrow and your body will be feeling as heavy as lead."

"Okay. I would appreciate it."

As Vivian dug her fingers into the smooth flesh, she divorced her mind from the act. It was harder though to ignore her body's potent reaction to the little moans of pleasure escaping from Claire. But she managed. As she performed the final sweep over the shoulder blades, Vivian took a big breath. It was sinful how good the woman smelt, a mixture of lavender soap and her own sweet alluring scent that couldn't be replicated in a bottle.

"That should do it," she said. She hoped Claire didn't notice how husky with emotion her voice sounded. "If I were you, I'd soak a little longer. The cold water will do the bites the world of good. And make sure you take another antihistamine before you go to bed, otherwise you'll be scratching all night."

After Claire moved away downstream, Vivian sank beneath the water. Her body surrendered to the coolness and her aches and pains gradually eased. It had been a gruelling day, mentally as well as physically. But worst of all was the absolute horror she had felt when the wasps attacked Claire. She had once seen firsthand how vicious they could be when stirred up. A swarm had killed a kangaroo rat right in front of her eyes. With the number of times Claire had been stung, if she had been even a little allergic to wasp venom, she would have been in deep trouble.

Those wasps. Not for the first time did she ponder their significance. There was no doubt in her mind the whole episode was engineered. Someone meant them to run into the bush. But why stop them that way? A knife or gun would be faster and more effective. Something wasn't adding up. What terrorist would bother snaring lizards and skinning pythons? And it was back to the question that had been bothering her since she found the body. What was he doing in the mangroves?

Trying to relax, she pushed away the problem. But with the release of tension, her thoughts focused straight back on Claire. She closed her eyes. The thought of Claire's body under her hands sent her pulse racing. Her nerve endings tingled and a throbbing began in her nether regions. It gathered intensity until automatically she slid her hand downwards.

She snapped her eyes open. *Hell, what am I doing?*

She hurried from the water. Vivian dressed quickly as Claire floated in the water with her eyes closed. She banished the erotic thoughts, conscious of the need to check the perimeters before nightfall. She slipped into the forest and pressed against a tree to listen. Only birdcalls and the buzz of insects. Satisfied, she did a quick sweep of the area before she returned to the camp.

"Where did you disappear to?" asked Claire.

"I was making sure there were no unwelcome visitors nearby. We'll eat our food cold tonight. No smoke."

"Should we take turns with guard duty?"

Vivian ran her fingers through her hair with a frustrated sweep. "We should, but that would only slow us down tomorrow. This humidity and heat are taking too much out of us as it is. We need a decent sleep to function properly."

"Okaayyy…" said Claire. "But if we don't, we'll be vulnerable. Sitting ducks, in fact."

"We'll set up a dummy camp with the packs in one of the tents." Vivian gazed up at the sky. Clouds had rolled by all afternoon, but now they formed a thick blanket over the forest. "It's going to rain tonight, so we can't sleep outside. We'll both have to sleep in the other tent. It'll be a tad squishy, but we've no other option. I'll camouflage our tent, and make the other one look pretty obvious." She looked anxiously at Claire. "Are you fine with that plan?"

"Of course. I really need to get my rest, 'cause I feel I'm holding you up as it is."

"Nonsense. You're coping well, much better than I thought you would considering you're not used to this heat. At least the rain will cool everything down so it shouldn't be too hot jammed up together." After their frank talk, she was relieved Claire was pragmatic about the bed sharing.

As quickly as she could, Vivian set up the mock camp, conscious a heavy tropical shower wasn't far off. She inflated their tent amongst the trees, covering it with fronds of the giant ferns that grew in abundance on the forest floor. By the time she'd finished, Claire had hydrated two packs of beef and vegetables and mixed pannikins of orange sports drinks. Army rations, not exciting but sustaining.

"Here," said Claire, passing over the tin plate. "We'd better eat before it rains."

The first warning drops came as they finished washing up. "Into the tent," Vivian called out, making a dash up the bank. After Claire crawled in, she zipped up the flap and switched on the penlight.

The ultralight one-man tent had enough room if they slept pressed together. Vivian placed her revolver under the pillow, aware that Claire, who had spread out gracefully on the mattress, watched her in surprise.

"I didn't know you had a gun."

"I brought my old service pistol along. We have to have some protection, and I *will* use it if I have to."

"I wasn't judging you. In fact, I'm pleased you did. I have a small one in my pack too," Claire responded lightly.

Vivian noted that in the torchlight the agent looked even more appealing. *Damn, this is going to be a long night.* She cleared her throat and gave a small cough. "Right, the only way this is going to work is to be on our sides. If you roll over, I'll lie down with my back against yours."

They shuffled into place. After a minute, Claire muttered, "It's uncomfortable. I'm jammed against the side of the tent. And you must be too."

Vivian nearly groaned aloud. Her libido was going to be stretched to the limit tonight. "Do you want to face my back?"

"Since you're the tallest, it would be better if you snuggled into mine."

Vivian heaved over without a word. Any argument would be pointless. There was no doubt it would be the best position in the confined space to make a comfortable fit. She winced when Claire wriggled back into her and pulled her arm over until it rested against her stomach. Then she held it. "That's better," Claire said brightly. "Comfy?"

"Uh-huh…Oh, yeah, sure."

"Are you tired?"

"Uh-huh. Big day. You must be knackered after what you went through with the wasps."

"I'm a bit too keyed up to go straight to sleep. Do you think we can talk for a while to help me settle down?"

Her answer was cut short when a sharp shower of rain pelted down. The tent swayed and dipped with the force. Automatically, they pressed closer together. When it eased off, Vivian said soothingly. "Don't worry. It's made to withstand more than that. Now, what do you want to talk about?"

"Tell me about the women who have been in your life."

"Good god, woman, you certainly go for the jugular."

A laugh came. "It'll be more interesting than hearing about what movies you like."

Vivian echoed her laugh. "Don't count on it. My love life will be sure to put you to sleep."

"Nothing juicy to tell?"

"Hardly. I was socially awkward as a teenager then joined the service. I never had a long-term lover until I was in my mid-twenties. Her name was Beverly. After twelve months' dating, we bought a house in Sydney together and lived there for four years. It wasn't what you would call an exciting relationship…I guess it suited us both to share a house and companionship. Because I was away a lot of the time and she was building her career, the passion and common interests that we had in the beginning just drifted away until there was nothing left. When I came home from the German hospital after being shot on assignment, she had gone."

Claire gave her arm a comforting squeeze. "That's sad."

"It was both our faults. We didn't work to keep our relationship alive. I'll never make that mistake again." She gave a little cough. "That is if I meet someone special."

Claire lightly brushed her fingers across the top of her hand. "What about Madeline?"

"Ah, you remembered what Gaby said."

"Well?"

"Madeline owns a boutique in Cairns. She's funny and gorgeous."

"So she likes you…or…or is it the other way around?"

Vivian's heart gave a little skip as she caught the slight peevish note. "We had a brief romance and I called it off. The thing I was looking for just wasn't there between us. A pity, because she really is a special woman."

Claire seemed to relax minimally. "And that's it?"

"Yep. I don't do one-night stands—they tend to make loneliness worse for me. What about you?"

"Oh I've had lovers, but no one for any great length of time. As you know, it's difficult being away on assignments to form a lasting relationship."

"No one waiting at home?"

"Not really."

"What about Ruby?"

Claire stiffened and shrank away. "How do you know about Ruby?"

Vivian pulled her back into her arms. "You talk in your sleep, Claire. How long have you been having those nightmares and, more to the point, have you seen someone about them?"

For a second Vivian thought she wasn't going to answer, but then she went limp. "To answer the first question, Ruby has been a casual lover for over nine months now. A friend to help me de-stress. It's a mutual arrangement. That's all."

"Huh! Poor old Ruby. I bet she doesn't look on the relationship quite so analytically. And she wouldn't have a clue what to do about it."

"What would you know about it? And who are you to judge me? You're not exactly an expert on love," Claire snapped.

"No, but I know when someone has unresolved issues. Been there, done that! Even though you were asleep the other night, you were in a great deal of pain. You've got to get your head around those problems before you can move on emotionally." She stroked Claire's head with her free hand. "It might help to talk about it."

"Why the hell would I want…" She broke into a sob. "I… maybe…oh, why not. You're right. The whole thing has come back to haunt me and I thought the nightmares had gone. It happened over seven years ago."

"Sometimes PTS can lie dormant for years. Then suddenly it manifests itself as bad dreams or erratic behaviour. If it was severe enough, it may never go away without constant support. Can you tell me what happened?"

"I hadn't been long in the missing person's bureau when a small boy disappeared from his home," she began in a quiet voice. "His name was Edwin Stonehaven."

"Ah," interrupted Vivian. "I remember that case. He was an only child."

"Yes, and the parents were older than most. To cut a long story short, we missed a vital clue soon after he disappeared. We picked up the paedophile in the first raid, but we didn't investigate him thoroughly enough. We let him go. Mind you, there were quite a few of the usual suspects brought in for questioning that night. But we hadn't been notified that a neighbour had phoned into her local police station and given the number plate of his car. She had seen it parked near the house. We found out later that Edwin was still alive when we had the perp in custody. The bastard went straight home after we let him go and killed the boy. He buried him in a state forest and disappeared. He was caught six months later and I was one of the officers sent to find the body." She started to shake. "It was horrible and the parents never forgave us. It haunted me for a long time and now it's come back again."

"You'll need more therapy when you go back home. But I can tell you what you are feeling is a natural reaction. Time does heal, but every now and then you should talk about it with someone."

"I know," Claire replied. "Even saying it out aloud to you has eased it a little."

Vivian slipped her arm tighter over her abdomen. "Now try to get some sleep. We're quite safe here."

"Okay," mumbled Claire. "I always feel safe with you."

CHAPTER SIXTEEN

Vivian woke to find a head buried beneath her chin. During the night, Claire had turned and was half-sprawled on top of her. Vivian lay there for a minute to savour the moment. *Sugar and spice*...the nonsense verse repeated in her head. Reluctantly, she shook Claire's shoulder. "Time to get up."

Instead of displaying any embarrassment, Claire merely rolled off with a moan. "Do I have to? I had the best sleep in months and would like some more please."

Vivian chuckled. "You wish."

"Pretty please."

"Up with you now. So no nightmares last night?"

A shy smile flickered over Claire's face. "None. I guess I have you to thank for that."

Vivian bent over and gently kissed her forehead, letting her lips linger. "You're welcome." She cringed. What had she just done? She usually avoided outward displays of affection. They always made her feel awkward. She was relieved to note that Claire looked pleased with the gesture. Without another word, Vivian crawled out of the tent.

The morning was bright with light. It glowed over the little clearing, sparkling on the newly washed leaves and dancing like diamonds on the water. The scene mirrored her good mood. After a bladder stop, she ambled down to the water for a wash. Since Claire hadn't yet appeared, Vivian headed for the other tent to retrieve the backpacks to prepare breakfast. As always, she scanned the earth for any disturbance, a routine that had saved her life more than once. If she hadn't been so thorough, she would have missed them: faint boot prints in the loam. An attempt to conceal the marks had been made, though it was half-hearted. Vivian surmised whoever it was, probably thought the heavy rain would wash away any traces.

With a great deal of caution, she approached the tent. The flap was slightly undone at the bottom, a fact that sent alarm whistles beeping. It had definitely been fully closed last night. She poked her head inside and started in horror when a snake's tail protruded from under a pack. She inhaled a long breath. The thought of a snake crawling over them in the night sent shivers down her spine. She realized what it meant. This was no accident. The floor and wall of the tent were joined. The only way in and out was through the flap. She could see Claire descending the bank and called out, "There's a snake inside the tent. Grab my staff, please?"

In a jiffy, Claire was by her side with the stick. "You're not going in there, are you?"

"Hardly…I think it's a brown. The space is too small to get a good swing at it. We're going to have to jiggle the tent and make a racket."

"Will that work?"

"It should. Snakes don't like us any more than we like them."

"Have you got a plan B?" asked Claire.

"We'll think about that if this doesn't do the trick."

"Let's hope it does then."

It took five minutes before Claire exclaimed, "There it goes." She stiffened. "There're two of them." She turned to Vivian, her eyes narrowed. "How did they get in the tent? You zipped it up."

Vivian stepped away from the tent to watch the snakes disappear into the vegetation. They were definitely browns. If bitten so far from medical help, they would never have made it out alive. "I found faint boot prints. Someone put the snakes in."

"That's attempted murder," Claire said bleakly. Her face had turned paler, but Vivian could see why she was considered a good operative. She had digested the information without panicking.

"Yes, it is. Let's pack up and get out of here. I'll pull the packs out with a hooked stick in case there are any more. We'll find somewhere not so exposed to eat." Fear rose in Vivian, not for herself, but for Claire, who probably had little experience fighting jungle warfare. Vivian hoped she'd be able to protect her now that things were this serious. If only she knew the enemy and where it was holed up.

An hour later in a secluded pocket between thorny rattan palms, they stopped for breakfast. Vivian held up her hand, listening intently. She relaxed and said softly. "We'll have to keep our voices down. Once we move again, only speak if you have to. Now we'd better make a plan."

Claire inclined her head and waited for her to continue.

"After the wasp incident, I thought whoever was in here was trying to just chase us away," Vivian continued, "but now we know someone wants us dead. I've been thinking about that. Let's examine your terrorist camp theory first."

"It's not *my* theory. It's one I was given."

"Okay, but if there were militia here, they could have sent men in with guns to kill us. Nobody would have heard the shots—we're miles from civilization."

"Yes, but if we didn't return, the place would be swarming with cops in no time."

"Exactly," said Vivian. "So, owing to the fact that someone is trying to kill us, we can assume your cover is blown. Two agents on their doorstep must indicate that the authorities know, or at least suspect, something illegal is going on. It's a lose-lose situation for them. The only choice now for the terrorists is to get out. Pack up and go. Live to fight another day. They would have a contingency plan in place to disappear."

Claire frowned. "So what are you inferring? Are you suggesting there's no terrorist camp?"

"I am. As I've said all along, the local grapevine would have noticed strangers as soon as they arrived."

"So what *is* going on?" Claire blew out a sharp breath, her frustration becoming more evident. "Is Dane Ahmed even here?"

Vivian's expression grew sterner. "Oh, yes. He's here all right. Think about him, Claire. What did he study?"

Claire's brow furrowed. "Wildlife Science."

"That's why he was recruited. And he's a thief—he stole his father's credit card."

"I'm afraid I don't understand," Claire muttered. "What are they stealing?"

"I think we've stumbled on an organization dealing in black-market native fauna. Wildlife theft is a multibillion dollar industry in Australia, third only to drugs and human trafficking. And it's so easy. You can sell anything: lizards, birds, eggs, snakes, python skins. One adult black cockatoo is worth thousands of dollars overseas." Vivian suddenly snapped her fingers. "Of course…that's why the dead guy was in the marshes. He would have been after birds' eggs, or…dare I say it…crocodile eggs."

"Oh dear, and the croc got him," said Claire. "Okay, I'm getting it. If they shoot us or we disappear without a trace, then it's the same scenario. Cops will come in and their trade is finished. So…?"

"So they make it look like the wildlife got us. A snake bite, wasps stings—they'll keep going until we're eliminated. We'll be found dead. Just two hikers out of luck. No suspicious circumstances. Then all they'll have to do is to wait for everything to settle down and they can go on as before. It'll actually help their cause. Word will get out how dangerous it is in here and tourists will avoid it like Ebola."

"But what about Ross?"

"They can't kill him. If something happened to him in town, there *would* be a hullabaloo. Besides, he has to be alive to organize a search party, which they probably wouldn't for at least a week after contact with us was lost. It buys the organization time to get rid of all traces of their illegal activity and get their people out."

Claire scratched a bite on her arm idly with a fingernail as she gazed at Vivian with concern. "Then I vote we head back as quickly as we can. You didn't sign up for this, and bringing Dane back is not worth your life."

Vivian pressed her hand firmly to emphasize the point. "It's too late now, Claire. They can't let us go. We've seen too much. I'd say our fate was sealed when we found those pythons. If we hope to survive, we'll have to outfox them."

"That won't be easy? We don't even know how many there are."

"I imagine not too many yet. Reinforcements would take some time to organize, and they'll have to hike here too. We've only got a small window of opportunity to escape before they arrive." Vivian spread the map out on the ground. "First, we organize this like a tactical operation. Evaluate the force, form an action plan, execute the plan." She looked up to find Claire smiling at her. "What?"

"You're quite impressive in combat mode."

"Huh! Be serious. The first thing is to eliminate *our* weaknesses. So your pack has to go. Only carry the water pouch on your back. You'll have to move faster. We'll take only what's absolutely necessary from mine and ditch the rest: a spare set of clothes each, the food, one set of eating utensils, the medical kit and basic toiletries. No tent. We'll sleep under logs or bushes, though I'll put in the piece of plastic and sheet in case it rains. Keep the repellent in your pocket. There will be insects where we're going. I'll give you an EpiPen. If you get bitten again by a wasp, use it. You could be more allergic to them now. Any small incidentals like a penlight, keep in your pockets. Leave your jeans and wear your cargo pants. They have more pockets."

"Fair enough. Do we go on, or go back the way we came?"

Vivian pointed to the map. "We go on. Either way, won't matter now they're after us, and we may still be able to get Dane. But it'll be by force now unless you're good enough to get him to come voluntarily. I'll pack the rope if we have to tie him up. There's a swamp to the west about two kilometres from here. We'll go there first."

Claire raised her eyebrows. "That doesn't sound too safe."

Vivian gave a wolfish grin. "It's not. It's notorious for being full of crocs, snakes and flaming big insects that really can bite. *We're* going to make the terms of engagement now."

"God, I hope I don't hold you up."

"You won't. I'm going to stash you somewhere safe and go it alone. That's what I'm best at."

Claire stared at her. "I can't let you go by yourself. I'm not a waste of space. I mightn't be as fast as you, but I am trained in the martial arts."

"You've got to go with me on this one. I don't want an argument. Together we'll be too easy to track. It'll be the only way we're going to make it out of here alive. These people have a lot to lose and they'll be playing for keeps, so I'll have to disable some of them. Now get on the two-way to Ross and fill him in. Give him the coordinates of the swamp, get him to organize some backup and tell them to start out immediately. If they hurry, they can be here by tomorrow afternoon. We'll wait for him."

"What about Sergeant Hamilton?"

Vivian hesitated then she shook her head. "We can't risk it. I haven't a clue who's involved in the town, but I imagine there'll be a few of them. Until we've identified the enemy, everyone is under suspicion."

Vivian worked quickly, ruthlessly discarding superfluous items. She could hear the anxiety in Claire's voice increase as she repeated continuously into the two-way handset, "Ross, are you on channel? Ross, are you on channel?"

Eventually, she returned the device to her pocket with a bald statement. "We're too late."

Vivian forced back her own consternation and gave Claire's shoulder a comforting squeeze. "We had to expect this. They wouldn't have hurt him, but must have found some way to disable the base set." She hoisted the rucksack onto her back. "Let's get going. I have to do a few things to lure them to the swamp."

Claire rose wordlessly.

As they walked west, they skirted boggy areas. The vapours that drifted from the quagmires carried the pervasive stench of rotting vegetation. They passed through dark gullies veiled with hanging vines and damp moss. Dismal places that made them shiver as they pushed on. Finally, when they came to a ridge of firmer ground, Vivian spied what she had been hoping to see. In between crops of spreading fan palms, stood an old bottle tree with a hole in its broad trunk. Hibiscus covered a portion of the entrance in a blaze of orange and red flowers. She made her way through the palms to the tree. Carefully she pulled aside the flowering branches and shone the light inside. The cavity was large enough to take two people comfortably. An ideal hideout.

"What are we doing here?" asked Claire.

"This is where I leave you. You'll be safe inside this tree until I return."

Although she knew Claire would be reluctant to stay, Vivian hadn't anticipated the force of her anger. Ramrod straight, she spat out. "I'm not staying."

"Yes, you are. It's the only way."

Claire's lips thinned; her cheeks blotched red. "*No!* You listen to me. You are not going alone."

"It's for the best."

"You are not in charge. You're my employee and you will do as I say."

Although Claire spoke emphatically, Vivian didn't miss the tremor in her voice. "You must, honey. I know jungle tactics."

"Don't *honey* me, Vivian. You can't expect me to stay in hiding while you go to fight by yourself. Don't be so damn arrogant. You're not...not invulnerable."

"Hey, look at me," said Vivian and reached out to stroke Claire's arm in a soothing rhythm. "I'm trained for this and I know the rain forest. I'll be back tonight."

"And if you aren't?" asked Claire bitterly.

"Then at the crack of dawn, you head east to the coast as fast as you can. I'll put the coordinates in your GPS. I'll leave you the gear and the food. A couple of protein bars will be enough for me."

Claire glared at her, but her eyes communicated more than anger. They were alive with worry, and Vivian sensed it was more for her well-being than Claire's own. "Okay. I'll wait here, but don't think I'm going to desert you." She grasped Vivian's shirt with both hands and gave her a little shake, "So you better get back, do you hear."

Vivian nodded with a reassuring smile. "They won't even see me. Come on, let's go in."

The inside was hollow to the ground. She pushed against the wall. It felt solid. She was pleased too, to see the top was still intact which made it weatherproof. She flashed the light around to make sure there were no unwelcome residents lurking in the dark corners, then threw the backpack onto the dirt floor. She glanced across at Claire studying the space with a discerning eye. For a second Vivian thought she would start protesting again, but then her face changed into a professional mask. "It's a good spot out of the weather. Will we be communicating on the two-ways?" Claire said.

"No. I'll take mine though it'll be turned off for the time being. I'll have to be silent."

Claire's face became stonier. "Then I just sit here and wait for you to come back?"

A chill pervaded the air now, one that was far more off-putting for Vivian than anger. "That's the idea."

Claire seemed to slip further into herself. "What weapons are you taking?"

"I've got two knives and a wire garrotte as well as the gun."

Claire handed over her GPS without another word. Vivian tapped in the coordinates and passed it back.

After she had taken what she wanted out of the knapsack, Vivian attempted a smile. When it wasn't returned, she rose awkwardly. "Right, I'll be off."

"Good luck," Claire offered, though she didn't meet her eye.

"Now don't sit here and worry. Take the opportunity to have a rest."

At this remark, Claire whipped her head up to glare at Vivian. "I get that you think I'll be in the road. And I get that you're used to being in charge. I really do. I've worked with people like you before. But contrary to what you think, I do know how to look after myself and I'm much stronger than I look, so please don't presume to tell me what I should do or how I should feel."

Ouch! "Sorry. I didn't mean to…" The rest of the sentence was cut off by a pair of soft lips suddenly covering hers. She sank into the kiss, emotion swelled in her chest as their bodies slid together. She clutched Claire's hips, though more to hold herself upright than to deepen the embrace.

But all too soon, Claire pulled away with a little hitching breath. "I'm sorry too. I'm usually much more professional. I seem to lose my objectivity when it comes to you. Just…just be safe. Please…"

Vivian nodded. With a quick press of her hand, she slipped out into the hibiscus flowers.

CHAPTER SEVENTEEN

Completely in the combat zone, Vivian ignored the heat as she moved through the underbrush. She didn't try to cover up her tracks, but made sure she left enough obvious signs so that she could be followed easily. As she hurried along, she kept her eye out for small mammals. There were plenty native to these tropics: possums, bandicoots, wallabies, rats and the yellow-footed antechinus. Her main plan hinged on finding one. During the previous days they seemed to be everywhere, but now when she needed one, not one of the little buggers were in sight. Typical. It was a pity possums were nocturnal, for they were pretty prevalent.

Just as she thought she was going to remain out of luck, a musky rat-kangaroo appeared on a mossy limb. From a vantage point behind a bush, Vivian watched it closely as she silently unsheathed the knife. But as quickly as it had popped into view, it disappeared from sight. With an irritated jerk, she slipped the knife back into the pouch.

Damn!

Time had all but run out when she caught sight of a small female swamp wallaby chewing on a native jasmine. She froze, this time determined not to scare it off. It raised its head, sniffed cautiously and went back to eating. Carefully she took aim, and with a practiced flick of her wrist, threw her knife. It struck it through the chest. The animal flopped over onto the ground. She wiped the blade, jammed the carcass into a large garbage bag and continued on her way.

Half a kilometre on, she reached the swamp. The vegetation here was different from the sclerophyll forest with its towering figs, eucalypt and acacias. This one was a tentacle forest, where vines coiled like leafy serpents up every tree, smothering the bark in a tangle of limbs. Gnarled trees grew on at the water's edge, their huge buttress roots creating an intricate pattern through the mud and leaf mulch. Dirty white rocks were scattered like dinosaur bones in the sludge at the water's edge.

Vivian sat on a root to study the swamp. It was a brooding place, its surface covered with a brown scum dotted by a few iridescent green patches. It stank of vegetative decay mixed with something that smelt suspiciously like raw sewerage. Even though the surface water was motionless, occasionally bubbles of gasses popped on the top. It was the habitat of a diversity of reptiles: goannas, snakes and the grand masters of them all, the saltwater crocodile. And it was common knowledge that there were plenty of them here. Nobody in their right mind would camp by this swamp.

She snapped to attention. Now was not the time to dawdle. They would appear soon. With quick strokes, she cut the wallaby into pieces, capturing its blood in the bag. Once she was finished, she stuffed the pieces back into the plastic bag. She covered her face and arms with mud and waited. Mosquitoes swarmed in a cloud from the stagnant water. She swatted irritably at them and slathered on more mud. Even combined with the repellent, the insects were hard to deter. Seconds later, there was no more time to dwell on them when faint sounds echoed in the distance. Swiftly, she trailed the blood and animal parts from the water's edge to the spreading roots of a Blue Quantong tree on top of the bank. Then she climbed the tree.

They were indefinable at first, just faint ripples in the murky water. Before long, Vivian was able to pick out the scaly backs floating like logs towards the bank.

One. Two. Three. Four. She grinned as she counted—more than she had hoped for.

As the first crocodile, a three-metre female, crawled out of the swamp, three men walked in single file over the top of the bank. The first two Vivian recognized immediately: the two Mooney brothers who owned one of the fishing trawlers in town. Phillip, a thickset dour man and the elder, led the way. As yet he hadn't seen the croc, which had stopped to devour the first piece of flesh near a rock. The next animal to emerge was more aggressive as it rushed out with an angry swish of its tail. From her perch in the tree Vivian heard the snap of its heavy jaw.

And so did Phillip. "Shit. Crocs. Get back," he yelled and abruptly turned.

Vivian threw her knife, her favourite weapon in her active days. This particular throwing knife had been weighted and specially designed for her personal use. She felt a sense of pride to see she hadn't lost her touch. With a perfect trajectory, it pierced Phillip's leg just above his kneecap. He collapsed with an agonizing cry. By this time, all four reptiles were on land, fighting over the remains of the wallaby. At the sound of his cry, their malevolent eyes all turned towards him. The largest male swung its tail savagely and began to waddle up the hill. It slid over the mud, using its legs to push itself along on its belly, the hind ones moving together to propel it forward. For a few seconds, it was distracted by a piece of meat, but swallowed it whole and turned its attention towards the wounded man on the ground again.

His thigh was bleeding profusely, the coppery smell of blood pungent in the thick air. He screamed, clutching his leg. "Get me the fuck out of here."

The other two men ran to his side. Vivian got a clear view of the third as they grasped Phillip under the arms and half lifted, half dragged him to the top of the bank, out of reach of the seething crocs below. It was Dane Ahmed. Before they disappeared back into the forest, Vivian heard something zing into the tree root above the crocodile's head.

She sat on the limb, impatient to be gone, though there was no way she was going down with the reptiles waiting underneath. After they'd devoured the meagre meal and slid back into the water, another precious twenty minutes had passed. On the ground again, she looked out over the water. The swamp had turned dark grey, the remaining summer light drowning in its depth. She pivoted quickly, conscious the sun wasn't far off setting. Should she follow them or go back to Claire? She had to go after them for a while at least. This opportunity couldn't be missed. It would be hard though to navigate back to the bottle tree in the dark, but she had the GPS. As she turned to go, a shaft of glistening metal caught her eye. She pulled it out of the tree.

An arrow. A big piece of the puzzle slotted into place. The bow hunters' club. She knew now the organization they were contending with.

For once, something went her way. Their camp was only a kilometre and a half from the swamp. The men were easy to follow—they had no time to hide their tracks as they hurried back to base. It was nearly dark when Vivian caught the glimpse of something white through the trees. She snapped into action mode and dropped to her knees. With infinite care, she wriggled the rest of the way on her belly until she reached a point behind some bushes where she could observe the camp. Four tents filled a small clearing. A young man around Dane's age was busy cooking over a campfire, the rest were nowhere in sight. Vivian guessed they were attending to Phillip in one of the tents. She watched as Dane came out and spoke to the cook. When ten minutes later nobody else came out of the tents, she concluded four were all there were. She smiled to herself—and one was severely disabled. The others would have their hands full.

She tapped in the coordinates.

Time to get back to Claire.

It was much harder going than Vivian had anticipated. With nightfall came nearly total darkness under the tree canopy. The moon wasn't due to rise for another hour. If it weren't for the GPS, she would have been completely disoriented. She plodded on with the light of her pen torch, often stumbling over obstacles that seemed to pop up out of nowhere. She had to ignore the thorny branches she seemed to be forever brushing against. At one stage, she had to steady herself against a tree, dizzy from straining to focus. Only for the fact Claire would be worried, she would have stopped somewhere for the night.

When the moon's glow finally arrived, the light was soon dimmed by rain. What started as a light shower became a downpour. Skin-soaking rain, with drops the size of ten-cent pieces. It pelted down nonstop for half an hour before stopping abruptly. Then after a too-brief respite, more heavy clouds drifted by and dumped their loads on the oversaturated forest. Vivian cursed at the heavens. Her clothes were drenched and she was hellishly uncomfortable, but at least the mud was washed off her arms and face. She walked on. At times, she heard strange noises in the brush. The sounds came and went. Probably animals foraging, she told herself. Though she knew darkness magnified fear, she still felt prickles of it.

Finally, after what seemed like hours, the GPS gave a beep. There was a moment of panic when the spot looked no different from the kilometres she had just traversed, but eventually the beam of the torch picked out the red and orange hibiscus flowers. As the round shape of the bottle tree came into view, a wave of enormous relief washed over her. Anxious to get to safety, she ran through the flowers and stepped into the hole. At the touch of cold steel pressed against her temple, she took in a sharp breath and wheezed, "It's me, Claire."

The gun was pulled away and a light shone in her face. "Vivian. For heaven's sake, don't you have a tongue? I nearly shot you."

"A bit trigger happy, aren't you?"

"You would be too if you'd been sitting in this crappy place for hours wondering what the hell was happening and if you were ever coming back," she snapped. Then her voice softened to a whisper and she pulled Vivian into a hug. "I'm glad to see you. I've been so worried."

Nestled in the embrace, the events caught up with Vivian. She suddenly felt raw and vulnerable. She wasn't as young as she used to be when on active duty. Her body ached all over and she was emotionally drained. All she could do was bury her face in Claire's shoulder and cling to her.

CHAPTER EIGHTEEN

Claire pulled her in tighter. The feel of Vivian in her arms brought a peace she couldn't describe. She'd never felt such affinity with anyone before. As instructed, she had remained in the crude hideout, but by nightfall had been nearly at screaming point. By then it had felt like a prison. Not that it wasn't surprisingly comfortable. It even remained dry through the tropical downpours. Plenty of room to stretch out for a sleep, which she tried to do unsuccessfully. Worry had gnawed at her. Even though she conceded it was logical for Vivian to go on alone, Claire still felt hurt and abandoned.

But as daylight vanished and the night wore on, the worry spiked into real fear. And the rain hadn't helped. She was dry, but the atmosphere had turned moist and gloomy. Eventually, she had grappled with the inevitable conclusion that Vivian couldn't find her way back in the atrocious conditions. She was hopelessly lost in this inhospitable nightmarish fucking forest, wandering aimlessly around at the mercy of every animal that bit, stung or sucked. Then a thought had hit like a sledgehammer. And that one really sucked. *Was Vivian still alive?* Claire had pushed the death scenario firmly out of her mind. It was the last place she wanted to go.

She felt helpless and isolated, and she hated it. In previous assignments, it hadn't been a problem to divorce her emotions from the task. It was all about control. With Vivian, all that had flown out the window in a flurry of disappearing good intentions. Her heart had latched on to the woman, something Claire couldn't ignore. It just was. And so quickly? It was ludicrous! But still, here she was, clutching Vivian to her bosom with her body wanting, *no demanding*, more. What was wrong with her?

With a concerted effort, she pulled away and tugged at Vivian's shirt. "You're sopping wet. Get changed and I'll get you something to eat. Then you can tell me what happened."

"It'll be a relief to get my clothes off. Is there somewhere I can hang 'em?"

"There are pieces jutting out of the wall high up that should hold them."

As Vivian stripped she sighed, a low hissing sound like air escaping from a tyre. "God that feels good.'"

Claire nearly groaned aloud. The thought of Vivian next to her so scantily dressed, sent her libido spinning. "Here're some dried meat and a peanut bar. Now tell me what happened."

While Vivian related her day between mouthfuls, Claire listened intently without interrupting. "So it was a very good day for the good guys. We now know their numbers, where their camp is and what group in town they belong to," concluded Vivian.

"You had lady luck on your side with those crocs."

"I know."

"So what would you have done if the plan hadn't worked?"

"Stayed in the tree until they passed, then followed them. It wasn't far off dark so they would have headed home soon enough."

Claire looked at her curiously. "Those men tried to murder us, Viv. Why did you aim for his leg? You had the right of self-defence to do serious damage."

She shrugged. "I don't kill unless there's no other alternative, and there was only a need to disable. Besides, it's better this way. The wound is deep and I imagine the tendons are damaged. Not an injury to have in the wet tropics, especially somewhere so isolated. They'll have to get him medical help as soon as possible."

"Will they wait for the others to get here, do you think?"

"They know the climate. They'll start carrying him out on a stretcher."

"So what's our next move?"

"We track them and pick off Dane," replied Vivian gruffly. "The game is on our terms now. I didn't recognize the fourth bloke, so I'm guessing, because he looked in his twenties, he's one of Dane's mates." She wiped her fingers on a tissue. "It'll be easy. There's only one fighter worth anything amongst them." She paused and stared at Claire.

"What?"

"You look different tonight. The torch glow is reflected in your eyes. They're flecked with gold. And your skin has turned a silvery colour. You look like an angel." She let out a sharp cough. "Damn. Sorry. I just got a bad case of foot and mouth."

Claire passed it off with a giggle. "Well, honey, to quote Mae West, *I'm no angel.*"

Vivian laughed. "Me neither. Have you ever had to kill anyone?"

"Nope. And I hope I never have to."

"It's something you never forget," Vivian murmured, lost in her memories. "I've had to...a few times...four to be exact. You asked me before why I didn't kill Phillip. I vowed I'd never again. It's one reason I'll never go back to my old job. Now, enough of being maudlin. We'd better get some sleep." She stretched out on the cover and patted the space beside her. "We're lucky it's roomy enough for both of us to lie down."

"I'm coming," whispered Claire not so sure about the luck part. It was going to be an unsettling night with Vivian so close.

With their bodies touching, Claire felt awkward. And judging by the way Vivian remained stiff, Claire knew she felt the tension too.

The rain fell harder. It hammered against the old tree and raked loudly down its sides. Automatically they reached for each other to seek comfort as the sound reverberated in the shell. When Vivian wrapped an arm around her waist, Claire snuggled into her body. As if choreographed, they shifted their heads simultaneously to find each other's lips. The kiss was tentative at first, a fleeting meeting of mouths. But as they moved into a rhythm it deepened, and their tongues curled together in an explosion of sensation and taste. Claire felt a wave of arousal. She trembled with the effort to control herself. She lost the tussle. With a strangled moan, she crawled on top of Vivian to get even closer.

Strong hands lifted her up. "Whoa, sweetie. Are you sure about this? It's probably a reaction to the stress. Don't do anything you'll regret later."

Claire settled back on her elbows. "I find you an exciting and attractive woman, and I'm not ashamed to admit how much you turn me on. I need to forget for a while…we both do. It'll just be comfort sex. No strings. But I really…really would…" She brought her face down until she could feel Vivian's warm breath. "Please…You do like me, don't you?"

"Oh yes, Claire, I like you. I like you a lot. You send me wild." As Vivian whispered the words, she flipped Claire over onto her back. Then with a growl, she crushed Claire's mouth against hers, and slipped in her tongue. Possessively she swirled it in all the warm wet places, while she moved her body over Claire's and began to slide against her with a steady rhythm. She thrust in a thigh to open Claire's legs and nudged it firmly into her centre. Lowering her head, she sucked down her neck and lightly bit down on the soft flesh at the base. Then she grasped Claire's backside, kneading it until it stung.

Claire felt her sex heat, her flesh tingle, her breasts swell. She was past surprise, hanging on for the ride. On fire. No one had ever touched her like this. She had unleashed a tiger in her bed. It wasn't the vanilla sex of her past lovers. Elegant women, with elegant quiet tastes. This was raw and wonderful, and Claire felt herself responding as she had never done before. When Vivian tugged down her bra and fiercely sucked a nipple into her mouth, Claire arched in to give her better access. With a quick twist at the back, Vivian had her bra off and impatiently rolled off her to strip off her knickers. Then she was back on top again. Her mouth consumed the other nipple, stretched it out, nibbled it and suckled it. Claire grasped her head with two hands to massage her scalp, loving how Vivian moaned when she lightly tugged her hair.

She struggled to focus when Vivian ran her fingers over her abdomen until she reached her mound. With her palm, she began to massage it and whimpered, "I love that you wax."

"Please...I'm dying here. I need you lower," gasped Claire.

"No. I'm not done here yet," she whispered and threaded her hot centre over Claire's thigh.

Claire felt the pressure rise in her as Vivian circled the heel of her palm into the pelvic bump in sync with her steady rubbing against Claire's thigh muscles. Moisture leaked through Vivian's panties, coating Claire's skin. Claire bucked, desperate for a touch. Vivian, at last, relented and lowered her hand. She began to stroke, lightly at first, then with more authority.

"I...I want you so...oh, God...there...yes..." Claire knew she was babbling. She didn't care. She was beyond coherence now. Her wild need consumed her. As the crescendo built, her clitoris began to pulsate, to throb. She dug her fingers into Vivian's shoulders and spread her legs open further. "I need you inside me, luv. Please..." She was nearly sobbing with desire now. Vivian pushed two fingers in and thrust in and out. She pumped her centre against Claire's thigh in time with the thrusts.

"Come with me, sweetie, come...ahhh...I'm there." As Vivian climaxed, she raked her thumb over Claire's distended clit and her orgasm rose as well. It was blinding in its intensity. She convulsed as the waves of sublime pleasure rolled through wave after wave leaving her trembling and weak.

With her eyes closed, she sank against Vivian and exhaled. "Phew...I've never come like that before. It was awesome."

Vivian brushed a stray strand of hair off her face. "I wasn't too rough, was I? You were so hot and receptive that I kinda got a bit carried away."

Claire could barely reply she was so tired. "You were just what I needed. I'm sorry, but I can't keep my eyes open any long…"

* * *

Claire woke incredibly refreshed. A fully-dressed Vivian stood at the entrance looking out. Claire felt suddenly shy, remembering the night before. Never had she felt so close or responded to anyone like she had with Vivian. Last night had been much more than just sex for her and she hoped Vivian felt the same. It had been mind-blowing special. "Good morning," she called out.

When Vivian turned, she smiled a welcome, but her eyes were wary as she looked down. "I let you sleep in."

Claire glanced at her watch. "Heavens, it's past eight. You should have woken me."

"No need to hurry. I've been studying the map and worked out which way they'd be most likely to go. They have to move east, so we can pick up their trail when they get closer. They won't be near here till about noon."

Claire waggled a finger at her. "Come over here then and give me a kiss. Maybe we can take up where we left off?"

"Er…There's a pool of water from the rain just down from here where you can have a wash. I've topped up the water bags."

Claire's heart plummeted. The night had meant nothing but a one-night stand to Vivian. "Then I'd better get myself presentable, hadn't I," she muttered. She heaved herself up, grabbed some clothes and pushed past her out the gap.

It was a fine day, the clouds had disappeared and the air was crisp. It looked like the rain had cleared away for a while. Her mood, though, wasn't on the same barometer. It had deteriorated into *Storms Likely*.

By the time she returned, Vivian had a meal prepared outside. Claire took the plate and sat cross-legged on the ground with her back against a tree trunk. She looked over at Vivian. She was studiously studying her meal, not meeting her eye. *Well, bugger you, buttercup. We're going to talk whether you like it or not.*

"So," Claire began in a clipped voice, "how did you pull up this morning?"

"Fine. I slept like a top."

"I did too. Best sleep I've had for ages."

"Good."

Claire slammed the plate down. At the clatter, Vivian raised her head, her eyes like a startled owl. "Are we going to talk about it?" Claire growled out the question. "That's what adults do."

Vivian made a huffing sound. "Why do you have to analyse everything? It was just sex. No big deal. You said so yourself."

"Yes I did," snapped Claire, really annoyed now. "And to me, it was pretty impressive. Since you barely acknowledged me this morning, I guess you were disappointed. Be it as it may, we have to work together so please don't damn well ignore me."

Vivian's head whipped up. "Is that what you think? That I was disappointed?"

"What am I supposed to think? You acted like I was a casual lay and you couldn't wait to get me out the door."

Vivian rose and marched over to her. She towered over Claire with her hands on her hips. "For your information, that was one of the best nights of my life. But I can't do a repeat performance, Claire. I'm going to get hurt if we continue. You made the rules: no strings, just sex. But it didn't seem like that to me. We seemed to click, to connect."

"I know," whispered Claire. "I felt it too."

"I'm…well I'm not nearly as sophisticated as you. I've only been with a few women—my job took up most of my time. I don't do casual. If I get in any deeper here, it's going to be difficult for me when you leave."

Claire squeezed her eyes shut. What had she done? She had only thought of her own pleasure. She got to her feet and took Vivian's hands. "I truly am sorry. It was a shitty way for me to behave. I should have respected your feelings more. Will you forgive me?"

Vivian looked at her sadly, her eyes glistening. "There's nothing to forgive. But I don't think you quite understood what I've been saying. I *liked* the way you behaved. I would *love* to do it again. I'm honoured you even wanted to have sex with me. I think you're one of the hottest, smartest women I've ever met. But it can't happen again because you're goddamn leaving as soon as we get back and I'm stuck here in the sticks with my market garden."

Claire's heart gave a little skip. She broke into a wide smile. "Really? I think you're wonderful too. But you're right—it can't happen again. We're what the dating scene would call geographically unsuitable. I think we're mature enough not to pander to our hormones and just be friends. Now show me the route you think they'll take."

As Vivian turned, Claire added quietly. "You know what I regret most of all?"

"What?"

"That I fell asleep too soon. I never got to touch you where I wanted to."

CHAPTER NINETEEN

Vivian swallowed the lump in her throat. Why had Claire said those last words? Now the thought of Claire's hands over her body was imprinted on her brain. A gaudy technicolour version in bright lights. She nearly sobbed with frustration, but it was pointless to dwell on it. What she had visualized beforehand had been nothing like the real thing. As soon as Vivian took her into her arms, it seemed so right. And Claire had been so responsive and passionate.

Vivian closed her eyes. Regret was going to be a big burden to carry, but it was better than getting involved any further. The woman was dangerous—she stole hearts. Nope, she had to be firm. No more fantasizing on something that she could never have again. Even if they did see each other in the future, Claire was so much classier. Blue chip, and Vivian certainly wasn't born the top apple on the tree. She wasn't Mayfair material and never would be.

She could and would move past this.

With a determined set of her shoulders, she went inside for the map.

* * *

"Damn you, Viv, you nearly gave me a heart attack. I didn't even hear you."

Vivian chuckled. Claire had taken her instructions to heart. Every part of her exposed skin was covered in dirt. "That's the general idea in jungle tactics. I was right about the route they'd take. I found them on this track, heading this way. In half an hour tops they'll be here. Let's get the surprise ready, and don't touch the leaves."

"What's this tree called?"

"It's the dreaded stinging tree and the one plant to be avoided in the rain forest. The leaves and stems are covered by thick hairs that inflict a painful sting. The toxin is savage, been known to kill a horse. It can last months and there's no effective antidote. If the nettles become embedded in your flesh, the only way to get them out properly is to use wax strips and yank out the stingers just like you would hairs. That in itself is painful enough!"

"Never fear then. I'll leave it to you."

Once she was finished, Vivian stood back to admire her handiwork. *Perfect.* "That should do it. Now let's get back into position."

"I hear them now," whispered Claire.

Vivian pushed Claire's head down. "Keep out of sight."

Three figures, the last two carrying a stretcher, came into view. They moved past a fig tree some twenty metres away. Owen Mooney led the way. He was thickset with a disfiguring cleft lip scar. Vivian knew him well. He came with a red flag attached. A kick boxer with a giant chip on his shoulder about his looks, he needed to be avoided. She would have to disable him efficiently the first time because she doubted she would get another chance. At least he was in the lead, which made it easier.

They came nearer. She sensed rather than felt Claire tense beside her. When Owen reached the mark, Vivian slashed the razor-sharp blade across the vine. Released from the constraint, the stinging tree branch whipped through the air like a slingshot and lashed across Owen's upper torso and face. He gave a startled yelp, slapping wildly at the limb. When the thousands of hollow hypodermic-like fine silica hairs embedded in his flesh, the nettles injected their poison. By the look of horror on his face, he knew what it was. With the stretcher poles still held in their hands, the two younger men stood gawking.

What happened next took her by surprise. Owen must have seen where the branch had come from, for he charged towards them. As he crashed through the shrub, Vivian smelt him before he hit. His body odour was atrocious. She had just enough time to call urgently to Claire, "Get Dane before he bolts. I'll handle Owen," before she braced herself for the onslaught.

He hit with a crunch, ramming her backward into the open. Then he swung a clenched fist. His punch hit the bridge of her nose hard and she sprawled onto the ground. Warm blood spurted over her mouth. She gagged at the metallic taste and spat. He kicked out. The boot sunk into her side. She ignored the pain, rolled over and jack-knifed upright. His mouth pulled into a macabre grin when she took the fight stance of a kickboxer. He was proficient at the sport, so she knew what was coming wasn't going to be pleasant. He jabbed a stiff flat palm at her. She blocked and counterpunched.

With a sharp rotation of his body, he kicked out. She weaved to the side, half-squatting, before she launched her own attack. They continued to punch and kick methodically, searching and prodding for the elusive opening. The blood streaming from her nose was hampering Vivian. Her hands were slick with it. She began to tire—her training snapped in. She pushed aside fatigue and continued to block and jab. Then she stumbled on a loose rock. He pressed his advantage, landing a kick to the kidney. With a swivel, she got a good kick into his solar plexus. He doubled over but retaliated quickly with a jab to her abdomen. She wheezed, trying to hold on. It was becoming harder. He was too strong.

Hang in there. The poison will work soon.

And then it did. He began to falter, becoming uncoordinated and erratic. She stepped away to watch as he screamed and collapsed on the ground. It was a particularly severe reaction to the venom by the way he was jerking, but she studied him dispassionately. She felt no sympathy. It was what he deserved. She sank to her knees and squeezed her nostrils together to stem the bleeding. It stopped after a minute and she gingerly climbed to her feet.

Claire stood to the side, her gun pointed at the two young men. Both looked the worse for wear. The stranger had a limp and Dane was nursing his arm. Vivian guessed Claire hadn't been exaggerating when she claimed she was trained in the martial arts. Vivian tried to muster a smile but failed.

"Lord, your face is a mess. Are you all right?"

"He punched my nose but I'll be fine." She pointed to the man groaning on the ground. His face and arms were already covered in swollen red welts. "But Owen's not. The nettle poison has taken hold. It'll keep him out of commission for days. Now we haven't any time to spare so grab the gear and let's get going." She turned to the young stranger. "You try to follow us and I'll shoot you. Now where's my knife?"

He flinched and pointed at the backpack beside the stretcher. "In there."

Phillip looked like he'd been drugged, but he still managed a glare. "You won't be getting out of here alive, Vivian."

"Wanna bet, asshole." She reefed opened the bag. Her throwing knife was wrapped up in a piece of felt on top. With a flourish, she waved it in front of his nose. "You won't be forgetting this in a hurry, will you? You tell your mates when they get here, that they'll get the same treatment if they come after us."

Vivian pointed a finger at Dane. He stood silent, his face pale, but his expression held a slightly defiant look. He was handsome in a boyish way and tall like a basketball hopeful. His full sandy beard needed a trim, his fair hair was tied back in a ponytail and his left eyebrow sported a silver stud. "You're coming with us. Get your gear."

"Like hell."

Vivian wasn't in the mood for resistance. Her patience had worn out long ago. Ignoring the warning look from Claire, she grasped him by the shirt. "You listen to me, you little shit. We came to get you, so move."

He wilted back into a little boy. "Can my friend Ian come with us? He came up here with me."

"No. He made his bed so he can lie in it. And these two bastards will need him. Now I won't tell you again. Go and get your backpack. We have to get out of here."

He didn't argue this time. He grabbed his bag and placed his hand on his friend's shoulder. "See you, mate. Ring me when you get out of this."

"Okay. Be safe."

With an impatient wave of her hand, Vivian called out, "Follow me," and walked briskly towards the east.

Ten minutes later, she called a halt. "That should be enough in this direction."

"Why? Which way are you planning to go?" asked Claire.

Vivian hauled out the map again, handling it carefully. It was getting tatty around the edges and they would need it for a while yet. "South and we'll come out at the back of my place. They would expect us to go east, the quickest route out of the forest but we wouldn't have a hope in the open country. They'd just pick us off."

"We could try the two-way again to get Ross."

"We could, but I've got a bad feeling about that."

"What do you mean?"

Vivian ran her hand through her hair. "Well, if I was those bastards, I would make sure your agent was otherwise occupied. And they could be listening in. The two-way is hardly private if you know the channel."

"Ross is a veteran agent, not a gullible amateur. His sole purpose in this venture is to protect me and Dane."

"I'm not taking any chances. He could have contacted us too, but he never did. Something's wrong…it has to be."

Claire slapped her hands hard against her thighs. "Without him, we'll never get out."

"Trust me…we will. We'll sneak out of town. The bow hunters club has twelve members, but it's not a Mickey Mouse show. They'll have contacts to move their contraband out of the country, so there'll be a network of people to support them, which will make it difficult. I have an idea how to get out without them knowing. You can hole up in Cairns until you can get on a plane. Once there we'll call the police. We'll talk more about it later. Now I'll show you the route we're going to take."

Dane peered over her shoulder and traced a finger along the map. "You're going to have a problem in this area. They're dangerous wetlands, very boggy and the sand flies will eat us alive. And it's full of crocs. We'd be better travelling southwest into the mountains to skirt it. It'll be a longer route but safer."

"How much longer will that take?"

"Another day's walk. There's climbing involved."

Vivian sat back on her heels to study Dane. He seemed genuine enough, but why the sudden turnaround? She was about to ask the question when Claire beat her to it. "Why are you so willing to co-operate, Dane?"

His face turned ugly. "'Cause you're fucking dragging me along with you and I don't want to go that way."

"But you have been there?" persisted Vivian.

"Duh! Of course...a couple of times. Why do you think I don't want to go there?"

Claire raised her eyebrows at Vivian for her decision. Vivian knew they had no option. They didn't have the luxury of time. If Claire and Dane hoped to get out of town, they needed some element of surprise. The longer they left it that would vanish. "We'll go through the lowlands. I'll be looking to you to guide us through, Dane, so don't stuff me about or you'll regret it."

Dane looked like he was going to protest but then rolled his shoulders into a shrug. "It's your funeral."

Vivian smiled, though it didn't reflect in her eyes. "No mate, it's *our* funeral."

They turned to the south and Vivian hid the signs of their change of direction as best she could. Claire hummed a cheery tune as they kept up a steady pace, while Dane, to Vivian's surprise, occasionally crooned along with her. But by midafternoon, the terrain began to change and they fell silent.

Where they had travelled before, the forest had been majestic with its towering trees and ferny undergrowth. Now swamp oaks, turpentine and oily tea trees grew thick, clogged with vines and covered in moss. The understory had changed into reeds and dank bushes.

Vivian let Dane lead the way now. Little by little the wetlands grew more tangled, the water darker and deeper. Dane steered them onwards, at times up what seemed dead ends. Yet he always managed to find tracks, sometimes thin as garden hoses, through the maze of olive grey pools. Vivian could see Claire glancing around cautiously. She didn't blame her. It looked like a set out of a movie, where crazy swamp people with missing teeth drank moonshine and puffed on corncob pipes. *Deliverance* country.

Vivian felt a twinge of guilt as Claire continuously swatted her arms and neck. Sand flies swarmed in the thousands on her.

"Hey, stop for a minute," Vivian called out. She dived into the pack for the citronella. "Put this on as well as the repellent. It'll help keep them off."

Claire took it gratefully. "God, I hate them. Will we be stopping soon?"

"As soon as we find somewhere that remotely looks like a decent camping spot."

"There's a dry place not much further on. That's why I've been hurrying," called Dane, and for the first time Vivian gave him a genuine smile.

CHAPTER TWENTY

A hundred metres on, a small stand of pines came into view. They looked so incongruous amongst the tropical species that Claire wondered how the seeds had landed there. Birds, humans or animals? But whatever, they were a godsend. The ground underneath them was covered by a dry thick blanket of pine needles. So much more inviting than the dank country they'd just trekked through. She sank down and propped herself up against a tree.

"Savour the moment," muttered Dane. "We've got some way to go before we get out of this hellhole."

Claire flashed him a grin. "Killjoy." She was pleased to see him respond with a half-smile.

"I'm going to. Keep an eye on junior here, Claire," announced Vivian. She bound his hands together with tape, ignoring the glare he shot her. "That should clip your feathers. And if you play up on her, you'll be answering to me."

Claire raised her eyebrows at the tape but merely said, "Take your time. I want a private word with Dane." After Vivian disappeared through the trees, Claire turned to Dane. "Sit down. Please. I want to talk with you."

"Why should I? She fucking tied my hands up."

"Shush. Don't argue. This is important."

"Look, lady…"

"Call me Claire, Dane. I'm a friend of your father."

He raised his eyes to stare at her. She had his full attention now. "*Dad* sent you?"

"No, but if we don't take you home, he can't clear his name."

"What's my being up here to do with him? He doesn't even know where I am."

"That's not what the Federal Security team thinks."

Dane squirmed, frowning angrily. "What do you mean?"

"They think you're in a terrorist training base and he sent you there."

He paled. "What! They think Dad organized me to join a terrorist camp? That's crap! My father is as right wing as they come. He'd no more support Islamic State than fly to bloody Mars. Conservative doesn't begin to describe him. Why would they think that of him?"

"The authorities suspect he's funding ISIS. He was caught fraternizing with suspected terrorists."

"That's bullshit."

Claire eyed him intently. "It's not and he *is* under surveillance. It would go a long way to convince them that he is innocent if you go home. You know how the terrorism threat has accelerated. It's got everyone spooked. Hell, you can't turn on the TV without it being splashed all over the news. You have to come home voluntarily with me, Dane, and tell them the truth…that there is no terrorist camp up here. Do it for your father."

"Then I'd have to explain what I was doing up here."

"Yes. But yours is a far lesser crime."

A mosquito landed on his arm. He tried to swat at it with his tied hands. "The mozzies have started. Can you spray some insect stuff on me, please?"

Claire rifled in the bag for the repellent. Big Scotch Greys had appeared from the stagnant water now the sun was setting.

She slapped the one on his arm, then liberally applied the bug spray and gave herself an extra squirt as well. "Why did you get into this business? You're bright and your parents have money, so I can't fathom what made you do it."

Dane looked at the smudge of blood on his arm. "That insect was a parasite." He grew quiet for a moment before he continued. "Dad called me a parasite when I used his government credit card that time."

"Why did you do that?"

"Because my mates wanted me to. It was just a bit of fun that got out of hand. But after that, Dad came down on me like a ton of bricks. It didn't matter what I did, he was never happy. So in the end, I thought, *stuff you*, and came up here with my friend Ian."

"How did they recruit you?"

"An uncle of a friend of mine lives in the Bay. I didn't realize they were so organized until we got here. It sounded like good money for what we had to do."

"To catch wildlife?" asked Claire.

"Yeah. And collect birds and crocs' eggs. Skin a few pythons...whatever customers wanted. Snakes and lizards are easiest to transport because they don't make a noise, so we trap a lot of them. I knew it was dodgy, but up here nobody really cares."

"Weren't you afraid of being caught?"

"Naw. It's usually only a fine if you're nabbed." He narrowed his eyes. "How do I know *you're* telling me the truth?"

Without hesitation, Claire fished the photograph of the senator with the three men out of her pocket. She had already decided to show him if she needed to. "Take a look."

An expression of surprise, fear—and anger too—passed over his face. "Where was this taken?"

"Overseas. In Europe."

"And they think he's tied up with them?"

"This is only part of the story. The rest I'm not at liberty to discuss with you. But it would go a long way to helping him if you return to explain what you've been doing up here," Claire said, careful not to push him too far. He was the one who would have to make the decision.

"Why are you making *me* decide? You could force me back."

"Because I want you to do it out of loyalty to your family. For your mother and your sister's sake, I don't want to take you back in cuffs. Besides," she added, "it's going to get dangerous when we reach town. This is a large-scale operation, and there's a lot of money at stake. Big bucks. They won't let us go without a fight and I'd prefer not to have to worry about you escaping. We could do with an extra man too."

"I realized they were playing for keeps when they put those snakes in your tent. We were planning to get out as soon as we got a chance." He chewed his lip. "Dad would never sell out his country. He's a ferocious nationalist."

Claire placed a hand on his arm. "Do you trust me?"

"I guess."

"Then come back with me. You know as well as I do what would happen if the press got a whiff that you were suspected of terrorism activities. It would take ten minutes for it to go viral on Facebook. Your father's career would be flushed down the toilet just as quickly."

Dane's eyes strayed to the mozzies buzzing in the air, then focused back on Claire. "Okay. I guess I have to. I'll go with you voluntarily on a couple of conditions."

"And they are?"

"I want you to treat me as an equal. I had enough of demeaning shit from my father. I also don't want to be tied up and I want you to keep that hellcat away from me."

Relieved, Claire laughed with a newfound respect for the young man. He wasn't a pushover and she knew instinctively he would never go back on a promise. "Thank you, Dane. I'll try to keep Vivian at bay, but that may take some doing."

"Yeah, she's pretty fiery when she's worked up."

Claire gave him a wink. "Most of the time she's a big teddy bear. Now put out your hands and I'll take off the tape."

She had just finished cutting the bindings when Vivian arrived back. A discernible heat built in her gaze as she took one look at the unfettered Dane. To avoid the inevitable confrontation, Claire said firmly, "Dane and I have come to an understanding. He's agreed to come with me of his own accord."

"And you got that impression in what…ten whole minutes?"

Claire muttered a curse under her breath. As if they didn't have enough worries without Vivian questioning her ability to do her job. "Trust me on this one. He'll stick to our agreement. Now let's have some dinner."

But Vivian wasn't going to be fobbed off that easily. Glaring, she walked over to Dane. "How come you're co-operating so easily?"

A mulish expression settled over his face. He turned to Claire with a frown but said nothing.

The last of Claire's sense of humour evaporated. "Lay off him, Vivian. I'll take responsibility for him."

"Now that'll really put my mind at rest."

"There's no reason to be sarcastic."

"For god's sake, have you listened to yourself?"

"Yes, well, let's put it this way. That's how it's going to be."

Vivian threw her hands up in the air. "Okay. I'll step away and let you two have your little lovefest. Don't take any more notice of me."

Claire rolled her eyes. Vivian sounded a little jealous. "Come on, Viv. Don't be like that. It'll make things a sight easier if you gave Dane a chance to redeem himself."

"Huh!"

"Do you think you could at least try?"

She hunched her shoulders forward. "I suppose so."

Claire beamed at her. "Great. I knew you'd be fair."

Vivian gave a wisp of a smile. "I hate it when you take the moral high ground. You're so smug about it."

* * *

Claire couldn't stop moving restlessly. She was exhausted but too keyed up to sleep with Vivian so close. She cursed the fact they'd had to discard most of the bedding. Once again, they had to share their one sleeping mat. As well, to keep out the insects they had to cover themselves with the only sheet. The smoke and citronella mostly kept them at bay, but there were still some persistent little buggers. Dane was in his sleeping bag on the other side of the campfire, snoring softly. With her back to her, Vivian was puffing through her mouth, compliments of the blow on the nose.

The darkness seemed to magnify the noises in the swamp. The buzzing of mosquitoes, croaking of frogs and high-pitched screeches of bats merged in an unsettling symphony. But when the gurgling growls began, Claire shuddered. She snuggled into Vivian's back for comfort, no longer careful not to touch.

A hand reached over and patted her hip. "It's the crocs. Don't worry—we're far enough from the water. We're perfectly safe here."

"I hope you're right. They sound awful."

"They'd give anyone the heebie-jeebies. Now get some rest. It'll be a tough day tomorrow."

"I know, but I can't sleep."

"Try."

"Yeah…as if. I've got Buckley's chance now those damn crocs have started up."

Vivian swivelled round to face her. "Think about something else."

"I can't." She plucked a piece of camouflage shirt material in her fingers. Vivian was sleeping in her fatigues. "On the other hand, maybe I can. Your uniform sure is an aphrodisiac."

"Claire! Remember what we decided."

"Hmmm…I know."

"Do you want to swop stories for a while?"

"Goodie, this can be a girl guides' slumber party."

"Do I detect sarcasm from you now?"

Claire laughed softly. "You do. Lying next to you like this, I'm hardly feeling virginal. Soooo, can I at least have a kiss goodnight." Without waiting for an answer, she dragged Vivian's head down and carefully avoiding her nose, brushed her lips against hers.

For all her words to the contrary, Claire had only intended it be a friendly peck. But as they leaned into each other, the kiss deepened. When Vivian pulled her tight into her arms, a warming arousal spread through Claire. She slipped her fingers under Vivian's shirt to feel her skin. It was smooth as silk. She could feel the heat of her and her own body began to flicker with a burning flame. It rippled down between her thighs and she gasped in anticipation. With the sure movement of a lover, she brushed a thumb under the swell of a breast. But as she began to tweak the nipple, Vivian pulled back with a groan. "No...no, please...we'd better stop. We...I can't do this again."

Claire blinked, for a moment not comprehending what Vivian had said. Then when the words sank in, she slowly withdrew her hand, took a long swallow and tried to calm down. It was nearly impossible with the way her body was throbbing. "Dear god, I'm sorry. I...I should have left you alone like you asked me too." She threw an arm over her eyes, her body taut as a bowstring. "I never meant to force myself on you. I just can't seem to..." she turned over abruptly. "Oh hell. Goodnight Vivian."

After a moment, Vivian rubbed her shoulder. "Come on. You didn't force anything. I was there too, Claire. But I...I just can't."

"I know you can't."

"No, I *really* can't."

Claire jerked her shoulder away. "Okay, you've made your point. You don't want to be touched. Just go to damn sleep." She knew she was being irrational, but she didn't care. Her arousal was so acute that she was humming with frustration.

She stared for a while into the darkness before she closed her eyes. But it was over a half an hour later before the sounds of the swamp finally faded into the background and she fell asleep.

CHAPTER TWENTY-ONE

Vivian opened her eyes to see Dane was still asleep and Claire was nowhere in sight. She got up, cricked her neck and stretched. Every muscle screamed—the hand-to-hand combat had caught up with her. And she was nervous. Claire's cold shoulder was likely. She wouldn't blame her. Vivian had sent her all the wrong signals with the kiss and Claire hadn't deserved such a harsh snub.

By the soft light filtering through the trees, she guessed it was around five thirty. Dane woke, rolled upright and combed his tousled hair with his fingers. He looked just like any healthy young man in the morning: fit, cute and sleepy. Vivian felt a touch of compassion for him. He should be out there tossing a football, flirting with girls, and not holed up in this godforsaken place in the company of crocodiles. *Ah, the choices we make.* Maybe Claire was right. He should have another chance.

"Morning. Come and have a sports drink with me," she called out cheerily.

Though he looked hesitant at the offer, he ambled over. "Thanks. Where's Claire?"

"Gone for a walk and a wash, I suppose. I've just woken up myself."

They sat in silence for a while, content to keep the fragile peace intact. Then she put down the mug to spread out the map. "Where do you think we should go from here?"

"You want *me* to choose?"

"I value your input." She fiddled with the corner of the map, in two minds about how to approach him. Maybe just go for it. "Look, Dane. If Claire trusts you, then that's good enough for me. We can't be at each other's throat in this environment. It's tough going and we need each other's support. I'm sure she's explained that we have to move as quickly as we can."

"Fair enough," he began and added hesitantly. "I just want to say that I had nothing to do with those snakes in the tent."

"I hope you didn't, because that was a whole new ball game: attempted murder. You do realize they'll never let us out of this rain forest alive if they catch us?"

"I know. They were planning a few more surprises if the browns didn't bite you."

"Like what?"

"Quicksand, crocs, there's lots of options in here. We were waiting for a chance to bolt."

Claire looked at him curiously. "You didn't catch on before this that they'd go to such lengths to protect their investment."

Dane blushed. "Pretty naïve, eh? We came up here for a bit of fun and the pay was good. They pay in cash…no tax. We've been camping since we arrived. After we made enough money, we were planning to backpack in Europe."

"Did you ever come across a guy with a beaked nose and droopy brown moustache? Aged around thirty to forty?"

Dane's eyes widened. "That sounds like Ollie. What's he done?"

"You were friends?" said Vivian cautiously.

"Yes. He'd already been trapping for eight months when we got here. He worked nonstop to make the money he wanted and left not long ago. Where did you run into him?"

"I found him dead in the mangroves. I'm sorry."

Dane slumped forward. "Oh damn. Poor Ollie. He had been saving to get a permanent visa to stay in Australia, and then he was going to bring his wife out from Greece."

Vivian felt some relief at those words. Madeline hadn't been lying. She put a hand on Dane's shoulder. "When we get out of here, I want you to give the police his wife's address. I recovered the money and there's no need to tell them where it came from. What's done is done. If he'd stayed in this damn rain forest for that length of time, he earned it. She'd be better off with the cash than letting it be sucked up into the government coffers."

"You don't like politicians?"

"Not much."

Dane laughed. "Me neither. But we won't tell Dad that." As he sipped pensively, he cast a timid look. "Um…Viv. Do you know if Claire's got a guy waiting for her at home?"

Vivian's stomach did a slow roll, followed by a stab of resentment. She studied him seriously now, noting that if he tidied himself up, he would be rather spunky. "I wouldn't know," she said gruffly.

"I'll just have to see then," he said with a grin. "Thanks for the drink. I'll get cleaned up before breakfast."

As Vivian watched him stroll off for privacy, words echoed in her head. *You pushed her away.*

Vivian was halfway through doling out three portions of rations when Claire appeared through the trees. Though she was looked reasonably fresh, Vivian noted the bruised patches under her eyes. With a cool nod, Claire said, "Good morning," and began to fold their bedclothes into the rucksack.

"Come and have some breakfast," said Vivian with a bright smile. Inwardly she cringed. The icy greeting hurt more than heated words. "It's the last of our porridge."

"Thank you." Still no warmth.

Claire began to eat without further comment and Vivian searched for something say. Tongue-tied, she shovelled a spoonful into her mouth. The sound of Dane's footsteps felt like a reprieve, but the smile died on her lips. He had shaved and his hair was pulled back neatly. His straight teeth shone pearly white against his bronzed skin. His buff body glowed with youth and vitality. *Crap! A Brad Pitt look-alike.* Vivian suddenly felt old.

"Hi Claire," he called out, his voice husky.

Vivian glowered.

Claire returned his smile affably. As they chatted on, Vivian tried to tune out. Heaviness settled over her. The closeness she and Claire had shared was drifting away like seaweed on an ebbing tide.

With an effort, she heaved herself up. "Get your gear together—it's time to go."

It was going to be a long, long day.

The weather grew hotter as they hiked. Vivian was content to follow Dane as he wove his way through the labyrinths of swamps. The terrain was even worse than yesterday—she hadn't thought that possible. The timber grew denser, vines and bushes literally clogging up the ground. To avoid the thickest areas, they were forced to wade through shallow water to continue. With an eye out for dangerous wildlife, Vivian followed in the rear to help Claire navigate the most difficult sections. Her admiration for the agent grew. Not once did she complain, although by lunchtime Vivian could see she was struggling to keep up.

"We'll find somewhere to have a short rest," she called out to Dane.

He glanced over his shoulder, though didn't break his stride. "Not here. There're a couple of crocs just over yonder."

Claire quickly picked up her pace. Vivian looked over the green slimy water. Sure enough, two brown logs were floating towards them. "Hurry up. They're coming. Get out of the water. We'll have to push our way through if there's no gap in the vegetation."

Even Dane, who so far had seemed at home in the surroundings, quickly scrambled up the bank and into the bushes. Ten minutes later, the large protruding roots of a fig tree provided a welcome seat.

Claire's breath hissed out like a kettle letting off steam. "This place is the pits."

"You're not wrong," said Dane. "That's why I didn't want to come this way."

"How much further until we're out of the swamp?" asked Vivian.

"Three hours or so, but we'll have to move. We must be out by dusk or we'll be in trouble. There are snakes in here as well as crocs, and there's a damn sight more water ahead."

Vivian turned to Claire, proffering a protein bar. "How are you feeling?"

She shrugged. "Fine." But her hand was shaking.

Vivian gave her arm a squeeze. "You're doing great. Hang in there."

Her lips tightened as she held Vivian's gaze that revealed both pain and determination. "You don't have to worry about me. I'll keep up."

The next hour proved horrendous as they pushed their way through walls of vegetation. Wild creepers spilled across matted tree limbs, forming at times nearly impenetrable barriers. Having gained little ground that way, they went back to wading in the perimeters of the murky waterholes. There were very few dry areas as they traversed the wetlands proper. Eventually, Dane called a halt on the edge of what looked like a small lake. Pandanus trees, their roots snaking out of the mud, were the last of the thick vegetation. A fine mist hovered over the water, blurring its surface.

"Our only option is to go through this," said Dane.

"Is there no other way?" asked Vivian.

"None. But this is the last big hurdle. Once across, we climb to drier country. It'll take us no more than fifteen minutes if we hurry. Be careful to follow in my footsteps. There's a shallow route across, but if we stray off that track it's deep in places."

"We'll be at the mercy of the wildlife," said Vivian flatly. It was more a statement than a query.

Dane shrugged. "Yes. It's not hard going but don't make any waves. We should get across before anything catches on we're in there."

Vivian raised her eyebrow. "Really?"

"That's the theory anyhow," said Dane. "Whether you like it or not, this is the only way."

Claire swallowed, alarmed. Hairs rose on the back of her neck and fear trumpeted in her head. *Hell!* What would they do if crocodiles found them when they were halfway across? Vivian must have been thinking the same thing because she undid the clip on her knife pouch. Suddenly a loud squawking chorus shattered the silence. A flock of black cockatoos, their feathers dappled with brilliant red, wheeled overhead in a flurry of wings.

"I'd like to scream too," Claire muttered as she watched them disappear into the north.

"One of those birds is worth thirty thousand dollars on the black market," Dane remarked. "Are we ready to go?"

Claire squared her shoulders. "I'm ready."

Dragonflies buzzed around her head as she followed Dane into the water. The ground was spongy but firm enough to support them. With water up to his midcalves, and even though it was difficult to hurry, Dane didn't waste any time. Claire followed doggedly, urged on by the thought of what lurked hidden in the depths. She was wary, but hearing Vivian behind gave her some comfort. Ten minutes across Dane veered sharply to the left. Taken by surprise, Claire kept going forward and lost her footing in a deep hole. As she splashed down, the scum on top disintegrated into a mass of small green frogs. She flailed wildly to push them away before Vivian clutched her arm firmly. With a swift pull, she yanked her upright and admonished sharply, "Careful. You're like a threshing machine. You may as well put out a sign 'come and get us.'"

Claire jerked her arm free. "You try swimming with the slimy little buggers."

"Come on, ladies," called out Dane. "Hurry up! We're nearly there."

If she weren't so het up, Claire would have appreciated the view ahead. A blanket of water lilies spread out over the water in an effusion of colourful lilac and pink blossoms. But her mind couldn't register the beauty. Her eyes were too busy darting back and forth, searching for anything hiding amongst the shiny round leaves. As she turned to follow, she caught a glimpse of a brown snout edging through the lilies. If she was frightened before, she was terrified now.

She jabbed a finger at it wildly. "Look there. A croc's coming towards us."

"Then hurry up," yelled Dane.

Too eager to be gone, she stumbled. Then Vivian was by her side shouting, "Go! Go! Faster!"

"I'm trying…I'm trying," she screamed then staggered again.

With an exasperated snort, Vivian hoisted her up in her arms and powered through the water. In a few strides, she was behind Dane who was climbing up the bank. Once on dry ground, he reached out. Vivian pushed Claire at him and began to scramble onto the muddy fringe. As Dane hauled her to safety, Claire watched in horror as the reptile launched at Vivian. It splashed down in an effusion of spray, its massive jaws open.

"It's just behind you," Claire yelled, staring at the huge mouth full of razor-like teeth. The tremendous power of the reptile was terrifying, yet fascinating in a macabre way.

"Duck," Dane called out. As Vivian quickly crouched, his backpack whistled over her head. It landed in the creature's mouth and the teeth snapped shut with a crunch. Vivian clambered over the mud and reeds and flopped panting as the knapsack was shaken furiously.

"Come on," screamed Dane. "It's realizing it's not a juicy leg."

"I'm right behind you," Vivian croaked.

Desperate to be away from the lake's edge, Claire galvanized into action. She dashed through the marsh grasses, only stopping when she was completely enclosed by trees. Her heart rate gradually returned to normal, the scent of warm earth and leafy mulch a blessed relief from the rancid stench of the water. Now in a safer area, she wrapped her arm around Vivian's shoulders and pulled her close. "Thank you," she said, though it seemed inadequate. There was no way Claire could have outrun the crocodile. "That's the last time I'm going near any water, even if I have to walk a day to go around it," she announced firmly.

"Don't worry...I was as scared as you were," Vivian said, rubbing her cheek against the top of Claire's head. Reluctantly Claire let her go, feeling at once the loss of security.

Vivian turned to Dane. "Thanks mate. I owe you one."

"No worries." Dane smiled broadly. "You can buy me another backpack though."

"I reckon. That's the second time I've nearly been a croc's dinner. It's becoming a little wearing."

"That's the last we'll see of them. Up ahead the forest reverts to the tall trees."

"I wonder where we are," said Vivian, pulling out her GPS. She studied it for a moment then gave a little fist pump. "Good news. We're not too far from the back of my house. It'll be wiser, though, to camp in the forest for the night. But I'm going to sneak home as soon as it's dark to make a phone call."

CHAPTER TWENTY-TWO

In the failing light, Vivian searched the forest floor. The track she was trying to find was easy to miss. Eventually, she caught sight of the moss-covered stepping-stones that led to her backyard. The house was in darkness as she prayed it would be. It hadn't been invaded yet, though she knew it would be when they realized they weren't going to catch them in the rain forest. She stepped gingerly into the open and reached the back door without a sound. As well as the ability to move silently, the art of blending in with her environment was ingrained by so many years undercover.

At the end of the landing, she fumbled under the yellow flowering bush for the key. The breath she was holding puffed out when she felt it nestled against the trunk. Carefully she fit it into the lock, turned the key and slipped inside. The tight muscles in her neck gradually relaxed when all was quiet. She couldn't wait to be free again to open all the windows to let a breeze in. The air already had the slight musty damp smell of a house locked up in the wet tropics. She edged into her study, delicately pulled the drapes across the window and searched for a number in her phonebook.

After two rings, a voice answered. "Hello?"

"Elaine, it's Vivian," she said in a low voice.

"Viv. This *is* a nice surprise. How are you?"

"I'm fine but…"

"Are you planning another visit? I've got a new house so you're welcome to stay anytime."

Vivian took a deep breath. It was going to be a lot to ask of her friend. "No…no, I'm not coming down. I've…um…got a favour to ask. A big one."

"Oh? I'll try to help if I can. What is it?"

"I can't tell you all the details, but there's a lot of shit happening up here. I have to get two people out of the Bay without anyone knowing."

"So what can *I* do?"

Vivian felt a moment of doubt but plunged on. "Do you think Robyn could round up a contingent of her HOGs to come up here first thing in the morning? And bring two spare leather jackets and helmets. Tell her to ride around the town as if they're on a sightseeing trip before they head back to Cairns. We'll meet you at that rest stop on the edge of town and my two friends can hop on the back of the bikes."

"It's sounds very secretive. By the sound of your voice, it's *really* important."

Vivian forced herself to calm down, not realizing she was grinding out the words. "It is. Do you think Robyn will do it?"

"She's here. I'll put her on."

When Robyn fell silent after she repeated the request, for a minute Vivian thought she was going to refuse. Then a deep chuckle echoed into the phone. "I think I can manage to get a group together. It'll be an adventure…we haven't been up your way before. How long will it take us to get there?"

"About three hours. What time do you reckon you can get here in the morning? It's imperative Claire and Dane leave as soon as possible."

"We can be on the road at first light…say five thirty."

"That would be fantastic," replied Vivian, feeling a heavy weight lift off her shoulders. "You'll have to make a show by driving around the town and perhaps get a takeaway coffee from the café. That'll make you seem legit."

"Okay, then we'll meet you at that rest stop on our way back to Cairns. Where is it exactly?"

"You can't miss it. It's at the entrance of the town. We'll be hiding in the scrub behind the cement toilet block. How many riders do you think you'll be able to rustle up?"

"About eight for sure at such short notice. There're some retirees amongst the gang. But maybe more if any can get time off work."

"Okay, then we'll see you around about nine thirty. When you get back to Cairns, take them to Madeline and tell her to get them on the first plane out. She's got connections everywhere and a good security system on her house." Overcome by the woman's generosity, her voice quavered a little. "I really appreciate this, Robyn."

"Hell Viv. Elaine thinks the world of you so that's good enough for me."

"You really like her, eh?"

"Oh yeah. Do I ever."

Vivian chuckled. "Hang on to her. She's a keeper. See you tomorrow then." Left with the dial tone in her ear, she sat back in the chair for a welcome respite. After a few minutes, she forced herself to get up, though reluctant to leave the calm sanctuary so soon. But there was no time to linger. She had to get back or the others would be worried. Conscious someone could be watching the house, she resisted the impulse to raid the fridge for some decent food and tiptoed out the back door.

* * *

Claire rested back against the log, surrounded by a cacophony of night sounds, the heartbeat of the forest. For a while, she simply listened. Now that Vivian had returned safely, everything was on an even keel again, and what once had seemed frightening, was familiar and comforting.

It was surprising how easily she had adapted to this isolated place so far removed from her life in Canberra. The smell of warm earth no longer brought back unwanted memories— they had disappeared, at least for the time being. She glanced across at Vivian who sat cross-legged on the ground. They'd finished their meal—time to discuss tomorrow's plans, something they all seemed to be avoiding. She guessed Dane was visualizing his father's reception and Vivian had been unusually quiet since her return. The problem of getting out of the Bay was turning Claire's stomach in knots.

She managed to project some professionalism into her voice and asked, "Now what's happening tomorrow, Viv?"

"It's all set up."

"So…?"

"Friends of mine will be taking us out."

"What about Ross?"

"No Claire," said Vivian with conviction. "We can't take the risk. Once you're safely out of the Bay, we'll call him."

Frustration bled into Claire's words. "He's my team. I have to keep him in the loop. I wish there was a damn mobile phone reception here. Talk about a third world country with its communication network."

"Please, trust me on this one."

Dane sidled over closer to them. "Who's going to take us out? There's only one road in and they'll be watching it. There're a few kilometres where it's hemmed in between the ocean and cliffs, so they'll know if we tried hiking out."

"Friends on bikes are taking us. We'll be wearing helmets with visors and leather coats so we won't be recognized. They won't be expecting us to go by road, although they'll watch it. They'll be guessing it'll be by sea or plane, but not until the day after tomorrow. Or at least tomorrow night. They'll know by now we went south, but they should expect us to skirt those hellish wetlands."

"We can ring the Cairns's police," said Claire. "They can send a patrol car to take us out."

Vivian's voice roughened. "I want you and Dane safe. That means sneaking out of town. We can't take the risk."

"Oh for heaven's sake," snapped Claire. "I have a professional agent here and the town has police, yet you won't use them. That's so damn stupid."

"We'll let them know when you're out of the place. I've survived in tight places because I took no risks and didn't do the obvious. Can't you just swallow your pride and do what I suggest?"

Claire grew tense as hurt rushed through her. "Pride? Is that why you think I'm objecting to your plan?"

Vivian threw her hands up in the air. "You're just used to being in charge."

"And you're not? Pleaseee!"

"Hey," exclaimed Dane, "quit squabbling. If my opinion's worth anything, I vote we go with Vivian's plan. The least number of people who know what we're doing the better."

"Okay," said Claire, not trying to hide her bitterness. "Do what you like. It seems I'm outvoted." She lurched to her feet. "I'm going to clean my teeth and have a wash."

The narrow gully had barely a trickle of water, but it was enough to rinse off the crust of dried perspiration and dirt accumulated over the day. And far enough away from their camp for privacy. Once ready for bed, she sat on a log, taking the time to bring her emotions under control. She couldn't afford to let the pain surface. Vivian's remark had cut deeply, but Claire knew it was more than that. It was nearly impossible to release the ache in her chest that welled up at the thought of never seeing her again.

She didn't know exactly how long she had been sitting gazing into space, but when her mind focused back to the present, the forest had taken on a primal glow. The air glittered with moonbeams, small golden fragments of light filtering down through the tree as if the heavens had thrown fairy dust over the land.

She felt hands on her shoulders and heard Vivian's voice in her ear. "I'm sorry."

Claire sniffed, fighting off the tears that seemed to come out of nowhere. She didn't turn—better to show anger than the emotion threatening to overwhelm her. "Leave me alone. You got your way."

Vivian ran her hand down her arm and said in a rough whisper, "Don't be like that. I'm just doing what I think is best. I couldn't bear it if something happened to you."

As much as she tried to ignore it, when Vivian began to stroke her hair desire shimmered through Claire. She was unable to suppress a moan as the fingers pushed errant strands back from her forehead and then fluttered gently down her cheek. When a fingertip reached her lips, she couldn't resist giving it a flick with her tongue. Vivian pressed close, her arms slipping around her waist. Claire remained still, resisting the urge to turn around. But when Vivian trailed her lips down the side of her neck, all resistance collapsed. A burning pulse began to throb through her body and her flesh seemed to ignite. It was something she was getting familiar with—this pent-up need to taste Vivian, to claim her.

She swivelled around to face her and stood up. The log was between them, the final barrier that had to be crossed. "Don't continue to do what you're doing unless you mean to carry it through. There's just so much I can take, and I've never wanted anyone like I want you."

"Oh honey, do you think I want you any less? I know you'll be taking away part of my heart but I don't care anymore. I won't let you leave without showing you how I feel. If we had the chance to get to know each other properly, I have no doubt I would fall in love with you. But we know that'll be impossible, so I'm going to take what I can and stash it away in my memory box."

With her palm on the top of the mossy wood, Vivian swung her legs over the log. As they stood looking at each other, Claire moved first. She grasped her shirt, yanked her forward and murmured, "My turn this time." She devoured Vivian's mouth, tasting her, drinking her in. Lost in the kiss, the perfume of the forest mixed with Vivian's earthy cinnamon scent sent her senses reeling. As she swirled her tongue, they pulled each other closer, desperate to join. Impatiently she pushed Vivian away and began to undo the buttons of the camouflage shirt. It felt too slow, so she pulled it over her head.

She nearly sobbed with arousal when there was no bra impeding the breasts. They were swollen, tight, the nipples hard dark pink buds standing erect in the puckered brown areola. She'd never seen anything more beautiful. Her mouth took in a nipple and Vivian swayed into her. Claire sucked hard, lightly nipped it and sucked again. She lavished each breast thoroughly, massaging the silky flesh as she sucked. The need to consume was overpowering.

Vivian dug her fingers into Claire's shoulders and begged, "Please honey, I need you. Please…I really do."

Claire gave a little laugh and trailed her moist mouth over the abdomen. When she reached the scar tissue, she ghosted kisses lovingly over the damaged skin while she unzipped Viv's pants. Then she slipped her hand down until it slid into the hot wet centre. With whispered words of love, she began to stroke, relishing the moans that wrenched out of Vivian.

"Do you want me inside, love?"

When a strangled "Yes…oh God yes," came, she eased two fingers inside, curling them as she pumped until Vivian groaned, "That's the spot. Please…don't stop."

Claire felt her own libido building to a climax as she steadily brought Vivian to her orgasm. She'd never felt so powerful, yet humble that this vibrant woman wanted to share this with her. Then as the muscles around her fingers began to contract, she pushed her thumb into the bundle of nerves. When Vivian began to spasm and shudder, Claire couldn't help uttering a triumphant, "Yes!"

Vivian sagged against her, her breathing ragged, the pulse in her neck pounding. Claire held her tightly, nurturing her, murmuring sweet nothings in her ear. Then Vivian's body began to firm in her embrace and before Claire knew it, her knickers were off and Vivian was kneeling in front of her. Without a word, Claire spread her legs. In a moment her throbbing centre was consumed, Vivian's mouth and tongue doing the most wonderful things to her already over-sensitised sex. Deftly

Vivian pulled Claire's leg over her shoulder to give her better access. Claire leaned back against the log, now engulfed in the orgy of sensations as the mouth ravaged her. She hung on as her orgasm rose in a torrent, spreading through her body in waves of exquisite pleasure until she could barely gasp out a word.

Vivian let her down slowly, but with arms either side, kept her trapped against the log. Claire looked at her in confusion, not knowing why her body still screamed to be touched. She rarely had more than one climax, and never one so forceful. Vivian seemed to understand completely. She quickly wriggled out of her trousers and pulled Claire down on the ground until they were stretched out, bodies touching. "This time, we do it together, sweetheart."

Vivian manoeuvred her legs so their centres were pressed together and with growing excitement Claire felt each sharp thrust. Slick with perspiration, they pounded frantically until finally they could only clutch each other, overcome by the explosions of intense rapture. As the last trembling waves subsided, Vivian began to brush her fingers through Claire's hair with slow languid strokes. Claire hummed, enjoying the quiet connection almost as much as the intense release she had just experienced. A new peace enveloped her. *My heart is home.*

She placed a finger in the cleft of Vivian's chin and gently turned her face towards her. "That was really special."

Moonlight speckled across Vivian's face as the magic dust continued to float down from the stars. "Yes," she said huskily.

But as Claire reached over to press her lips again against the mouth swollen with her kisses, awareness of what she was doing sank in. With a sob, she scrambled to her feet.

"What's wrong?" cried Vivian in alarm.

"I...I...oh hell, Viv. What did we just do?" A tear leaked down her cheek.

"It was wonderful. Why are you crying?"

Claire looked at her in agony, stifling tears. "That's the problem...it was. We didn't just have sex, we made love. I've never felt so close to anyone in my life, and...and we've got to say goodbye in a couple of days."

When Vivian touched her on the arm, Claire reared backward. "Please don't touch me. It'll only make things worse." She hastily pulled on her clothes, looked wildly at Vivian and stumbled back to the camp.

Dane was asleep as she stretched out on the ground and wriggled into a bed of leaves to get comfortable. Still awake when Vivian gently settled down beside her, she turned without a word and took her in her arms. With a soft sniffle, Vivian nestled her head on her breasts. Claire stroked her back soothingly, pulling her in closer. "I'm sorry," she whispered.

Tomorrow she would reap what she had sown. Tonight she would forget there was going to be a tomorrow.

CHAPTER TWENTY-THREE

The forest was still in shadows when Claire woke. Tenderness tugged at her heartstrings as she gazed at Vivian stretched out on the ground, her face peaceful in sleep. *How stunning you are.* The memory of how desperately she had given herself the night before quickened her heartbeat until the blood pounded in her ears. And just the thought of Vivian's response sent ripples of arousal surging through her body. But reality tamped down her desire—the piper had to be paid. They'd formed a connection that now could not be broken without heartache on both sides. They'd played with fire and had to bear the consequences for being so blasé about their feelings. The *no strings* fiasco would come back to haunt them.

With gentle strokes on Vivian's arm, she coaxed her awake. Her eyes fluttered open, no longer dark but warm as if the sun had spilled its golden light into their depths. Without a thought, Claire brushed her lips against her mouth. Vivian smiled and pulled her head down again for another deeper kiss. Their tongues slid together in communion, but hearing Dane stir, they pulled back reluctantly.

"I guess we'd better get up," said Vivian. "We have to be at the entrance to the town by ten and we can't walk in the open."

Claire groaned. "How far?"

"About six kilometres, so as soon as we have breakfast we'd better be on our way."

As they ate the last of the dried cereal, the forest came alive. A flock of crimson rosellas flew overhead, calling their brassy "kweek kweek" as they disappeared into the treetops. A grey goshawk swooped down, snatching a small rat-like marsupial in its beak. Colourful butterflies fluttered amongst bright tropical flowers bursting from lush green plants, while small brown lizards skittered up tree trunks, melding into the bark. Spiny crickets and stick insects clung to bushes, while longhorn beetles and centipedes scurried across the leafy floor.

She looked at Vivian, surprised to see she was taking photos with her phone.

"Smile," Vivian called out.

Claire's natural instinct was to turn away—she hated her photo being taken—but not wanting to be a killjoy, she gave a lopsided grin. When Vivian kept snapping, she shooed her away with a wave. As she reluctantly rose to her feet, Claire realized sadly that she was going to miss this world. "What do you have a phone for if you can't get reception?"

"It's a prepaid for when I go away. And it's handy for taking photos."

While Dane cleared up, Vivian shouldered her backpack with an obvious lack of enthusiasm. But the relaxing interlude was at an end—it was time to move. "Okay…let's go," she said.

They walked through the more sparsely spaced trees and ferns at the edge of the forest, though deep enough inside not to be visible from the grassy plains. At one stage Claire touched Dane's arm and pointed. Its distinctive blue neck vivid against the green foliage, a cassowary peered at them through a white Hazelwood shrub. "I've never seen one before," she murmured.

"There're only about fifteen hundred left in Australia and all live in North Queensland," said Dane. "They're on the endangered list."

Vivian stopped at a small pathway and waved at it. "This leads to my backyard." Without another glance, she continued pushing her way through the undergrowth. Further on she halted and cocked her head. "You hear that?"

"Sounds like those damn hornets," Claire muttered.

Vivian grinned. "That's the bike crew coming into town." She glanced at her watch. "Right on time."

An hour later, she stripped off her backpack and pointed to the east. "Just through there should be the back of the rest stop."

They moved to the edge of the trees where a large mown area was partly cordoned off from the main road by a log fence. A blunt concrete toilet block stood at the back, its walls streaked dark grey by the overflow from the gutters. In the middle of the small park was a simple structure covering a long slab table and bench seats. A small rainwater tank, with a chipped enamel pannikin hanging on the tap, was attached to the roof by a tin pipe. After a quick visual assessment, Vivian led them to the back of the toilet. "We'll wait here. They shouldn't be long."

"What if someone else comes in?" asked Dane.

"Most unlikely this time of year, but if anybody does, they wouldn't come round the back here."

They sat against the wall, content to rest in the shade in the peace and quiet. The clouds had cleared away and there was something welcoming about the cloudless sky. A slight breeze blew with a whispering sound that tickled Claire's ears. It carried the salty scent of the sea, a change from the ripe pungent smell of the rain forest. Overhead, a plane droned by. Vivian sat close, her arm so warm and smooth against hers that Claire wished it could be like that forever. Dane gazed at them occasionally with a quizzical expression, but whether he guessed they were more than friends he gave no a sign.

Traffic on the road was never busy and today was no exception. Only two cars drove by before the roar of motorbikes could be heard in the distance. "Here they come." Vivian rose, though she remained behind the wall.

Soon the park reverberated with the loud rumble of engines. A minute later a figure in black leather appeared around the corner. "Hi Viv," said Elaine with a wide smile.

Vivian pulled her into a hug. "Hello, yourself. Am I glad to see you! Wow, you look the part in black leather. Where's Robyn?"

"Coming in a sec. She's getting the gear off the back of the bike."

"Meet Claire and Dane, Elaine."

Elaine pushed her sunglasses on top of her head and clasped their hands. "It's a pleasure."

"How many was Robyn able to rustle up?" asked Vivian.

"Eighteen. Lots jumped at the chance to come." Elaine looked around as a tall figure came into sight with an armful of riding accessories. She quickly performed the introductions.

Claire shook her hand with approval—Robyn looked like she could kick ass.

"Okay," said Robyn, all business. "I brought two sets of jackets, gloves, shin guards and helmets. Put them on before you come out. Two of the men have offered to take you on their bikes."

Claire frowned. "We need three sets."

Vivian cleared her throat. "I'm not going."

Thrown off-balance, Claire pivoted to stare at her. "And when exactly did you decide *that*?"

"There's not much point in me going. Once they know you managed to get out, the game's up for them. I'll go back home through the trees and wait it out. Ring your boss to get the police up here as soon as you're within phone range."

"Don't be ridiculous. They're not going to let you get away scot-free. They're…"

Obviously aware a real argument was coming, Vivian interrupted firmly, "I've no intention of leaving my house unprotected. They're likely to trash it in spite."

"For heaven's sake, they've already tried to kill you. What's to stop them finishing the job?" Claire felt like taking her by the shoulders and shaking her, but with an effort managed to stay controlled. "Come with us…please."

"Don't worry—they won't get me. Anyhow, I can't come. I haven't a helmet."

Claire glared at her, her old festering wounds resurfacing. Once again she was going to be responsible for a death, only this time it was someone she was really attached to, which would make it infinitely worse. She should never have insisted Vivian be their guide. With an anguished cry, she reached forward to clutch her hand. "Don't be silly, Viv. They'll kill you and feed you to the sharks or crocs. If there's nobody, then how can anyone prove you just didn't disappear on your own accord? You said yourself you've severed all ties with your old life." She bit back the threatening tears. "Nobody will look for you."

Vivian smiled. "Don't write me off yet. I'm not that easy to catch. Besides, you forget Ross is still here. Now get dressed and get on the road. The sooner you're out of here, the sooner I can relax."

Conscious the others were staring, Claire took the protective clothing from Robyn with no further protest. Once the borrowed jacket was zipped up, she clipped the leather guards around her calves. A second later two low whistles suddenly pierced the air galvanizing Robyn into action. "Quick," she said. "Get your helmets on and follow me. That was a warning sign... someone must be coming in." She looked at Vivian. "When I give a whistle, bolt for the trees."

All Claire had time for was a frantic good-bye before Robyn jammed the helmet firmly on her head and flipped down the visor. Then she placed a hand on Claire's back and propelled her towards the two closest bikes. Without a word Dane leaped upon one, which gave her no option but to throw her leg over the other. "Put on your gloves," ordered a male voice.

She complied then settled on the leather seat, the curve making it easy to clasp her hands around his waist. The powerful engine throbbed into life at the first press of the starter button, and instead of letting it idle, her driver took off immediately to join the stream of bikes making their way out of the rest area. A white cruiser nosed its way into the park as they roared by. Claire stole a glance over her shoulder—the last few bikes had stopped in its path. By this manoeuver, she guessed Robyn intended to block the view of the toilet to give Vivian time to disappear back into the forest.

Time went by in a blur. The vibration of the machine under her was anything but calming. It mirrored the throb embedded in her skull. Though worry for Vivian's welfare gnawed at her, she could do nothing but agonize over it. The way they had parted left a hole she was sure would never be filled. And as the distance away from her lengthened, the loss became harder to bear. The day that had started with so many possibilities had turned hopeless. They hadn't even had time to swop contact details. Or kiss good-bye. Or damn anything.

She sniffled, trying to concentrate on the ride. The Harley moved along at a cracking pace, her rider handling the huge machine with such ease she at no point was worried about her safety. But her physical wellbeing wasn't the issue—it was her feelings that were battered. Fear for Vivian's safety began to take second place as bitterness coiled within her like an ugly serpent. She had wanted a last kiss.

A surge of anger came, hot and heady. What right did Vivian have to play with her affections then discard her so easily? She could...no *should*...have come with them. Then the recriminations faded as quickly as they had surfaced. Claire hadn't had a chance to say good-bye, but what could she have said? *It was nice, but now I have to be going back to my life where you'd never be happy.* She shuddered, hating how she could hear her mother's disapproval in her head. Vivian would loath all that pretentious shit.

Suddenly she felt deadly tired and all she could do was hang on. The lonely road finally ended at a T-junction and the long snaking line of motorbikes roared south. As they neared the built-up areas, the lead bike turned off into a large BP service station on the side of the highway and the rest followed it in. When the machine came to a stop, Claire swung off the seat, slightly unsteady. Her body felt coiled and stressed like an overwound clock. With a long stretch she eased some of the tightness out of the knotted muscles along her spine, and for the first time had a glimpse of the man she had clutched for so many kilometres. When he took off his helmet with a broad smile, she couldn't help but chuckle. From the feel of his firm abs, she had not been expecting to see a nearly bald man with a neatly trimmed white beard, who looked to be well over seventy.

Her hand was taken in a firm grasp. "Hello. I'm Fred."

"I'm Claire, Fred. And thank you for the ride. You sure know how to handle the bike."

"I've been a HOG for many years now. There's nothing like the buzz astride a Harley. Now I'm going to top up with fuel so you can get a drink and something to eat if you like."

A sense of urgency rushed in. Vivian's life was at stake, she had no time to waste. "Thanks. I have a call to make first." When she was far enough away for privacy, she pressed the number listed in her phone.

A feminine voice answered, "Colinton Enterprises. How may I help you?"

"It's Claire. Is the commander in?"

"Claire! Thank goodness. Where have you been? He's been trying for days to get on to you and he's not in a good mood. I'll put you straight through."

An icy shiver flickered through Claire—that meant Ross hadn't called in either. Where were they? When the deep voice came on, she felt as if everything was closing in on her. "What's happening up there, Claire? And why did communications cease for so long?"

"I'm nearly at Mossman, sir. I have Dane and he'll be on a flight out tonight. Hasn't Ross called in?"

"No. Don't you know where he is?" The words were barked out.

Claire shoved her free hand in her pocket to stave off the disquiet as she gave a brief summary of the events following their arrival in Ashton Bay. After she had finished, there was a momentary silence at the end of the line. Then with no preamble, the commander stated, "I'll get the Cairns's police to get a squad there immediately. I'll also notify the coast guard. How long does it take by road?"

"About three hours if they hurry."

"Right. Since at this stage they think you're still in the rain forest, it will give the police the element of surprise. Vivian Rathbone...is she with you?"

"No, she stayed in the Bay to protect her property."

"A wise move. They'll be sure to target her home once they know you got the boy out."

Claire made a small sound of disgust. "Not so wise. They're dangerous people."

"Judging by her service record, she'll be able to handle herself well enough. I'll tell the inspector to get someone out to her house immediately after they arrive. Have you any idea what could have happened to your protection detail?"

"No. Vivian doubted Ross would be harmed. Somehow he must have been persuaded to go somewhere with no communications. It's got me beat."

"He's got a mobile hasn't he?"

"There's no coverage up there. Only landlines."

"What about the satellite phone?"

Claire let out a frustrated sigh. She wasn't in the mood for the third degree. "We didn't take one into the rain forest because the tree canopies are too thick for decent reception. The two-ways were the better option. There's a radio tower on the mountains which services the fishing trawlers."

"Humph! How's young Dane holding up?"

"He's fine. Anxious to get back to explain he wasn't in a terrorist camp and worried about his father. He's a good young man," said Claire. "Just a bit misguided, but I think his actions in helping us out under the most trying of circumstances have more than exonerated him." She hesitated before she plunged on. "I would like to go back with the police after I put Dane on the plane, sir."

"Definitely not. That isn't our business. Your assignment was to find Dane and bring him home. We'll book your flights now. There'll be a car waiting at the airport. Oh, and well done, Claire. I'll be in touch."

Claire jabbed the *off* symbol with a snarl, letting frustration surface now she was disconnected. How easy for the commander to divorce their agency from the battle that was about to erupt up there. Get in, get out...take no responsibility for anything but your target. She'd heard it all before, but this time, it didn't sit well with her ethics. Surely they had some responsibility to see justice done. Taking deep breaths, she fought for some internal calm before she faced the others. Once she had herself under control, she walked quickly past the bowsers to the shop.

Elaine looked up with a smile as she stepped through the automatic door. "Everything okay?"

"I'm afraid I can't tell you much for security reasons, only that my boss is organizing a police raid as we speak. They should reach the Bay by late this afternoon."

Elaine shepherded her over to a corner table and dropped her voice to a murmur. "You look disheartened."

Claire tried to smile, but could only manage a grimace. "I'll be fine. It's just...just that..."

"I know. You worried about Viv, aren't you?"

"Yes, I am."

"You like her, don't you?"

Claire could feel the blush rising and was helpless to stop it. "Is it that obvious?"

A tinkling laugh echoed from Elaine. "You'd have to be blind Freddy not to notice. And Viv looked like she was having a tooth pulled when you left. I've been waiting a long time to see that happen."

"You sound really fond of her yourself."

"She's a wonderful woman and I count her a very good friend. She deserves to be happy."

Claire gazed at her curiously. "And she hasn't been?"

"Not completely, no. She's been satisfied enough with her life, but every time we talk, I get the impression she's searching for something that she knows is missing. Like a piece of a puzzle that has been misplaced. She never gives me the impression that...well, that she's whole if you know what I mean."

"I do know. I'm much the same. Coasting along but never quite fulfilled."

Elaine peeped at her under lowered eyelids. "Maybe you're Vivian's missing piece."

Claire felt a crushing weight on her heart. She knew Vivian was *hers*, but it wasn't going to do any good. It wasn't going to happen. "Perhaps, but we won't be seeing each other again," she replied, fighting to keep her voice emotionless.

Elaine began to say something then fell silent. "Come on, we'd better get on the road," she said after a long pause.

"Will we be going to your place?"

"I offered, but Viv thought it would be better for Madeline to have you in Cairns. It's all teed up with her. She has connections at the airport, plus an A1 security system on her house. You'll be safer there."

"Madeline?"

"A friend of ours. Just a word of warning there. She's… um…more than a little taken with Viv."

A spurt of jealousy shot through Claire. "Oh?"

Elaine patted her on the arm. "They were lovers briefly a couple of years ago, and Madeline has been trying extremely hard to reestablish the connection. She's a difficult woman to say *no* to, for she's gorgeous with a likable, lively personality."

Claire narrowed her eyes, hating the woman already. "Then I shall have to be noncommittal about our relationship."

"Best of luck. She's nobody's fool."

CHAPTER TWENTY-FOUR

It was just after one o'clock when Vivian followed the path to her back garden. The blades of the long grass around the entrance were sharp, baked brittle by the blazing sun. She stood still for a moment to listen. Crows cawed in the distance. She hoped they weren't feasting on the ripening pawpaws. After a visual check over the yard, she ran to the back door and dug out the key from its hiding place. When the door clicked open, she slipped over the threshold. Even though the inside was overheated, she refrained from turning on the air-conditioning—the hum would advertise someone was home.

Ten minutes later, satisfied she was alone, she made a jumbo sandwich and cup of coffee. Once entrenched in her office with lunch, she scrolled through the photos on the phone. Moisture shimmered in her eyes. It was too much. Vivian shut down the phone as the longing wrenched at her. She'd had no concept of how much it would hurt to see Claire disappear around the corner of that cement block and out of her life. And she hadn't even been afforded the luxury of watching her drive away, let alone to say a proper good-bye. Instead, she had to huddle out of sight until the 'all clear' whistle came, after which she had bolted back into the trees, not caring that the spiky branches tore at her body. She just wanted to stop the heartache. By the time her feet stopped pounding, her arms and hands were streaked with weeping scratches, her breathing laboured and painful.

With an effort, she forced her mind back to the present. There would be many lonely days to relive the past, now it was time to concentrate on the present. She swivelled in the chair, trying to formulate a plan.

What do I do? Go to the police station or wait it out? First things first, though…a shower and clean clothes.

The bedroom air was so stale she opened the long glass doors to the balcony to let in the warm sea breeze. It was good to be home, but as she stood staring out over the railing she felt oddly displaced. A big house like this should be shared with someone. What was she doing at her age living like a nun? Damn Claire. Why did she have to come into her life like a mini cyclone, making Vivian feel more alive than all the time she had spent in this…this mausoleum? She shook her head ruefully, knowing she was being melodramatic but couldn't help herself. Only half a day and she missed the woman fiercely.

Irritably she stripped off her army fatigues in the bathroom—she'd burn the damn things later. Not only were they ingrained with dirt, they smelt of Claire. As the hot water scalded away the layers of grime, she couldn't stop images of Claire flickering through her brain like a slide show: her head back, laughing, wisps of white hair caressing her cheeks, eyes the colour of crystal bluebells, pale eyelashes catching the raindrops, lips swollen from kisses. A wave of anguish roiled through, cramping Vivian's stomach. She slumped forward with her hands against the tiled wall, bitter tears joining the water streaming down her face.

Finally, she managed to get herself together to get out and towel dry. She dressed in a plain black outfit with her most comfortable pair of joggers, and from the safe bolted to the wardrobe floor pulled out a wad of money and her credit card. As she tidied up, the phone on her bedside table began to ring. Though tempted, she let it go to the answering machine.

The caller didn't leave a message.

After a last look around, she was shutting the balcony doors when the hairs on the back of her neck began to prickle. She dipped her head on the side to listen. Nothing. Then she twigged what had caused the feeling. Everything was *too* quiet— the crows had stopped squawking. Something or *someone* had frightened them away. Vivian dashed to the cupboard for the shoebox on the top shelf for the silencer cylinder, wrapped in the oiled piece of cloth. She hurriedly tucked the box back before hurtling down the stairs to her office. She took out her revolver from the backpack, screwed on the silencer and after she checked that the clip of bullets was full, tucked the weapon under her belt of her jeans.

She placed the pack behind the chair in the corner—at a later date, she would send it to Dane. He would appreciate the state-of-the-art rucksack and her debt would be paid. And as an extra bonus, he would be getting something free from the organization that had been sent to drag him home. She wondered how his reunion with his father would go. Hopefully, the senator would think more kindly of him now.

When she inched out of the back door, her eyes involuntarily blinked shut against the glare. Heart thumping, she pressed back against the wall, waiting until her pupils adjusted to the light before checking the surrounds. Once satisfied all was clear, she crawled behind the hedge to the corner of the back wall.

Vivian saw them immediately. Two figures at the edge of the orchard, one carrying a jerry can, the other a bow fitted with an arrow. Her heart sank. *Damn!* She knew them well—the two youngest members of the bow hunters' club, Nick and Pete. She waited while they walked up the driveway until they were near enough to be easy targets. Automatically her training kicked in. *Don't hesitate…if the enemy is armed then disable immediately.* She squeezed the trigger. The armed boy collapsed on the ground, dropping the bow as he clutched his boot. Even though she regretted it, she still felt a flicker of pride. She hadn't lost her touch—the bullet had precisely hit the top of his foot.

His companion looked round wildly. The jerry can clanged onto the stony ground as he hunched into a crouch beside his friend. Vivian remained in her hiding spot, exhaling a relieved breath when he slowly raised his arms above his head. The last thing she wanted was to have to shoot him too.

"Bring Nick over to the house or the next bullet will be yours," she ordered sternly. To get her point across, she fired again.

A puff of dust exploded centimetres to the side of Pete's boot. He didn't hesitate, half carrying, half dragging his mate along the gravel path to the front porch. Vivian could see their utility parked behind the orchard. She strode towards them, feeling more disapproval than anger. God, they were no more than kids—Nick played football for the local team and had just celebrated his twenty-first birthday, while Pete was twenty, a geeky young dork. She had not long ago gone on a fishing trip with Nick's father, and Pete's mother was a good friend. The whole rotten business was a damn train wreck.

Never in her wildest imagination could she have foretold that this little backwater would be harbouring a crime syndicate. She had chosen to come here because it wasn't a tourist haunt. The summers were hot, long and wet, the town had almost nothing to offer in entertainment except fishing, there were no cinemas or supermarkets and the Internet was tediously slow with limited usage. The road out to the main highway was unsealed and there was only a bus service to Mossman, Port Douglas and Cairns twice a week.

As she approached, Pete looked up warily, the whites of his eyes stark against his tan. Nick sat propped up against the awning pole next to the bed of pink azaleas, blood leaking from his damaged boot. He was moaning loudly. Any empathy vanished from Vivian—in its place came a quiet rage. "Get him inside," she ground out, fighting the urge to hit Pete. Once they were in the kitchen, she jabbed a finger at the chairs. "Sit down. Who ordered you to burn my house? I want an answer...*now*."

For a moment, Pete looked like he wasn't going to reply, but then the fight flew out of him, leaving a frightened little boy. "Bruiser. He told us you went psycho and attacked someone in the forest, and if we burnt down your house you'd have to leave town."

"And you believed him?"

He shrugged.

Vivian gritted her teeth. Whether the boy was telling the truth or not didn't really matter. The fact that they were willing to destroy someone's home on the word of that drop-kick Bruiser told volumes of their mentality and morals. "Well, I can assure you I'm quite sane. Though now I'm thoroughly pissed off. You tangled with the wrong person, so now you're going to bear the consequences."

Their fear was tangible as they stared at her. No longer moaning Nick quietly shivered, Pete was pale and sweaty.

"Whatcha gonna do?" Pete panted out.

"For a start, I'm going to tie you both up." She gestured to the bottom drawer of the long kitchen cupboard. "There's a roll of duct tape in there. Get it. Try anything and I'll shoot another one of Nick's toes."

Tentatively Pete sidled past her, fetching out the tape.

"Turn around and put your hands behind your back." For a second Pete looked poised to bolt, but then his body slumped in defeat. Once he was trussed up on the floor in the corner, she turned to Nick who was swaying on the chair. As quickly as she could she eased off the boot, bound the foot with a crepe bandage and passed him three painkillers. The bullet had blown the top off the big toe; the bleeding had stopped with the pressure but he was going to need medical attention. After she wound the duct tape firmly around his limbs, she bared her teeth in a wolfish smile. "Now I'm going to have great pleasure in burning your car."

"Shit! No!" yelled Pete. "It's Dad's."

"Too bad. They expect to see smoke so they're going to get it. Now I'm out of here. Start praying someone finds you soon." She turned back as she reached the door. "And if any of your mates turn up before I get back, tell them I've activated the outside cameras. They feed back to a central base. Which means, if your limited intelligence can understand, if they finish the job you were sent here to do I'll have them on tape."

With a load of satisfaction, she poured the whole jerry can of diesel over the new Nissan utility. A toss of a match and fire began to flicker, followed by a massive *whoosh* when the diesel fully ignited. The flames leaped skywards in a jet of pure fury. Black smoke billowed into the air. The rush of heat forced Vivian backward, but fascinated by the display, she watched the machine burn to a shell before turning towards her garage.

To stay in the house much longer wasn't an option—it was more than likely someone would come out shortly to check on the two arsonists. She looked at her truck but decided on the motorbike. It could go into tighter places, and with her helmet on she may not be recognized immediately. Her old truck was a town icon—they'd see her coming a mile away.

She glanced at her watch. Claire should be with Madeline by now. Should she ring or shouldn't she? Okay, Claire was going back to her real life, but it wouldn't hurt to see if she arrived in Cairns safely and if the police were on the way. And it would be nice to hear her voice. Before she could talk herself out of it, she dialled the number from the phone extension in the garage.

The familiar warm voice answered. "Hello."

"Hi Maddy."

"Viv. How are you?"

"I'm fine. Have they arrived yet?"

"They got here in one piece a while ago. They're booked on an afternoon flight out."

"I really appreciate this. Claire and I have become…um… really good friends. I'm glad she has you to take care of her. She's been through a tough time, poor kid."

"Kid? She's hardly that."

Vivian chuckled as she visualized Claire's curves. "No…she's definitely not that. I tend to be a bit too protective around her. Can you put her on?"

"She was exhausted and is in the spare room asleep. Do you want me to wake her?"

Vivian bit back her disappointment. "No…no. Let her rest. Did she say if the police were on their way?"

"Yes. Her boss has teed it up."

"Good, then I guess I'd better go. Can you tell her I rang?"

"Of course. Oh and babe, I'm having a party Friday week for my birthday. I'd like you to come."

Vivian rolled her eyes. It wasn't a request, it was a royal command. She owed Madeline now and she wouldn't be able to wriggle out of this invitation. "I'll be there." *That is if I'm still damn well alive.*

"I'll be looking forward to it."

"I'd better go. Don't forget to say hello to Claire for me. Bye." Vivian slammed the phone back on the wall. So much for being able to say good-bye. And now she was obliged to go to Madeline's party. Socializing was the last thing she wanted to do in her present frame of mind.

Shrugging off annoyance, she put on her wind jacket and helmet and wheeled the Kawasaki out of the garage. Where to go was the problem. She would be too vulnerable back in the rain forest if someone came out to check on the fire. And besides, she'd had enough of the place. Logically she should drive straight to the police station. Claire would have organized the raid as soon as she was in range, which meant in another hour or two a police squad should be arriving. But if Joe Hamilton were out of his office now, she would be alone there. And something had to be wrong, for where was Ross?

It was too dicey to go to somewhere isolated. She would have no protection if they found her, and they had already proven they could kill. The best place would be somewhere public, somewhere with witnesses. And with luck, the cops would be in town before the bow hunters discovered she was there. The café was the best choice—the owners weren't part of the bow hunters club—hopefully neutral territory. The engine grumbled into life at the first turn of the key. She flipped down the visor, kicked the bike into gear and slowly drove down the driveway past the smouldering vehicle. A quick glance into the orchard put her mind at ease—nothing seemed disturbed in the trees. At the turnoff, she activated the small camera hidden on a nearby post before roaring onto the main road.

She sank back in the seat, relishing the wind blowing against her body and the power of the machine beneath her thighs. Half a kilometre on, an old green Falcon, practically an antique, appeared in the distance. She recognized it immediately as that of her neighbour, a crusty old bachelor who was even more reclusive than she was. It was doubtful he would be involved in the seedy business, but she kept her head averted all the same as he passed by.

There was no more traffic until she reached the built-up area of the town. Only a few cars were on the main street when she pulled up outside of the Olympia Café and parked the bike. She left the keys in the ignition in case she needed a quick getaway. After a swift pat on her pocket to reassure herself the gun was there, she placed the helmet carefully on the seat. Bracing herself, she pushed open the door.

CHAPTER TWENTY-FIVE

Claire immediately missed the rushing wind lapping over her when they pulled up in Cairns at the end of their journey. She wasn't sorry to dismount—her buttocks were numb and her hands cramped from holding on. They had left the long line of bikes at the botanical gardens turnoff to follow Robyn and Elaine up the mountain, eventually stopping at a very impressive house with a spectacular view over the city.

Fred, after a walk around to loosen up his muscles, settled back into the seat. "I guess I'll be off. You look after yourself now, Claire."

She reached over to give him a grateful hug—sharing the long ride with him had felt rather intimate. With a farewell wink, he gunned the engine and roared back down the road with the other bike in tow. She watched them disappear around the corner before joining Robyn and Dane on the garden path while Elaine rang the bell. When the door opened, Claire sucked in a sharp breath and could only stare. The woman who greeted Elaine was a full-blown exotic honey-haired beauty. Talk about sex-on-a-stick. *This* was Vivian's Madeline? *Hell!*

When Madeline said in a low whiskey-soaked voice, "Please come in," Claire felt like slinking under the carpet. She must look like she'd escaped from a refugee camp: no decent bath for days, smelly clothes and her hair plastered to her skull from the heavy helmet. With an attempt at a pleasant smile, she mumbled, "Thank you for having us."

"Anything for my Viv. Now, who else have we here?"

Dane was so overwhelmed his Adam's apple bobbed like a yo-yo when they were introduced. "He...hello," he croaked out.

"Well aren't you a good-looking one," Madeline purred.

He stuttered and blushed. Claire rolled her eyes; the poor sod was going to be devastated when he discovered she was a lesbian. Better not to tell him and let him have his fantasies.

With an appreciative eye, Claire noted the inside of the house was as stunning as the outside. "You have a lovely home," she said, then remembering her dismal state, continued apologetically, "We desperately need a shower."

"Of course." Madeline wrinkled her nose. "I'll find you something clean to wear. The bust may be a little big, though." She turned to Dane with a smile. "I have a polo shirt and tracksuit pants that should do for you."

He beamed, completely unself-conscious. "Cool."

"There are two showers near the pool, towels are in the cupboard. Go on downstairs and I'll fetch the clothes."

The hot water was heaven, something Claire had been dreaming about for days. After washing her hair with a divinely scented shampoo, she found a blow-dryer in a drawer under the basin, along with a spray-on deodorant and bottle of perfume. Dressed back in her undies, she was just finishing winding her hair into a loose braid when there was a knock on the door. Elaine poked her head in. "I've got the clothes."

"Come in. A clean outfit will be fantastic." Claire lowered her voice to a whisper. "I was hoping to talk to you privately."

"Oh?"

"Um...how well do you know Madeline?"

"Very well. I've attended many of her parties for our community. It gives everyone a social outing and a chance for the single ones to meet somebody."

"She's the local lesbian love guru?"

"Something like that. She gets a kick out of getting people together. Now put these on."

Claire held up the top to the light. "Nice," she said and flicked a look at the label, "*and expensive.* How…how close exactly are she and Viv? You said they had a fleeting affair, but the way she referred to Viv was rather…well proprietary." She pulled on the blouse while she anxiously waited for the answer.

Elaine straightened the fabric on her shoulder. "Jade suits you. You don't have to worry about Madeline, my dear. Viv has made it quite clear she's not interested, though I don't think Maddy has given up the chase entirely. It'll eventually sink in that it's a lost cause." She peered at Claire curiously. "Now *you're* a different kettle of fish. Viv really likes *you.* So what are you going to do about her? And don't give me that rot about not seeing her again."

"What can I do? I live in Canberra—she lives up here—so never the twain shall meet. Besides, we haven't known each long enough to…"

"Rubbish. As soon as I saw Robyn I knew. Either you're interested or you're not. If you think she's worth it, at least try. She's very shy so you may have to do the asking."

"Oh, she's worth it," murmured Claire.

Elaine gave a nod of approval. "There'll be nothing for you in that little backwater of hers, so you'll both have to work something out. Time away from her will tell if it's only a passing fancy."

"You make it sound easy, but I doubt a relationship between us can get past first base. There are other factors to consider like…Oh never mind, let's go eat." She spun around. "How do I look? I'd say Madeline hasn't worn this outfit for many moons. It fits me well and I'd be at least a size smaller than her."

"I'm afraid Madeline is in for quite a shock. You were rather bedraggled when you arrived, but now…well, now you look very fetching indeed. She's going to resent you."

"Why?"

"She already suspects someone has caught Viv's eye. You're the likely contender," replied Elaine.

"But she doesn't know I'm gay."

"She'll try to find out."

"Then I shall just have to let her know. I can be just as possessive."

"Word of advice?"

"Yes?"

"Give her back in spades what she's going to give you."

Her iPhone jingled as Claire was gathering up the dirty clothes. For one heart-stopping moment she thought it could be Vivian, but remembered they hadn't exchanged numbers. She flicked a look at the caller ID—the commander. With a waggle of her fingers at Elaine, she said, "I have to take this. You go up and I'll see you in a minute."

"Hi sir."

"Hello Claire. I've booked two business class seats on the four o'clock Qantas flight this afternoon to Sydney. The connecting flight to Canberra will be leaving an hour and a half after your plane lands. Your tickets will be waiting for you at the Cairns airport and a car will be at the airport to take you home when you get here. Dane will be delivered to his father's house. I'll expect a full report in the morning."

"Right. Any word from Ross?"

"None. The inspector is going to let me know as soon as he has some news."

"I'll see you tomorrow then, sir."

Claire punched the off button and hurried upstairs to the dining room. By the dumbstruck look on her hostess's face, Elaine was right. Madeline's probing gaze wandered over her, lingering at her chest before meeting her eyes. "Well, well, those old clothes did spruce you up. I must have been a bit thinner the last time I wore that outfit."

"I feel a new woman and, believe it or not, the bust isn't too big at all."

"No, it isn't. Motorbike jackets can certainly hide a woman's best attributes."

Claire chuckled. "But what fun uncovering them, eh?"

Madeline's eyes widened. "Ah yes."

"Good, then we understand each other. My boss booked us on a four o'clock flight out this afternoon. And thank you, this food looks wonderful."

"It is," Robyn piped in. "I bet you're going to enjoy every mouthful after living on dried rations."

"You bet I am. Viv didn't seem to mind, but I love my food too much."

Madeline raised her head from her plate and stared at her. "You two were somewhere where you had to live on rations for a length of time?"

"They came to find me in the rain forest," said Dane. "Vivian was a regular Tarzan in there. You should have seen her pick Claire up when the croc went for them in the waterlilies."

Elaine gave Claire a horrified look. "You had a run-in with a crocodile?"

"Yep. If it wasn't for Dane throwing the backpack in its mouth it would have got Viv."

"You sound like a good man to have around, Dane," said Madeline. She turned to Claire with a steely glint in her eye. "What do you think, *Jane*?"

"He is."

"And how long were you together on this little...um... escapade?"

"Quite a while. We even had to share a tent," replied Claire nonchalantly, taking another helping of salad.

"And Dane was with you the whole time?"

"Only the last couple of days."

"How cosy."

Claire let a ghost of a smile flitter around her lips. "Hmmm. At times it was."

"I expect..." Madeline's phone ringing brought her to her feet. With a quick look at the screen, she strode out onto the balcony.

Claire glanced around the table. Elaine was fighting to suppress laughter while Robyn had her head down, her shoulders shaking. Only Dane seemed oblivious to the tension as he attacked the food voraciously.

Elaine leaned over and whispered in her ear. "Don't yank her chain too much. She does have a bite."

Claire snorted but didn't comment.

Madeline glared at her with open hostility when she arrived back. The phone call had obviously upset her. It would probably be wise to be a little more conciliatory as they still needed her help. "About our flight, Madeline. Our tickets will be waiting for us at the airport. It's now two fifteen, so we're not going to have time to shop. Would you mind if we wore these clothes home?"

"Of course not. The clothes fit both of you nicely and I'd hate to see you miss the plane."

"Thank you. I'll send them back when we get home."

"There's no need. They are just some old things I had in the cupboard. We'd better be ready to go by a quarter to three. I'll organize a friend at the airport to pick up the tickets, saving you having to go through the check-in. When we arrive, she'll take you to a private room until your flight boards."

"I appreciate it."

"I'm not doing it for you, Claire. I'm doing it for Viv."

"Okay, but I still appreciate it."

Madeline gave her a hard stare. "If the others wouldn't mind tidying up, I'd like a private word with you."

Claire sighed resignedly. Madeline apparently hadn't finished the grilling session. "Let's go," she muttered.

She was led down the hallway to a sunny room enclosed by huge windows and long glass roof panels. White wicker furniture with colourful cushions stood on a polished wood floor, surrounded by hanging macramé plant holders and potted palms. A delightful décor, so reminiscent of colonial days. And her hostess looked like the quintessential lady of the manor as she reclined with elegantly crossed legs. Claire sank down opposite, waiting for her to get to the point of the little chat.

She wriggled uncomfortably. The way Madeline's green eyes focused on her was very much like how a cat watched a mouse. The analogy certainly didn't inspire any humour, instead, goose bumps prickled across her skin. She was, after all, the mouse.

"What exactly is Vivian to you?" asked Madeline abruptly.

Okayyy. Right to the point. "She was employed by our organization to be my guide."

"Don't treat me like an idiot. How close are the two of you?"

Claire blew out a hot breath. *Damn you, lady. Work for it.* "Define *close?*"

"Oh, for heaven's sake. Are you lovers?" Madeline snapped.

"What business is it of yours?"

Vivian sank back into the chair, tapping a long red-nailed finger on the cane arm. "I think the world of Viv and don't want her hurt. She's reticent when it comes to relationships, in fact quite naïve in lots of ways. She shouldn't be taken advantage of."

Claire leaned forward and ground out the words. "It sounds like you don't know Vivian well at all. She is anything but naïve. She's the worldliest person I've ever met and knows exactly what she wants. She's seen more shit in her life than you and I put together, and then some. Hasn't she told you anything about herself?"

Madeline blinked. "About herself? She doesn't talk about herself. I presumed she had a tough upbringing and was ashamed of her family. She never mentions them."

"She's a private person with a complex past."

"And why did she share confidences with you? I know her far better."

"Maybe because of your condescending attitude," Claire snapped. "The way to handle a woman like her is through respect."

Madeline reared back, a flush staining her cheeks. She clamped her lips together then replied caustically. "Maybe I should be thanking you for telling me how to handle her. Once you're gone, she'll be looking for comfort. And believe me, I intend to give her as much loving as I can."

That was the last thing Claire wanted to hear. Jealousy bubbled like acid in her breast. She leaned forward to spit out a retort, but at the last second managed to bite her tongue. *Whoa! Calm down, girl! Madeline's deliberately pressing your buttons.*

She took a deep breath. Time to get control of the conversation or they'd have a full-scale row. Answering in anger would only fuel the fire. And she had the advantage here. They both had a vested interest in Vivian, but it was Madeline on the back foot. Claire even felt a degree of sympathy for the woman—for all her charm and good looks she hadn't been able to hold on to the one person she wanted.

She said firmly, though not unkindly, "I'm sorry Madeline, but what Viv and I feel for each other is our own business, and that's all I'm prepared to say on the subject. Whatever happens between us in the future has nothing to do with anyone else, including you. I refuse to sit here any longer and bandy words with you, which would be upsetting for both of us and entirely fruitless. Whatever the future holds will be entirely up to Vivian. We can't pre-empt how she will feel when I go, but knowing her, she won't be manipulated. Now I'd like to have a few more minutes with Elaine and Robyn before we have to say good-bye." Without another word, she marched from the room.

Elaine looked at her questioningly when she joined them in the kitchen. Claire gave a half-hearted shrug though didn't offer a comment.

"I wouldn't worry too much about her. Jealousy was rearing its ugly head," said Robyn. Even though she looked tough, Claire suspected Robyn was a big ol' softie.

Claire touched her arm to reassure her that she wasn't too upset. "I guess it's time to say good-bye. I can't begin to thank you for what you've done for Dane and me. I can only say if I can ever return the favour don't hesitate to call me. Have you a pen and paper and I'll give you my phone number?"

Elaine dug into her pocket and produced her phone. "Put them in here."

"Would you pass it on to Vivian? We left it to the last minute to swop particulars and in the end didn't have time. Do you know her mobile number? I know her landline."

Elaine found a pen in her pocket and wrote on a slip of paper. "Here. It's a prepaid she uses when in Cairns."

Madeline appeared as they were hugging good-bye, so composed it was hard to tell she'd even been upset. She slipped back to her hostess role like a comfortable glove, kissing Robyn and Elaine on the cheek before they mounted their big black Harley-Davidson.

Claire licked her lips nervously. Now they'd left, she hoped there wouldn't be another outburst in front of Dane. She needn't have worried. Although she looked at Claire like she was barely a class higher than a bug, Madeline addressed her with a perfect civility. "The garage is on this level, out the side door past the kitchen. Are you ready to go?"

"We threw away our dirty clothes in the garbage bin. We're ready."

"Do you need money?"

Claire shook her head. "No, I had my wallet in my pocket. But thanks for the offer."

She shuffled Dane next to Madeline into the front seat of the silver-grey Volvo, relieved to rest quietly in the back. As they sped through Cairns's streets, Claire divorced her mind from the events of the past two weeks. There would be plenty of time to agonize over them in the coming lonely days. She prayed Ross was safe, but he wasn't her responsibility any longer. Her mission would be completed when Dane reached home.

Madeline and she barely spoke again, their farewell a strained formal handshake. Claire couldn't resist giving the shapely hand a "keep-your-cotton-pickin'-fingers-off-my-property" strong clamp. By the look on Madeline's face, she knew what it meant, though she didn't say a word.

And when a half an hour later she stood at the door of the jet, Claire took one last look at the far north before she stepped inside the plane. The air was hot and humid, and storm clouds were gathering on the horizon.

CHAPTER TWENTY-SIX

Vivian leafed through the magazine rack just inside the door of the Olympia until she found the latest edition of the North Queensland Register. With her back against the wall, she settled down to wait in the corner, her face turned slightly to the side for a good view of the front door. Three other tables were occupied: four young mothers with babies sat at the closest, while three elderly women talked over coffee next to them. But the man who was seated with his wife at the far side of the room was the worry. He caused her heart to race and made her wonder if she had been overhasty in her assumption that this was the safest place to wait for the arrival of the police.

Balding, overweight and wearing thick black glasses, he looked innocuous, but she knew that was very different from the truth. He was the best archer in the club, deadly from any range. Vivian didn't like hunting sports, but particularly despised bow hunting. Non-fatal wounding rates could be high, the time of death prolonged and animals usually remained conscious while they bled out. The compound bow, which had a finer accuracy, faster action, and a farther trajectory than the traditional longbow, was the most popular weapon. The poor animals didn't have much of a chance.

So far he hadn't noticed her, as he sat with his back to her table. She held up the paper to hide her face, and probably would have remained unnoticed except Francine Stavros called out from the counter, "Do you want your usual cappuccino, Viv?"

Without a thought, Vivian dipped the paper to peer at the café proprietor over the top of the page and nodded. Then she flicked her eyes towards the other side of the room, more of a reflex action than the need to see if he had taken note of the words. She knew he would have heard. And she was right. He had swivelled to look in Vivian's direction. When their eyes met, his widened. *Crap!* Now she was in for it. She was under no illusion that Thom or Bruiser would be notified that she was in the café, but had hoped the Cairns police would be in town before this happened. Just her luck a member of the club was at one of the tables.

With a whispered word to his wife, he scraped back his chair and without another glance in Vivian's direction, hurried from the room. She didn't look up again until the coffee arrived.

"I haven't seen you around, Viv. Have you been out of town?" Francine asked as she placed the mug on the table.

"For a while...yes."

"Your friend Claire has gone?"

"She was called away a few days ago." She studied Francine warily. There was nothing in her expression to suggest that the inquiry wasn't genuine, nor did she show any sign she knew the statement was untrue. So the drama in the rain forest couldn't be common knowledge—the café was the gossip hub of the town. "You haven't by any chance seen the bloke she came up with, have you? Claire gave me something to give him."

"He's in the Cairns hospital."

Vivian stared at her. "Hospital? We were under the assumption his arm had healed."

"Oh dear, you haven't heard. A few nights after he came back without you, he went for a drink in the hotel bar. Apparently someone spiked his drink and he passed out at the bottom of the back ramp. A delivery truck ran over his leg. It was a mess… multiple fractures. The ambulance took him to the Cairns Base Hospital." Francine blushed. "I must sound like an old gossip. Dee was in here yesterday keen to chat."

Vivian frowned. "How is he now, do you know?"

"Dee said he's getting better slowly, but still needed pretty heavy pain relief."

Things began to click into place. So that was why Ross left his post. The whole business sucked. But there remained a big piece of the riddle. Why hadn't he asked someone to contact them on the two-way? And why hadn't he organized a replacement with his boss?

But that puzzle wasn't going to be solved in the near future— there were more urgent things to attend to. Like how was she going to get out of this now they knew her whereabouts. To sit tight was the only option, for to go would leave her totally exposed. She smiled weakly at Francine and ordered a piece of apple pie. As the minutes ticked by, Vivian half expected any moment someone would burst through the door brandishing a weapon. The butt of her gun was pressed against a rib, giving some comfort. Not that she could use it with mothers and babies in the room.

When someone did arrive, she was nearly taken by surprise. Out of the corner of an eye, she caught a shadow slip out from the kitchen door across to the far corner of the room where the restrooms were situated. The person was gone before Vivian could turn her head. In the next instance, the front door opened and Thom walked in.

When he reached her table, he halted. "What are you doing here Vivian?"

She shrugged. "Having coffee." She tapped her watch. "Bit early for you to knock off work, isn't it?"

"Yeah…well…there are extenuating circumstances. Where's your mate?"

"Who?"

He leaned forward until his forearms rested on the table and whispered. "That blond bit of fluff you've spent the last week with. I'm going to show her a thing or two about pleasing a man. She'll be screaming for it by the time I'm finished with her."

Vivian quashed the urge to sink her fist into his stomach, instead gave a sour laugh. "God you're full of shit. Now run along and let me finish my apple pie in peace."

His eyes glittered coldly and the tip of his tongue slid between his lips like a lizard tasting the air. He crowded into her face. "And when I'm finished with her I'm going to take the skin off your back with that fucking knife you used on Phil."

Vivian leaned backward away from the smell of his breath, which was as overripe as her late summer fruit. *Phew!* "Get over yourself and get out of my face," she snapped, not bothering to lower her voice. "And chew some gum. Your breath stinks."

There were audible gasps from the mothers. Hastily they packed up the prams and disappeared out the door. Even though it was obvious that they had also heard the interchange, the three older women didn't budge. Vivian knew them well—not women who would be frightened by a public argument.

A drop of perspiration worked its way down the side of Thom's thick nose and from the glare he gave her, she was under no illusion he would do her some serious damage once they were alone. Without another word, he walked over to a spare table. It developed into a stalemate as they both sat quietly, but she knew once the three women left she was in trouble. No more customers had entered the café—she surmised someone outside was turning them away. She ordered another coffee. Eventually, when the women rose, someone in a hoodie darted from behind the screen and disappeared through the kitchen door.

Vivian didn't hesitate. She leaped to her feet to beat the women to the front entrance. She opened the glass door with a flourish and said disarmingly, "There you go. I'm on my way to the police station. Could one of you give me a lift please?"

"I'll take you," answered a tall thin woman with light auburn curls streaked with white. Vivian knew Carrie, the postmaster's wife, well. With a look of regret at her motorcycle parked beside the curb, she followed the older woman to a blue Camry.

Immediately after they were seated inside the car, Carrie came straight to the point. "What's going on? I was worried you and Thom were going to come to blows in there."

"It's complicated, but it really is very serious. Once you drop me off, don't hang around."

The woman's lips firmed. "Good heavens, if it's all that bad, I certainly won't be driving away until you're safely inside."

"Thanks." Vivian patted her hand to convey her gratitude. A ray of hope was on the horizon. In the rear vision mirror, she could see two cars following, but they wouldn't attack her with Carrie as a witness, and the station was a place they could not afford to violate. She might be able to stay alive until the cop squad arrived. It couldn't be too far off. When the car pulled up, Viv gave a hurried good-bye before leaping out. Once she hit the footpath, she pivoted on the balls of her feet, opened the gate and sprinted up the steps. A glance over her shoulder confirmed that this was indeed a safe haven. The two cars spun around, tyres squealing, and headed back down to the main street. She gave Carrie a wave before stepping inside.

The reception area was deserted. A sign on the counter informed customers to ring the bell for service, but that would have to wait. A toilet stop was needed urgently—two cups of coffee and jangling nerves had overtaxed even her hardy bladder. She was washing her hands over the basin when she heard someone come into the room. As she lifted her head to peer into the mirror, she felt the touch of cold steel on her neck. *Crap!* She had walked into that one—she hadn't even bothered to latch the outside door. Not only was she getting old but careless too. A rank amateur would have done better.

"Hello Viv. I've been waiting for you to turn up."

The voice was totally unexpected. She hadn't even given her a thought, even though she remembered hearing a plane while they were waiting at the road stop. Straightening up, she brushed her coat and swivelled her head to look into her eyes. "Well, well, Gaby, you're the last person I expected to be involved in this."

"Just keep your voice down."

"Or you'll do what? Shoot me? If I go with you I'm dead anyway."

A low chuckle echoed. "I'm not the enemy, big girl."

"No? You better explain then why you've got a gun stuck in my neck."

"Okay. This was only to stop you taking a swing at me. Now I'm going to put it away and I want you to listen."

Vivian turned around and pulled aside the coat flap to expose the revolver she was holding. "You're lucky I didn't shoot you. Now you'd better start talking."

Gaby eyeballed the gun. "That's a Sig-Sauer P229. You can't buy them on the street. Who the bloody hell *are* you?"

"I'll tell you later. Why did you highjack me in here?"

"To stop you from going into the office before I had time to warn you."

"Warn me? What do you know that I don't? And more to the point, who are *you*, Gaby."

"I work for the Department of Parks and Wildlife's security section. My charter business allows me to patrol the coastline under the radar, as well as bringing me a few extra dollars. We've been investigating suspicious activity in the town for a while now."

Vivian stared at her. This was a stranger, not the self-absorbed womanizer she had come to know. "You're a government agent? Damn you're good…you had me fooled. So how did you know I was in trouble?"

"I came to the Bay earlier on a charter and received an order to look out for you. I was told the police will be raiding the place," she glanced at her watch, "in about half an hour."

"Ah…Claire's boss must have had something to do with getting me protection. Now for the million dollar question… who's in the station office you're so worried about?"

"I think the head honcho of the syndicate."

"But I saw Thom drive away."

Gaby gave a derogatory snort. "It's a big business, too slick an operation for a yobbo like Thom to be the mastermind. He'd be as useless as an ashtray on a motorbike. All brawn and no brain."

"How come you know so much? I live here and had no idea."

"Francine Stavros was recruited by our agency over a year ago when we were approached by Customs. They suspected hosts of wildlife were being smuggled out. She kept us up to speed when the two agents arrived, and how you and Claire had disappeared into the rain forest. By the rumours buzzing around the town, she guessed there was something going on in there. She heard you wounded one of the bow hunters, and that they were searching for you. When you turned up in the café, she notified me immediately. I came straight over, slipped into the back and heard you ask for a ride to the police station. Fortunately, after you left, Thom didn't bother to keep his voice down when he announced, with much delight might I add, that you were going just where they wanted you to."

"Francine was right. There *was* plenty happening. They tried to kill us, so I knifed Phil Mooney and swatted Owen with a stinging tree branch."

"If you got the better of those two, then you're going to have to tell me after this is all over who you really are. Where's Claire?"

For the first time, Vivian smiled. "Gone to Cairns. By now, she should be just about ready to fly south. So back to business. How did you get here so quickly?"

She nudged Vivian's shoulder with a friendly shove. "On your bike, which you conveniently left outside with the keys in and the helmet sitting on the seat. I drove up the street at the back of the station."

"Thank the lord for small mercies. I thought I'd never see it again. So what's the plan? Do I go in or wait it out in the toilet? I imagine whoever's in the office knows I'm in the building. I hope they're not waiting to pounce on me as soon as I open the door. It's been very quiet in there."

"We better have a backup plan before you…"

The sound of footsteps thumping on the front steps made Gaby halt midsentence. Then she grinned. "Looks like the troops are here."

Vivian stood for a moment to breath in the sweet smell success. It was nearly over. The corridor was full of armed cops when she opened the door. From the look of their weapons, uniforms and protective gear, she assumed they were the Special Emergency Response Team. The squad certainly looked impressive and downright scary with their semiautomatic rifles trained on her as she very carefully stepped out of the restroom. The townfolks were going to have a pink fit. Gaby brushed past her, her badge held up to the light as she asked to see the officer in charge.

A broad-shouldered man with a distinct air of authority appeared from the sergeant's office. From the sudden smile that lit up his face, she guessed he knew Gaby well. A welcome relief, for the rifles that had been pointing at her, were now turned into the ground.

"Gaby, good to see you mate." He raised his eyebrows at Vivian. "Who have we here?"

"Vivian Andrews, Jack. She was the one who broke this case wide apart."

He took her hand in a strong grasp. "Ah, yes. Well done. We've instructions to keep you safe."

"Who was in the office, sir?" asked Vivian with a sinking feeling. It was becoming obvious that whoever had been waiting for her wasn't there now.

He gave a frustrated shake of the head. "Apparently someone saw us pull up and rang to warn them. The two men left via the back door before we could surround the place. We found Joe Hamilton's wife inside the office, knocked around a bit and quite shaken up. She was operating the station while the sergeant took a call. Now as quick as you can, jot down the addresses of the bow hunters and we'll start picking them up."

"Did Dee say who the two men were?" asked Gaby.

"She'd never seen them before. Apparently they were directing operations from outside the Bay."

Vivian groaned. *Damn it!* If she hadn't gone to the loo she would have seen them. But then again, she might also be fish food by now. "Give me a sec and I'll make that list for you. Better hurry 'cause they'll go bush once they find out you're here. Could you send someone to my house as well—there are two of them tied up inside. I interrupted their arson plans."

CHAPTER TWENTY-SEVEN

Dee was distraught. Normally in complete control, she was white-faced, whimpering, with blood oozing from a long slash on her forehead. A female officer had the first aid box open on the table, ready to treat the cut.

"Hi Dee," Vivian murmured softly.

Dee gave a wan smile and two tears crept down her cheeks. "Hello Viv. I'm afraid you've caught me at a bad time."

"Scary shit, eh."

"Very. I'm just sorry they got away."

"They weren't locals?"

She shook her head. "No. I've never seen them before. They looked Indonesian, or maybe Filipinos…I'm afraid I really can't be accurate there." She sniffled. "They…they had knives."

"Where's Joe?"

"Out at the reef. He was called away yesterday to help a trawler in trouble. He radioed to say he'll be back in late tonight."

Vivian inspected the cut and gave her hand a kindly squeeze. "That'll need stitching."

The female cop nodded. "Yes, it will, ma'am. I can plaster it together until she can get to a doctor. Is there one here?"

"There's only a clinic on Wednesdays. She'll have to go to Mossman. Have you someone who can drive you there, Dee?" asked Vivian. "I'll take you if you haven't."

"I've already rung Marlene and she's coming to pick me up at home in half an hour. I might stay with a friend in Cairns for a bit…Joe will have to manage by himself for a while."

Vivian listened to the story sympathetically, but somehow it all seemed a little odd to her. Why did the mysterious Southeast Asian men come to the Bay now? Was it to check on their organization because of the events in the forest? But that would be counterproductive. If they were in danger of exposure, then surely they would keep out of sight, especially with an agent around. And there was still the puzzle of Ross. He was a consummate professional. After his operation, he would have organized someone to get word to Claire. And if he'd thought she was in danger, he'd get his boss to send help immediately.

Which could only mean that he thought Claire was in no danger. Someone had to be reporting that back to him. Vivian made a mental note to check the communication unit in the agent's hotel room as soon as she left the station. But it was time now to write down those addresses. She reached for the phone book.

Five minutes later with the list handed over, she looked at Gaby. "Ready to go?"

"You bet. Where to?"

"First the hotel, then would you like to come out home with me for a few drinks. I think we both deserve to relax and we probably should get out of the way so these guys can do their job. To be quite honest, I've had enough excitement for one day."

"Me too. A beer sounds good."

Vivian turned towards Dee, and as she leaned over the desk to say good-bye, the phone rang next to her elbow. She picked up the receiver with a gruff, "Ashton Bay Police station."

A female voice came on. "Marlene here. Would you tell Dee I'll pick her up in ten minutes?"

"Will do."

The phone clicked off.

"Marlene will be here in ten minutes."

"She's a sweetie," said Dee with a smile.

Vivian cradled the phone in her hand thoughtfully before she replaced it into its slot. She stared at Dee as the final piece of the puzzle fell into place as if drawn in by a magnet, and the whole rotten picture became as plain as day. She swept her eyes around the room again—it had to be somewhere.

"Come on, Viv," called out Gaby.

Impatiently, she muttered, "In a minute," and walked around the room. Now that she knew what she was looking for, she spied it immediately. Half hidden behind the police communication unit was a black compact two-way radio base receiver with the brand label *Bower and Wilkins*. She could see Dee fidgeting, half craning her head to try to keep her in view.

"I'm nearly finished, ma'am. I would appreciate if you would keep still so I can finish," ordered the exasperated medic.

Gaby tossed her head towards the door. "Are you coming?"

"Not quite yet." Vivian turned to face the woman in the chair. "Aren't you the devious one, Dee. Good ol' sergeant's wife, an upstanding member of our community. Does Joe know of your extracurricular activities? That you run one of the biggest wildlife theft syndicates in the country. Did *you* tell them to kill us in the rain forest?" Vivian stopped to curb her escalating anger. Once she gained some control, she poked an accusing finger into the air. "God you're a nasty piece of work. Theft is one thing...but murder? How could you have given that order? Hadn't you made enough money to stop for a while? Were you that greedy?"

As she spat out the words, the medic slowly backed away from the chair and unclipped her pistol holster. Dee, her face as pale as the cream-coloured wall, looked ill. With an obvious effort, she composed herself and muttered, "I don't know what you're talking about. I'm the victim here."

"No, you're not. I should have cottoned on straightaway. You're always in command, never giving an inch to anyone. Your little weeping act was too exaggerated to be in character."

"Is that all the proof you have to make such a preposterous accusation? For heaven's sake, I was assaulted. Haven't you any empathy at all?"

"It was the phone call that convinced me. You told the SERT officer someone rang to warn your assailants just before the team arrived. Gaby and I were next door, in the toilet. We didn't hear a phone ring."

"I doubt you would have heard it there."

Vivian leaned forward, not even attempting to control her anger now. "Of course, we would have! And we heard no screams. It must have hurt when they cut you. But what's going to nail you, Dee, is that flash radio communication unit behind the police set on the bench over there. It's the state-of-the-art one the agents brought with them—too expensive to be issued to small stations like this one." Vivian had to stop herself from shaking the woman until her teeth rattled. They had been hunted in that forest like animals so this bitch could make more money. Blood money. Just the thought of the wasps stinging Claire made Vivian curl her fingers into a fist.

Gaby clutched her arm. "Steady down."

Vivian shrugged her off, though continued less aggressively. "Ross left you in charge of our communications after he came to after the accident, didn't he? I've no doubt you rang him every day in hospital to assure him we were fine. Told him we were having a holiday in there. Is that how it went, Dee? He probably asked you to contact his boss as well. Don't you think it's strange that now he's out of commission nobody has been sent to replace him?"

"You don't know what you're talking about. And who are you to accuse me of anything."

"I'm the one you set your dogs on in the rain forest. That gives me every right. I imagine if we search hard enough in this room, we'll find a scalpel or razor blade you cut your forehead with. A good touch that. It gives you an excuse to get out of town immediately. You can't stay around because the game will be up when they speak to Ross. I imagine you were planning to just disappear, never to be sighted again." Vivian looked around to see the senior officer standing at the door. "Did you get that, Jack?"

"Most of it." He nodded to the medic. "Watch Mrs Hamilton and I'll take Vivian's statement at the front desk. The truth will be out when we talk to Agent Hansen. We'll contact him immediately."

Her formal statement completed, Vivian headed home. Gaby rode pillion. The town was practically deserted as they slowly drove through. It wasn't surprising, for the grapevine would have worked overtime—quickly and efficiently. The magnitude of the raid would have been enough for everyone to retreat into their homes and pull the curtains. At the side of the café, she spied armed police loading five men into an armoured wagon. It wasn't hard to recognize Bruiser and Thom amongst them. They were the two who were giving the most resistance. Thom caught her eye as she slowly passed by, and with a ferocious glare, spat on the ground.

"Up yours," she muttered and unable to resist, gave him the bird. And then she began to laugh, a hearty deep laugh that rolled out from her belly and floated joyously on the wind.

* * *

"I'll get us another beer," said Gabby, climbing to her feet.

Vivian sat back in her chair as she gazed out over her land. The last rays of the setting sun caressed the tops of tall mango trees in the orchard, and in the distance, the coconut palms flanking the road stood out like cardboard cutouts in the waning light. The police had removed the two arsonists from the house.

As the repercussions of the whole business began to sink in, she swallowed back pain and regret. As much as she wanted a choice, to stay in the town was a poor option now. The events had forced her into an untenable position. The damage had been done when she pulled the trigger, and it didn't matter that the boys had carried a weapon onto her land or that she was entitled to protect her property. To this close-knit community, she would be a pariah because she had fired on one of their own, one of their young, something that would never fully be forgiven or forgotten. The fact she had only hit his toe wouldn't come into the equation. Whatever the outcome, it would be better in the end if she sold out and moved on. For she would be ostracized, and the only thing she would be left with would be crumbling walls of self-righteousness and ghosts of the past.

Vivian tugged back emotion. What was there to remain for anyhow? Her house and gardens? Material things. It would be horrific to lose them but they were replaceable. And after meeting Claire, she knew she would never be completely happy living in this isolated place again. It was time to move on to make a decent life for herself and reconnect with friends of her past. She would fly to England to see her sister and get to know her kids. And there would be nothing to stop her going to Canberra to visit Claire...*would there?*

She was brought out of her musings by Gaby with the beers. "You look zoned out. Are things catching up with you?"

"Not really. Just contemplating my future."

"Your future? You thinking of moving?"

"I am. I'll hate to leave everything I've built up here, but it's time I made a better life for myself."

Gaby frowned at her. "You sound disheartened. Is it anything you want to talk about? I'm a good listener."

Instead of answering immediately, Vivian sniffed the wind. "It'll be raining before midnight. What about bunking down tonight in the spare room. You can avoid all the drama in town and I could do with some company...after the last hectic couple of weeks the house seems so damn lonely. I'll grill some sausages later."

"Okay. It'll do me good too. There's nothing worse than sitting in a hotel room by oneself."

Vivian looked at her curiously. "Why am I getting the feeling you're not really a womanizer at all. Is it all a front?"

"It's a con, a smokescreen for the job. I parade around as though I'm God's gift to women, straight and gay, and nobody takes me seriously. It's easy to get information when everyone thinks you're a posturing airhead who's only interested in the next lay. But I'm just like the rest of the poor schmucks out there, trying to find true love. I'm twenty-nine-years-old and I've never had a serious relationship. I just wish I had someone to come home to, but the nice girls avoid me like the plague. Nobody wants to be another notch on my bedpost."

"Cripes, you're more down in the dumps than I am."

"Yeah…well…you're rubbing off on me. Now tell me all about your adventures in the rain forest and how you managed to piss off the bad guys."

As she related the story, Vivian felt she was back reliving it, albeit from afar. She tried to avoid mentioning Claire too much but guessed she hadn't been too successful when Gaby remarked after she had finished, "Well damn me, foxy lady. Blondie has you hooked good and proper. You're not even wriggling on the line now."

Heat flushed across her cheeks. "Is it that obvious?"

"Uh-huh! What are going to do about her?"

"I can't do anything. She's gone back to her real life." Then a thought sent a cold shiver through her. *She'll be seeing Ruby.* She pushed away the panic and said with a little more cheer, "Come on. I'll light the barbie so you get those snags cooking and I'll make a salad. You can tell me all about your job while we eat."

As they ate together on the patio quietly talking, Vivian felt a measure of peace. She wished she had known the *real* Gaby before this. The pilot was a sensitive woman, much better company now she wasn't trying to be someone else. They chatted into the night and Vivian, knowing instinctively Gaby wouldn't betray her confidence, told her about her former life as an uncover agent. It felt liberating to be able to share secrets with a friend, something she could never bring herself to do before. She wondered if she had trusted Beverly enough to tell her what she really did, would it have made any difference to their relationship. She concluded it probably wouldn't have, because Beverly was too wrapped up in her own career to question hers. At no stage did she query the long stretches of time Vivian spent away. So different from Claire, who had in only a few weeks and with little effort broken down her barriers.

Finally, she got up and stretched. "It's time we turned in or we'll be zombies in the morning."

"It's been nice really getting to know the real you. We should get together again sometime soon."

"Madeline has a birthday party coming up shortly. If you're up this way on the plane, could I hitch a ride to Cairns sometime next week? It doesn't matter what day because I want to stay with Elaine as well."

"No problem…I'll be here Thursday week. Now show me which bedroom I'm in."

CHAPTER TWENTY-EIGHT

Two days later, Vivian was at the breakfast table when the phone rang. For a second her heart leapt to her throat. Could it be Claire? When a man's voice came on the line, she pushed aside her disappointment. "It's Ross, Vivian."

"Ross. How are you?"

"Still in hospital, but on the mend. The doc said I'll be able to fly home in a couple of days."

She didn't say any more, but waited for him to continue.

After a moment's silence, he said in a low voice, "I was a complete idiot."

"They slipped you a roofie. It wasn't your fault."

"I know. But my job was to protect Claire. I bombed out miserably."

Any animosity she harboured vanished into a wave of compassion for the man. He sounded completely broken. "For what it's worth, I can see why you were taken in by Dee. She can be very persuasive and *is* the police sergeant's wife."

"I hated leaving the communications with someone else, but my leg was badly smashed. Then for days I was so spaced out on pain drugs I didn't even care." His voice began to quaver. "She told me you were fine. She said she contacted my boss and a replacement was coming. How could I have been taken in like that?"

"So she rang you every day?"

"Twice daily. Said you hadn't come across any subversive activity. She made it sound like you were having a hiking holiday in there. Lots of waterfalls, animals, and exotic plants." His voice took on a hard note. "It was all lies…just fucking goddamn lies."

"Have you heard if Joe was in on it?"

"One of the Cairns cops filled me in yesterday. Despite him making a great public show of making sure the bow hunters kept to the hunting season, he knew they were going all year into the state forest and turned a blind eye. He's denying knowledge of the trafficking. Whether he was an accessory or not, will come out in the trial no doubt."

Vivian looked dubious. "It's hard to believe he didn't know his wife was up to something. What about all the money she made?"

"Maybe she salted it away in an account overseas and planned to leave him one day. We'll find out eventually."

"That we will. Thanks for ringing, Ross, and best of luck." Vivian hesitated then added. "Um…you wouldn't have Claire's address by any chance. I forgot to get it off her."

"Sorry. I've never visited her at home. We're encouraged to keep our personal lives separate in the organization. But if it's any help, her father is Patrick Walker, a solicitor in Canberra."

"Thanks. Take care."

* * *

Vivian put down the hoe and wiped her brow. Her heart was no longer in it. It was shaping up to be a bumper crop and she couldn't care less. The first of the summer vegetables would be ready to harvest in a month, but all she could do was to replay the time she had spent with Claire. It had been twenty-one days since she had left, days that had stretched into an eternity. Now all Vivian could do was wallow in self-pity, and pity was the mother of charity. Was that what she was becoming, an emotional charity case? So why was she still here? It was time to do something about it. An idea she had been working on suddenly looked a lot like it could be a solution to her dilemma. With renewed enthusiasm, she went inside to shower and make the phone call.

An hour later when she drove up to the small weatherboard house, Mary Graham was standing outside on her porch. "You wanted to see me, Viv," she said a little anxiously. "It's not Ned is it?"

"No...no, Mary, there's nothing wrong. I wanted to talk, but not over the telephone."

"That's a relief. Ned's been so much better since you've taken him under your wing. I'd hate for him to have ruined that relationship."

"He's a good kid, so there's no worry on that score."

"Come inside and we'll have a cuppa. What do you want to talk about?"

Vivian followed her into the house, which, though needing a coat of paint was spotless as usual. She settled into one of the pine kitchen chairs and smiled at her friend. "Are the kids still at school?"

"They're due home shortly."

"How are you managing really?"

A shadow passed over Mary's face. "I can't say it's not tough. Emotionally I'm getting better, but financially it's a struggle. But you'd didn't come to listen to my woes. Now tell me why you're here."

"I've got a proposition for you."

"That sounds interesting."

Vivian took a deep breath. Once she started this, there was no turning back. "I intend on leaving the Bay. I was wondering if you'd consider taking on my market garden. It's a viable concern and Ned has a good hold now on how everything works. You could lease the business or pay on a share-farming basis—that would be something we could work out together. I'll make sure it's a fair deal for both of us. You would have to stay in the house, though. Homes deteriorate if nobody lives in them."

Mary stared at her. "You're leaving?"

"It's time I moved on. I've been thinking about it for months, and the recent drama has brought it to a head."

"That was hardly your fault. They broke the law, not you."

"I know, but it's been the catalyst. Now you don't have to answer me today, but I'd like your answer by the end of the week."

"You know very well I'm not going to say no," said Mary with a chuckle. "I can't believe you're offering us that lovely home to live in. And a way to make a decent living. Not mentioning the fact the kids can work it with me."

Vivian smiled at her fondly. "Then come around tomorrow and I'll go through the finances with you and the terms of the lease. You may want to buy it from me one day."

* * *

The light plane touched down at the Cairns airport with barely a shudder. Vivian shouldered her backpack and followed Gaby to the end of the tarmac where Elaine was waiting beside her car. She felt a wave of happiness wash over her. She was somewhere where she was welcome.

"Hello luv," said Elaine and kissed her on the cheek. "Hi Gaby. Throw your bags in the boot. I'll drop you off at your flat on the way."

Vivian felt free for the first time since Claire left. She was going to spend a week with friends, something she hadn't done for years. Tomorrow night, though, she would have to do something she didn't relish: break the news to Madeline that she was leaving the north. It wasn't going to be easy to say good-bye to such a dear friend, and there was no doubt Madeline would be upset. Drops of rain splattered the windscreen as they made their way through the city to Elaine's home. Robyn was in the kitchen, putting the finishing touches to the meal.

After dinner when they adjourned to the living room, Vivian nestled into the leather comfy armchair, with her legs resting on the raised footrest. She loved talking with these smart, good-natured women, and as they conversed, something shifted inside her. The floodgates fully opened. She began to share confidences with them as she had with Gaby, anxious now that they fully understood what made her seek solitude in such an isolated part of the country. She was over wanting to maintain a distance, especially with Elaine whom she considered one of her best friends.

"What do you plan to do after you leave the Bay, Viv," asked Elaine, who now seemed a little in awe of her.

"I'm going to play it by ear. For a start I'm going to Canberra for a holiday, maybe stay there for a while."

"Claire's in Canberra, isn't she?" asked Robyn with a sly grin.

"Um…yes. I intend to look her up."

"Oh, I forgot to tell you. She gave me her mobile number to give to you."

Vivian felt a flush of pleasure so intense, she sputtered out the words, "She…she did? Great."

Elaine's eyes twinkled. "Now don't pretend you don't care. We're not falling for that baloney. And she likes you too…very much."

"Yeah…well…we did get on well."

"You're rapt in her. Anyone can see that. So you're going down to Canberra specifically to see her?"

A lump formed in Vivian's throat as she nodded.

"Just a word of warning," Elaine went on. "Madeline is not going to take it well, so how are you going to handle it?"

"Do I have to figure out a plan before I go?"

"Yes luv, you do. She's going to be extremely upset."

"I know. And I don't want to hurt her. She's a good friend, but I've never been able to reciprocate the feelings she has for me. I guess we can't help whom we love, can we?"

Elaine looked fondly at Robyn. "No, we can't. Word of advice?"

"Yes?"

"Don't tell her you're going to see Claire. Leave her with some dignity. A woman like her needs to know she's desired. Sometimes it's kinder to be silent."

"Okay...I wouldn't have known how to tell her anyhow. Hurting Maddy is the last thing I'd want to do. You're a good person, Elaine."

"Too right," chipped in Robyn.

"So when are you going down south?" asked Elaine.

"After my week with you, I'll head back home to settle Mary and the kids in. Then I'm going. Whether I stay there will be answered when I get there."

CHAPTER TWENTY-NINE

Vivian decided to walk from her Canberra motel to the Walker home. After a few blocks through cool, leafy-lined streets, she left the footpath to cut across a park, taking her time to enjoy the experience. She sat on the seat for a few minutes to admire the spreading trees that sheltered lovers and picnickers. Four joggers shuffled by, and two women came into view with three very busy little terriers on leads. They headed towards an area for unleashed dogs, distinctly marked to the last centimetre. She wondered how the Council could ever hope to confine an animal within such definite boundaries. She thought wistfully of Toby running free—it would be a crime to restrict him so rigidly.

At the end of the park, she caught her first glimpse of the house and eyed it appreciatively. It was a two-storied mansion, guarded from the street by a high wrought-iron fence covered in a thick cloak of ivy. When Vivian pushed open the gate, she could see an extensive colourful garden either side of a long paved pathway that led to a columned front porch. The garden was magnificent—such a display of flowers would have had to receive lots of TLC. An older woman knelt at a bed, weeding between rows of gladioli. She glanced up as Vivian approached. By the fine wrinkles scoring her face, she looked to be in her late fifties, early sixties.

She sat back on her heels, cocking her head to the side. "Hello. Can I help you?"

Vivian suddenly felt foolish and completely out of place. She hadn't expected the house to be so grand. It was only nine o'clock in the morning, a bit too early to visit in the city. She didn't know what she had been thinking. Maybe she should just go. She was getting ready to make her excuses when she noticed the woman flexed her spine with a frown. She squatted down beside her with a smile. "Here, let me help. I'm not doing anything this morning and I love gardening. I'm Vivian by the way."

"That's kind of you to offer, Vivian. I'm Camilla." She took off her glove and rubbed the small of her back. "I have to rest my back every so often when I kneel down, so I won't say no. I wanted to get most of the perennial seedlings and a bed of bearded iris bulbs planted." She waved a hand to the left. "There's a spare hat and a pair of gardening gloves on the seat near the fountain."

Vivian regarded her with some compassion. It was a large area for this woman to maintain. "Are you the only gardener they employ? It seems a lot for one person."

"No…no. A man comes once a week to mow the lawn and trim the hedges."

"Well, I'm at your disposal for the morning. Tell me what to do and we'll make a big dint in the work."

They worked all morning side by side, talking generalities, interspersed with some comfortable silences. By noon, the seedlings were planted and a good deal of the beds weeded. When Camilla pulled off her gloves and said in a pleased voice, "That should do for the day," Vivian felt oddly disappointed that the interlude was over. She had very much enjoyed the older woman's company and the chance to get back to nature.

"Come into the kitchen and the cook will get us some lunch," said Camilla and pointed to the end of the building. "There's a room just around the corner where you can wash up. After you finish, come around to the back patio."

"Sounds good."

By the time Vivian reached the patio the table had been set for two and Camilla was pouring iced lemon into long frosty glasses. As soon as she was seated, a maid appeared with a salad and a platter of meats. "Thank you," murmured Camilla.

Vivian looked at her sheepishly. "You're not the gardener, are you?"

Camilla chuckled. "No, I'm not. I'm sorry I led you on. I couldn't resist, and you were so good at the work I thought you might disappear if you knew. Now come on and eat."

Vivian needed no second urging—she was starving. Once they were finished with the meal and served coffee, Camilla sat back and studied her. Aware her hostess had been dying to broach more personal matters for a while, Vivian silently applauded her good manners. She could see where Claire learned her self-restraint. "You're not from Canberra, Vivian?"

"No. From a seaside town north of Mossman."

"Ah, that explains the slight drawl. And the wonderful tan. Now I *am* curious. What brought you to our house this morning?"

Tongue-tied for a second, Vivian eventually got the words out. "Um…I actually came to see Claire. We worked together and became friends when she was up north. She doesn't know I was coming." She added hastily, "This is the only address I knew."

"You haven't her number?"

Vivian winced, feeling a fool. The mother probably thought she was mad. "I have but…well…I just thought…"

"You'd surprise her?"

"Yes. I…I guess it wasn't such a good idea. I'm sorry. It was rude of me to turn up uninvited. To be quite honest, I didn't know if she would be particularly interested in seeing me now she's back here with her family and friends."

A slow smile spread over Camilla's face, lighting up her face. "I think she would like to see you very much, Vivian. You do yourself a great disservice if you think she could forget you that easily. She's away at a conference and won't be home until tomorrow lunchtime. Now tomorrow night we're having a little party to celebrate my husband's birthday. Why don't you come along? You can catch up with her then."

Vivian blinked. *Wow!* Did Camilla suspect they were more than friends? Somehow, Vivian got the impression she did. That would mean she'd just been given the royal stamp of approval from Camilla to see her daughter? She felt like giving a little skip, but curbed her delight and said in a quiet even tone. "I'd like to very much, Camilla."

"Good, then that's settled. Come around six. Oh, it's semiformal dress."

* * *

Claire shrugged into the satin Vera Wang, a long backless sleeveless cream-coloured evening dress, and twirled in front of the mirror. It wasn't as tight as the last time she had worn it. Her foray up north had taken off four kilos, which she didn't mind at all, although she could think of easier ways to lose weight. Seated at the dressing table, she had begun to battle with her hair when her mother appeared at the door.

"Let me give you a hand."

Without argument Claire handed over the brush and pins. It had been a long time since her mother had helped her like this and she welcomed the attention. Since she had come back from the north, she had felt off course, like a rudderless boat. She had tried to put Vivian out of her mind but it was impossible and getting worse as the weeks went by. Many times she had picked up her phone only to replace it without calling. Over four weeks and she hadn't been to see Ruby, who would be extremely hurt. She would be at the party tonight. What was she going to do? There was no way she could be with her after Vivian, but pressure would be applied to continue their casual arrangement.

Obligation—loyalty—compassion—all the big guns would be brought out to get Claire back into her bed.

Her mother brushed the long white hair then began to twirl it on top of Claire's head. "What's troubling you, dear? You haven't been yourself since you finished your last assignment."

"I know? I'm just a bit lost at the moment."

"Is it your work? Was your assignment difficult this time?"

"It was, but that really isn't the problem. I just feel... dissatisfied."

"Is it Ruby?"

Claire snuck a look at her mother's reflection in the mirror. When had Camilla Walker cared about her daughter's love life? She only acknowledged Claire was a lesbian because she didn't flaunt her sexuality, and chose acceptable women to date.

As if sensing her thoughts, Camilla went on, "I don't think she's the right person for you. You're picking the wrong sort of woman."

"Huh?" *Where the hell is my mother?*

"Close your mouth, dear. It's unbecoming to gape."

"So why the sudden interest in whom I date? You've never bothered before."

Camilla gave a little snort. "Because you need to start thinking about settling down. I do want grandchildren one day."

Flabbergasted, Claire stared. "I thought Ruby was the kind of woman you approved of."

"Good heavens, have I given you that impression? She's far too high maintenance. You're like me. You need someone to take charge occasionally." Camilla gave a little laugh. "Or let them think they're in control anyway." She patted her shoulder. "There, you look lovely. What do you think?"

"Great, thanks."

"I'll see you downstairs shortly then. The guests will be arriving in half an hour." She swept from the room leaving Claire slightly shell-shocked.

CHAPTER THIRTY

Vivian followed a stylishly dressed couple to the front door of the Walker house, which was lit up like a Christmas tree. She silently blessed Elaine for making her buy the light grey tuxedo from Madeline's boutique. "You'll have to take Claire somewhere nice on a date and your old clothes need to be retired," Elaine had said firmly. Vivian hadn't been game to argue. Though her credit card had been a lot lighter, from their expressions of approval the evening wear was worth every cent.

Tonight she had discarded the bowtie, opting to open the white silk shirt low enough to wear two chunky silver chain necklaces. A pair of polished black lace-up shoes completed the outfit. After a visit to the hairdresser, she felt she wouldn't look out of place in the birthday crowd.

Camilla and her husband were talking to guests at the door. Camilla spied Vivian, and took her hand, eyeing her appreciatively. "Oh my, you do scrub up well, Vivian. Someone is going to be really swept off her feet tonight. But come and meet the birthday boy."

Her husband wasn't a big man but had a presence. He looked to be in his midsixties, still handsome, with touches of grey at his temples and piercing light blue eyes. There was no mistaking Claire favoured him rather than her mother. He obviously had been briefed by his wife for as he clasped Vivian's hand, he shrewdly sized her up. "Welcome to our home, Vivian. Enjoy the night. I hope we can have a chat later."

Before she moved away, Camilla leaned over and whispered in her ear. "I didn't tell Claire you were coming. I didn't want to spoil the surprise."

The words were of no comfort to Vivian, but instead made her even more apprehensive. The last thing she wanted to do was embarrass Claire. As always before she entered, she looked around the room. The rich and powerful of the city were gathered in the huge lounge, spilling out onto an expansive balcony. Politicians were sprinkled in the crowd, as well as TV personalities, diplomats and a general who's who on the rich list. Then to her surprise, she sighted her old boss Quentin Harleton, who she heard had been promoted to the Director-General of ASIS. He hadn't changed in the six years since she had last seen him, though carried a little more weight. She didn't realize until that moment quite how much she had missed her colleagues.

"Viv, is that really you?" The genuine delight on his face eased her mind and she shook his hand warmly.

"Yes sir. It's me."

He held her hand while he scrutinized her. "You look tremendous. Have you healed completely? And none of this 'sir' business. You're no longer in the service."

Vivian smiled. "Okay Quentin. I'm fine now."

"Do you intend staying up north? I heard you helped that team get Dane home."

"I like it up there. No stress."

"Hmmm." He eyed her thoughtfully. "This is a stroke of luck running into you here. I've a position to be filled and I've been having a devil of a time trying to get the right person."

"Stop…don't even look my way. There's no way I'm going out in the field again. I like being my own boss."

"This doesn't involve undercover work and you'd work autonomously. Your experience would be invaluable. It's a diplomatic posting."

Vivian's first instinct was to decline, but the thought of a fresh start made her hesitate. Her future was up in the air now that she was leaving the Bay. It wouldn't hurt her to listen—it sounded intriguing.

"What about coming around to my office on Monday morning and we'll have a chat. Say at ten."

"Okay. I'll be there."

He gave a hearty laugh and threw an arm over her shoulder. "It really is good to see you. We've all missed you."

As he gave her shoulder a squeeze, Vivian caught Camilla staring at them. She chuckled. Claire was sure to be given the third degree about it in the morning.

Claire was nowhere in sight, so Vivian headed for the bar. She really did need a stiff drink to dampen the nerves. A woman was sitting on one of the barstools, sipping an exotic green cocktail with a piece of pineapple and a tiny umbrella perched on the rim of the glass. From the slightly glassy look in her eye, Vivian guessed it wasn't her first. When Vivian asked for a beer, she turned and murmured, "Well hi there. It must be my lucky day."

Aware she was being perused rather blatantly, Vivian said flatly, "Hello, I'm Vivian."

"I'm Ruby. I haven't seen you before, and believe me, I would have noticed. Do you work for the firm?"

Vivian hid the shock that felt like a sharp slap. *This is Ruby! Damn!* The woman was stunning, with long wavy jet-black hair curling to her shoulders, large brown eyes framed by long lashes and a full curvy figure. How could she ever hope to compete? "No, I'm Claire's friend."

Ruby's eyes narrowed. "Well, isn't she the sly one keeping you under wraps? She should have mentioned you, but then again, she's good at holding things from me."

Vivian frowned, annoyed. "I'm her friend, not a dirty little secret."

"Come off it. She's got something on her mind and you'd turn any girl's head."

Vivian caught the resentment in the tone. She couldn't help feeling relief that all was not well between Ruby and Claire. But then she forgot about Ruby when she heard the voice she had been longing to hear again. "My god, Viv...what are you doing here?"

She turned and all the old feelings flooded back in a heady rush. Claire looked sensational with her hair swept on top of her head and an exquisite evening gown moulded to her curves. And she was staring at Vivian, her face alive with emotion. At once, the people around them faded away into shadows, and the immediate space around them was the boundary of their world. It was all too much for her oversensitised heartstrings. With a strangled cry, she swept Claire into her arms, pressed her close and buried her head into her neck. When she raised her head, tears felt heavy on her eyelashes. She said huskily, "Hi, sweetheart. I had to see you."

"Oh...I'm so very glad you did. I've been so dreadfully lonely." Claire clutched her tightly with a little moan. When she finally stepped out of the embrace, she ran the tips of her fingers down Vivian's cheek, then straightened her collar and tucked back a stray strand of hair behind her ear. "You look fabulous. When did you get to Canberra?"

A hiss escaped from Ruby. Claire moved backward, a pink flush spreading across her cheeks. "Vivian and I met when I was up north, Ruby. We...ah...well became good friends."

"*Friends*? Come now Claire, I'm not an idiot. You're hardly the soul of discretion the way you're pawing at her. Is she why you haven't been to see me since you got back?"

Claire shuddered. Ruby was poised to make a scene that would be disastrous in this elite company. Her mother would never forgive her. "That's enough, Ruby. Please...let's go somewhere private to discuss this. It is Dad's birthday party so don't make a fuss."

Ruby screwed her eyes up until they were slits. Claire felt intense relief when the hissy fit didn't eventuate and Vivian took control. "Come on," she ordered in a voice laced with authority. "Where's the nearest private room?"

Claire pointed at a side corridor. "The library's that way. Second door on the left."

"Then let's go." Vivian moved off, leaving them to follow. Once there, Vivian slipped her hands into her pockets and leaned against the doorframe. Ruby stood with her hands on her hips. Claire knew this victim pose well. She had little defence against it and dreaded the fallout that was coming.

"Now you can continue your bitching," announced Vivian.

With a disconcerted look, Ruby sniffed. "Who put you in charge? Claire's *my* lover, which you seem to be unaware of."

"Let Claire have her say. Ultimately it's up to her how she wants her life to be in the future," said Vivian drily.

"She's right, Ruby. We both know we've been going nowhere with our arrangement. It was to our mutual advantage to have… um…a casual affair, but it was never meant to be long-term or monogamous. You made the rules. Now I want to move on."

Ruby jerked a thumb at Vivian, practically spitting out the words. "With her?"

Claire didn't even try to deny it. "If she'll have me."

"But babe," said Ruby, clutching her hand. "You can't throw away what we've got for someone you hardly know."

Claire jerked her hands away in exasperation. "Stop it, Ruby. You were seeing other people in the time we were together. I understood that."

"Only in the beginning. You did too."

"No I didn't, even though we agreed on *no strings*. Believe it or not, I'm the monogamous type. I tried to tell you before I went north that I was unhappy and wanted out, but you wouldn't listen." Claire began to feel desperate. If Ruby kept up the act of the slighted lover, Vivian might feel too disgusted and go. She wasn't the type of woman to condone this sort of drama. Claire felt like stamping her foot and telling Ruby to buzz off. But with an effort, she reined back her temper and tried again. "Let's not end it like this. Can't we be adults about it?"

Vivian coughed and Ruby whirled around to confront her. Then help came from the most unexpected quarter. Her mother swept into the room, took one look at the three of them and grasped Ruby by the hand. "Come, dear. I have something to show you." When Ruby began to protest, she tugged her gently towards the door. "It's time to leave these two in peace. They have a lot to work out, and there's one thing in life we all have to learn…when to concede defeat. Now you two enjoy yourselves." And they were gone.

"That woman was my mother if you don't already know. Or used to be. Now I'm wondering *who* she is."

Vivian laughed. "I think she gave us the thumbs-up."

"It would seem so." Claire took a deep breath as her face turned serious. "I'm sorry. I don't know what you must think of me. That display with Ruby…"

"There's no need to apologize. Very few people can be circumspect when it comes to personal feelings. Ruby was fighting to keep you, which was understandable. Her big mistake was to think that a 'no strings' arrangement could form the basis of a proper loving relationship."

"I can't blame that on Ruby. I needed someone to help me de-stress when I came back from an assignment, so I used her as much as she used me."

Abruptly, Vivian walked over and gripped Claire's shoulders. "You know what? I vote we forget all about Ruby. Personally, I never want to see the woman again, because I'm a little jealous you've slept with her."

"You've no need to be, sweetheart. I've never felt anything for anybody like what I feel for you. You make my heart sing."

"Then I've only one question. Will you have dinner with me tomorrow night?"

"On a real date? My, we are progressing."

Vivian pulled her closer until their bodies were touching. "We are indeed. And we have a great deal to talk about."

"We have," Claire whispered. "What about we have some practice before the date? I was planning to stay the night so I wouldn't have to drive, and there's a big bed upstairs that has never been used for any extracurricular activities."

"What never?"

"Can you imagine doing anything with my mother in the house? I'm sure she's got x-ray vision, as well as highly honed ESP. Superman's got nothing on her."

"I like her."

Claire looked at her curiously. "How does she know you? You must have made an impression to get to Dad's party. So where did you meet and how did you charm her so quickly?"

"I came yesterday morning to see you and offered to help in the garden—I thought she was the gardener. We spent the morning together and I found her great company. She's knowledgeable about world affairs, in fact she can talk on just about anything. Not that we agreed all the time, but she respected my opinions."

"She enjoys a good debate. Mind you she can be dogmatic, in fact downright aggravating sometimes."

"That's called 'mother and daughter syndrome," said Vivian with a laugh. "Now give me a kiss."

"Just one. I do have to get back to help Mum with party duties. We'll skip out after the speeches."

It was well after eleven when Vivian finally felt fingers brush against her arm and heard a whisper in her ear. "Want to get out of here? My room's upstairs at the end of the corridor."

"I thought you'd never ask." Vivian mutely trailed Claire to her bedroom, suddenly overcome with doubts. Waiting for Claire all evening hadn't been easy. Her libido was sitting on a volcano, and for all her bravado, she was nervous. It had been nearly a month. Would Claire still feel the same passion they had shared in the forest? Danger always heightened emotions.

When the door clicked open, she could see a king-size bed in the middle of a tastefully decorated room. It was so Claire, with pastel-coloured bedspread and pillows, and a huge contemporary abstract painting adorning the wall above the bedhead.

"How did you…?" The question was swallowed in a tangle of tongues when Claire threw her arms around her and kissed her. It wasn't sweet and gentle, but hot with arousal—a claiming kiss.

"I want you so much, darling."

The air crackled around them as Vivian eased Claire backward until her legs were pressed against the mattress. Then she quickly slid the zipper down her back and peeled the dress down her legs until it hit the floor. "Now the pants and bra," she ordered. They were dispensed with immediately and she raked her eyes over the naked body. "My god, you're gorgeous."

Claire gave a satisfied smile. "Now you'd better get that sexy tux off quick smart, otherwise, I'll have to tear it off you and it looks like it cost a fortune."

Vivian laughed delightedly. "Yes ma'am."

Later, completely sated in the glowing aftermath of their lovemaking, Vivian settled Claire against her and lazily stroked the curve of her breasts. "Now we should talk, sweetie."

"Yes, we should." Claire's voice gave a little hitch. "We've got to come to some arrangement so we can see each other. This last month has been hell, to put it mildly. The separation did nothing to dim how I felt about you. Instead, it was a case of 'absence makes the heart grow fonder.' Elaine gave me a word of advice. She said time will tell if what I felt for you was real. Well, it is. I want to give us a go."

"Me too. I missed you as if a part of me was pulled out. And just so you know, I'm the monogamous type too."

"Good, because I'm not going to share you with anyone." She lightly scratched the skin below Vivian's navel. "And that definitely means Madeline."

"Maddy? She's harmless."

"Huh! That siren's off-limits." Claire lowered her voice, serious again. "What are we going to do? I'm on long service leave, so I can go back with you, but I'll have to return in a month. How long are you planning to stay?"

Vivian leaned over and brushed her lips over Claire's mouth. "I'm not going back north to live. I've leased my place to a friend and her children. After I find an apartment, I'll go back to fetch my gear and get Toby from Ned. I'll look for a job this week as well."

Claire stared at her incredulously. "You're leaving your lovely house and gardens."

"It'll be a bit of a wrench but they're only material things. What's the point of having a great house if I haven't got you to share it with?"

"As least you haven't sold it yet."

"I will eventually. But for now, I'll wait to see how things pan out."

"With me you mean?" Claire sounded a little hesitant, so Vivian gave her a reassuring kiss on the forehead.

"With earning my living. There's already something in the pipeline, but we're going to sit down together and plan a future so we can have time for each other. That's important. We're going to be solid."

"We are. Have you heard what's happened to the members of the Bow Hunters?" asked Claire.

"Thom, Bruiser and the Mooney brothers have been remanded for trial. I believe Nick and Pete were let off with a warning, citing coercion from senior members of the club. Apparently the operation was extensive—millions of dollars' worth of wildlife had been smuggled out of Australia over a long period. The bust has been hailed as a giant step in breaking the wildlife trade."

"What about Dee and Joe?"

"Both have been charged, though, according to the grapevine, Joe maintains he didn't know anything about it," said Vivian, feeling the familiar rush of anger. "At least the whole rotten lot of them will be going on trial for attempted murder."

Claire rubbed her arm. "No they won't, Viv. I'm sorry. Our organization can't be caught up in a trial. Very few know we even exist. For all intents and purposes, we were never there."

"You're kidding me."

"No…you know how it works."

Vivian's shoulders slumped. "Yeah I know. I lived that life. I'm pissed off, though, that they got away with it."

"Me too. But if it's any consolation, they intend to come down heavy with the trafficking this time. I expect they'll get hefty jail terms." Claire wriggled in closer. "Now we'd better get some sleep."

"Hmmm. I got a lot of years to catch up on."

"Okay…maybe I'm not that tired," Claire whispered with a sultry smile.

"No? Then come here, lover girl," murmured Vivian, "Perhaps we'll stay here for a week."

Claire gave a saucy grin. "That *will* give my mother something to think about!"

Bella Books, Inc.

Women. Books. Even Better Together.

P.O. Box 10543
Tallahassee, FL 32302

Phone: 800-729-4992
www.bellabooks.com